Ruth Hay

With This Ring

by

Ruth Hay

Book V

Printed in Canada

ISBN 978-0-9867545-4-8

ruthhay@rogers.com

PRO2 16 05 12

*For all those women who hope
love can come again.*

"What counts in making a happy marriage is not so much how
compatible you are, but how you deal with incompatibility."

Leo Tolstoy (1828-1910)

One

Lynn Kyriakos closed her bedroom door and sighed deeply. Stavros was working in his office at the university and was unlikely to disturb her task until his daily quota of graduate student marking was completed. The house was quiet, yet she felt a tinge of guilt as she spread the jewellery out in front of her. Decisions had to be made soon and she did not want any member of her family to know what she was doing.

She could imagine Sarah's exasperation at the very thought of her mother assigning personal items to family members as if she was an old lady about to depart this earth. Lynn sighed again. She was an old lady in her own eyes every time she glanced in a mirror and saw the ravages of time on a face once thought to be attractive. Departing this mortal coil might not be in the cards at the moment, but departing this country for the annual Easter gathering in Greece was looming, and that prospect made her extremely nervous.

First there was the journey itself. The landing in Athens airport skimming past tall apartment buildings so close that, if she dared to look, people working in their kitchens could be seen clearly, was a nightmare. Then there was the family feasting that brought Stavros' relatives from all over Greece to a lengthy gathering on the tiny island of Paros.

Lynn had tried over and over again to fit into this group of voluble Greeks but she was now, and always, an outsider; the strange English woman who had married their brother, nephew, son, when he was far away in England as a young man. The unspoken comment, although Lynn's knowledge of Greek was so elementary that she could not be sure if the comment had indeed been spoken many times, was that she had stolen Stavros from his family in a moment of weakness while he was suffering from homesickness. Spending the month on Paros was for Lynn like being immersed in an alien environment where she was unable to communicate. On the few occasions when one of the younger members of the family tried to speak to her in English, Lynn found little in common to share, and the girl would soon melt back into the laughter and conviviality of her family reunion with no attempt to conceal her relief.

Lynn acknowledged much of this was her own fault. She dreaded the annual trip for months before it arrived and her mental attitude was tainted by these negative thoughts. In the early years when she was able to avoid the trip because her mother, Isobel, was so ill and required constant supervision, Lynn felt ashamed that Stavros expressed his sincere appreciation of her sacrifice. In fact, she was far happier supervising her mother's dementia episodes than pretending to enjoy the Kyriakos' celebrations.

Later, when Sarah was grown and married, she occasionally asked her mother to look after Caroline and Mike while their parents grabbed a quick spring break on their own. Lynn always eagerly volunteered to stay in Sussex with her grandchildren.

Stavros eventually realized his wife's participation in the annual event was not a holiday for her. He began to take her travelling with him for part of the month in Greece and Lynn found a different attachment for her husband's birth place when he revealed his love for the history and culture of Greece that was so much a part of his life.

These short trips helped Lynn's understanding of both the country and her husband, but did little to stem the nerves she experienced each time she contemplated the Easter family gathering.

She spread the rings out on the dark cloth she had laid over her bed. The camera was ready and she had a set of recipe cards and a pen nearby. She was determined not to leave the room until the job of choosing who would get each ring had been completed.

She knew this act was a reaction to the looming departure for Greece. There was always the fear that she would not survive another flight, so anxious did airplane travel now seem to her after many years of tension. But there was another reason for her haste, and this one was a constant worry.

Her mother Isobel had never been really well after Lynn's brother Philip had left home suddenly. The occasional depression from which she had suffered during her children's childhood became a mental deterioration that slowly developed into dementia. Having watched her mother slide into confusion and disassociation, Lynn knew how devastating the condition could be for any family member trapped in the home with such an illness.

When her mother died in the Mayfield Manor Nursing Home, it was an end to a saga of tragedy that set her daughter free but left behind a lingering suspicion that one day Lynn herself might succumb to the very same mental confusion and inflict the same trauma on her husband or on their own beloved child, Sarah.

The act of choosing and labelling her rings was an attempt to stave off that fear of dementia by preparing for a future when she might not be able to do such simple tasks. For the same reason, Lynn refused to let household junk accumulate in her home. She dreaded the thought of Sarah and Caroline forced to deal with boxes of papers, old ornaments and bags of used clothing.

Trips to the local charity shops were a regular occurrence in Lynn's life. As a result of this policy, Stavros kept his office at home locked and used the cupboards to store any comfortable older clothes he wished to save from his wife's grasping fingers. He thought she was afflicted with an obsessive need to tidy everywhere and she let him believe that was the reason.

Where to start? There was her mother's wedding ring. Lynn picked up the worn silver band and rolled it between her finger and thumb. Her mother had no engagement ring and this one ring was lost when Isobel stopped wearing any jewellery. A few weeks after her mother's move to the nursing home, when Lynn was digging in the garden to make the property more attractive to buyers, she had found the ring glinting in a trowel of dirt. The sight of this ring still evoked sadness. It felt as if her mother, by losing her wedding ring had deliberately cast away any last concerns for her marriage and consequently for her children. Lynn knew this was illogical, but the feeling persisted.

"I'll give this one to Philip, perhaps," she murmured. "He may never wear it, but he should have something of our mother's, now that he knows, thanks to Anna Mason's detective work, why she devoted so much of her life to his welfare."

She placed the silver ring to one side and picked up a chunky Scottish regimental ring that had been worn by her father, Kyle Purdy, during the Second World War.

"No point in this one going to Philip," she thought out loud. "His birth father was far away in Canada although he owed more than he ever realized to the man who brought him up and gave him a home." She made out a card with the name of her grandson Mike, and took a photograph of the signet ring and card together.

"That's done, for sure! Now, what about Caroline?"

Lynn had a great affection for her granddaughter. A lovely girl with talents and abilities in every field she cared to pursue, Caroline had endeared herself even more by taking on a role of caregiver and innovator in her great-grandmother Isobel's final months in the nursing home. Together with a group of college friends, Caroline had completed a project to brighten and improve the lives of all the residents in a variety of ways. Her current interest in local politics stemmed from those experiences. Lynn hoped she would live long enough to see what Caroline would do with her life. She suspected it would be something amazing for the benefit of society.

"Yes, this one!" She selected a beautiful amethyst ring with diamond shoulder stones and turned it to the light so that the stones glittered. She could not help smiling at the memory of the day she turned fifty and bought the ring on an impulse just because it made her happy to see it, and because she wanted to celebrate surviving to that advanced age.

"That was almost twenty years ago!" she exclaimed in amazement. "I still get a thrill when I wear this one and I know Caroline has admired it."

The third card was quickly written and photographed.

Her own wedding ring and engagement ring were removed from her left hand with the little tug that reminded her of the groove worn into that finger by so many years of constant wear. The pair was not a matched set, as seemed to be popular for today's young brides. Lynn's engagement ring was a second-hand, small, diamond solitaire, found in an antique shop in London, and labeled as an 'estate ring'. Stavros had offered to replace it with a larger, more imposing diamond when they had been married for ten years and accumulated some finances. Lynn had always refused to entertain the idea. The old ring was precious to her as a symbol of first love. At times, even now, she was astonished that the tall, dark, and handsome man who was her husband, had chosen her and given her this ring as a sign of his intent to marry. Her simple wedding band was similarly inexpensive. It had once had to have gold added where the metal had thinned with use, but it also held too many memories to be rejected in favour of more 'bling', as today's celebrities called it on TV.

These two would belong to Sarah one day. Lynn placed the rings back on her finger once the choice was recorded and prayed it would be many years before she had to relinquish them.

She had nothing left for her son-in-law, David. Perhaps Stavros would give his wedding ring or his university ring to David. She had no idea if Stavros would be willing to do this. Perhaps he intended to leave items to a favourite brother or nephew in Greece? Lynn had no wish to ask her husband about this as it would open up a whole discussion she wished to avoid at all costs. Although their life in the small town of Horam was convenient to Sarah and David's home in Uckfield, and within reasonable travelling distance from Stavros' teaching work at Sussex University, the topic of her husband's approaching retirement, and the location of their retirement residence, was the very worst of all her fears.

As a classics professor, Stavros not only spent his days teaching about Greek and Roman civilization, he also conducted courses in the summer months in Greece, where his graduate students and other members of the public who had an interest in archaeology, would tour the major historical sites and participate in digs in some remote areas.

Lynn constantly worried that the predominance of Greek relatives and his involvement in Greek studies would overwhelm the pleasant life they had enjoyed in England. When Stavros had the chance to choose, where would he wish to spend his retirement years? Many English residents, including couples who were friends of theirs, had fled the uncertain summers of England for the baking heat of France, Spain or Greece. It seemed inevitable that Stavros would follow their lead and return to his homeland.

The trouble was that Lynn had no desire to leave her own homeland. She hated too much sun exposure and was allergic to insect bites. She was most comfortable on cloudy days when the English sun played peek-a-boo and lit up the glorious, verdant countryside of the Weald.

How was this dilemma to be resolved? Lynn could hardly deny her husband the retirement he might choose and yet, she could not see herself accompanying him to an environment so far from her daughter and family, in a foreign land where she could never feel settled.

Casting aside these upsetting thoughts, she replaced the rings in her jewellery box and clicked the lid shut with rather more force than the task required. She had accomplished one item on her list of preparations for the Easter trip. If only she could lock away all her worries in a box and throw away the key.

Stavros would retire from his teaching job in the next few years and then the decision would be made, one way or the other. Until then she must try not to fixate on the uncertainties of the future and spoil what time might remain here, in England, with her family.

Two

Saving his notes on tomorrow's conferences with his graduate students, Dr. Stavros Kyriakos removed the memory stick from his computer and stretched his back to relieve the cramp hours over the keyboard created. He swiveled his chair around and rested his eyes on the fresh green leaves of the willow that brushed against his second floor office window.

He badly needed a few minutes to clear his head and organize his thoughts about his personal life before heading home to the quiet street in Horam where he and Lynn lived.

Although spring was usually a busy term at the university, this year was so much more complicated for him. The decision about whether or not to submit his resignation and collect his pension would have to be made before he left for Easter. This was a momentous choice and one about which he realized he was in two minds.

On one hand was the definite freedom of leaving behind university politics with its eternal meetings about budget and the competition for subject hours, office help, and classroom space.

For years he dared not miss a meeting in case a motion should be approved to cut his teaching hours or his research budget and cast his work back several years from which point he would have to struggle once again to reclaim lost territory. It was a battle he had fought too many times. The study of classics was not a priority in the university's lexicon. There were no grants attached to Ancient Greek and Roman courses but it was what he had always wanted to do with his life. As soon as he acquired the qualifications, he worked and waited until an elderly professor finally retired and relinquished the position to his younger colleague.

"Now I am the elderly colleague," he whispered with some chagrin. "Who is waiting in the wings to take over my position? Will the department seize the opportunity to close down classical studies completely if I leave?" He knew Latin had vanished from the curriculum in a similar scenario several years ago.

Turning his head to left and right and rubbing his stiff neck, he could not help noticing the bookshelves crammed with text books and even his own writing on Greek culture and civilization as the foundation of modern democracy. The books were interspersed with a finely sculptured head of Athena and a delicate pottery vase with the elegant paintings of heroes and monsters striving to win glory. There was also a collection of coins and potsherds and framed scenes of the many archaeological sites where he had laboured in the summers.

Would retirement also mean the end of these summer courses in Greece with his most promising young students and the adults whose fees for back-breaking work under the sun made the entire enterprise financially feasible?

This summer's dig in Aegina was fully subscribed already, although much of the travel and site organization was still to be finalized. Would this be his last chance to uncover something amazing hidden beneath the dust of ages; something that would make his name revered in the annals of historical research? If these summer courses were to be continued under his guidance, a part-time contract with the university would have to be negotiated soon; and with whom? Of late, deans of the university's departments had been falling like leaves in the autumn. Each summer meant the danger of new personnel; the new brooms who might wish to sweep clean the traditional, and uneconomic, areas of study.

"Damn it all!" he exclaimed, drumming his hefty fists against the oak desk. "I have other things to think about." He pushed himself up from the chair and moved to the wall where a map of Greece was pinned to a bulletin board beside a variety of timetables and department dicta.

Thrusting a finger at Paros, he pictured in his mind's eye the piece of land near the Aegean for which he had made tentative enquiries about purchasing a dilapidated house and several acres leading down to a curved and secluded beach. The whole parcel of land was sheltered by a headland on the west and the location was far enough away from any hotels or tourist areas to be not only reasonable in price, but also, as yet undiscovered by the casual traveller. His own intimate knowledge of the island of his birth permitted him to seek out such places only the locals would know about.

The entire world knew how desperate the economic situation in Greece was becoming. Any outside observer could see the dire restructuring of the society that must be put in place despite the strenuous objections of the Greek populace. Only in the current circumstances could Stavros consider making a purchase of land in his homeland. His teaching career had provided a decent income and lifestyle for himself and Lynn but they had had such a slow start in life because of delays caused by Lynn's family situation with her parents, that savings for the future were not a strong aspect of their present finances.

Now was the time to act on the dream of living in Paros far from the soggy English summers and the unpredictable climate. As a

Greek-born man he was confident in his abilities to negotiate a good price with the landowner. He was familiar with the legalities involved and knew how to circumnavigate the pitfalls that might trap a less savvy man.

The final price would have to leave in reserve enough money to rebuild the house and furnish a home that would delight his wife and persuade her to leave England at last.

There was another matter of concern, however. Stavros was tall and strong from years of digging and hefting rocks on archaeology sites in Italy, Turkey and Greece, but he was not a skilled builder. He was aware he knew more about taking apart structures than he would ever know about putting one together.

How was he to accomplish this task while teaching the planned summer course? Which team of local men could be trusted to take over this work unsupervised, so that the shell at least would be secure before the winter months?

It was abundantly clear that many decisions needed to be made. Stavros thought his dilemma was like a temple with slender marble columns supporting a pediment roof. If any one of these columns failed to stay in place, the entire edifice would rock on its foundation, bringing down every stone and shattering everything.

For this, and a dozen other reasons, he decided to keep the debate from his wife's knowledge for the moment. Surely she would be delighted to discover the completed plan when all was ready to be revealed?

Retrieving his laptop and the memory stick from his desk and stuffing them into his leather briefcase, he exited the office and locked the door behind him. By this time next week he hoped to be in a better position to steer a clear path through the morass of decisions facing him. Until then he would postpone any discussions with his wife.

Three

Anna and Alina had been back in London, Ontario, for just over three months. The winter had sped by with the demands of their A Plus internet business but there had been several discussions about other matters when time allowed. A favourite topic was the amazing sights they had seen on their Egypt tour.

On snowy days when they huddled around the gas fire, they pulled out the disks of photographs and watched the scenes of the Nile on the screen of the computer or on the television. They could almost feel the warmth of the sun on their faces as they saw the vivid colours and remembered the temples and tombs they had visited together on Alina's 'trip of a lifetime'.

"So," began Anna after another one of these evenings when the Egyptian photographs had taken precedence over the meager offerings on television channels. "What do you think now that you have had a chance to put it all into proportion? Was the trip worthwhile, Alina?"

"You know it was, Anna! I admit there were a few scary moments, particularly when Richard's wife made her appearance, but that could never overshadow the incredible things we saw. It was a dream of mine to go to Egypt and no part of the trip disappointed me."

"Well, I guess it was worth all the expense and trouble to have these extraordinary photographs to savour whenever we choose to."

"Not just that, Anna," said Alina with a sparkle in her eyes that revealed a youthful confidence which seemed to have appeared since the December holiday. "There are all the souvenirs we brought back and the fabrics I collected. They are permanent evidence of our adventures."

Anna looked around at the new shelf unit they had purchased in January to display the artifacts that had weighed down their luggage on the return trip to Canada. Admiring the hand-sculpted plaques and the replica head of Nefertari, together with smooth, carved, wooden symbols such as the ankh, and the small collection of sturdy canopic jars, she knew the extra baggage costs were well worth the money.

"Of course!" she agreed. "Not only these beautiful reminders but also the delicate crochet shrugs and wraps made from the multi-coloured thread you found in the bazaars, Alina."

Her companion shrugged briefly at this touchy subject. Alina's eyesight no longer permitted her to spend hours on the tiny stitches required by the fine threads. She had employed skilled workers to follow her instructions and create the garments, but it was hard for her to relinquish a talent she had always treasured.

Anna quickly changed the topic. "Another lingering effect of that memorable holiday was the connection you made with my half-brother, Philip."

"Oh, don't start that again, Anna!' She turned away so that her face was temporarily concealed. She was aware that a smile appeared automatically on her face whenever Philip's name was mentioned and she did not want to raise false hopes of some kind of happy ending in a situation fraught with problems.

Anna was glad to have distracted her friend from the worry about her eyesight issues but she was reluctant to let Alina pass off the unexpected link between her somewhat distant brother and her dear friend, who had rarely expressed any interest at all in a member of the opposite sex.

"Now, come on, Alina!" Anna chided. "You know I could not miss the phone calls. Have you two made arrangements to meet again?"

"And how would you expect that to happen? Philip is just finishing the hotel project in Luxor and *we* are immersed in the product lines for spring and next fall. The new cable-knit throws are really doing well and we have to coordinate supplies with our Scottish knitters. When exactly do you think such a meeting could occur? Not to mention where in all the world it might take place? Provided we wanted it to happen at all," she added hurriedly, afraid she might have revealed too much to the ever-aware Anna.

"Oh, I'm not pushing either one of you, my dear," said Anna calmly. "If you want a meeting to happen there's always a way. Just know I am happy if it makes you happy."

"Shut up!" growled Alina, as she gave a laughing Anna a mock push. "Change the subject, please."

"Well, I do have something else to discuss that relates to our trip." Alina settled back in a comfortable chair and gave Anna her full attention.

"You remember how I finally got the photographs of my Aunt Helen?"

"The ones George uncovered from the files in his office?"

"Right ! I had Maria's Paul send them to a specialist lab to enhance the colour and sharpness, and I must say the likeness to my mother in her later years was only increased when I received the finished copies."

"I did wonder what you intended to do with those photographs, Anna. We've never seen them enlarged on the screens."

"No. I had another idea for them. What do you think of this? There was once a large painting over the fireplace in the upstairs double bedroom in the Oban house. I saw the mark on the old wallpaper where it hung. Although the room was freshened up with new paint and paper I was never able to find the right picture or mirror to put over the mantel there."

"Are you telling me you want to make an arrangement of Helen's old photos to hang in that room?"

Alina sounded doubtful about the effect of that idea, but Anna shook her head.

"No, I want something more appropriate. I think I will look for an artist to work from the photos and any other shots of my mother I can find, and paint a proper portrait of Aunt Helen. After all, she should be represented in the house that was her gift to me, don't you think?"

Alina paused and a vision came unbidden to her mind, of the ashes floating on the breeze from the Nile as Helen's sad diary pages disappeared forever.

She shook her head to dispel the scene and replied to the question.

"I think it's a fine idea, Anna. It will be a fitting tribute to that lady who spent happy years in the McCaig Estate Farmhouse. Do you have an artist in mind for the job? It won't be an easy assignment."

"Not yet, I wanted to see what you thought about the plan. I'll start to investigate possible candidates soon. I want to be able to take the painting with me on my next trip to Scotland."

"When were you thinking of going?"

"No plans at the moment. I am happy to stay put here until the weather warms up significantly."

"Speaking of that.....I was thinking of heating up soup for supper and toasting that whole-wheat bread. Let's have it by the fireplace and close the drapes so we don't see or hear the windy weather."

"Sounds, perfect!"

The search for a portrait painter was more complicated than Anna had expected. Although she managed to track down a couple of candidates, neither one was comfortable working from photographs of dubious quality. It soon became obvious to Anna that a special kind of artist was required; one who would allow her to be an active part of the process.

A retired London teacher, who now worked as a volunteer docent at the Museum, supplied a short list of artists who worked in water colours or oils. Anna was of the opinion that a woman would be easier to deal with so she discarded the males on the list and set about contacting the two remaining names.

The first of these was no longer living in the city. The landlady informed Anna that the woman had left for Toronto to live with a friend.

The remaining candidate's phone number went immediately to an answering service so Anna left a brief message, leaving her e mail and phone number and asking the artist to contact her as soon as possible. A week went by and Anna was on the point of calling again when she received an e mail asking her to send more details of the work she wished to have done. After some consideration, Anna composed a reply and sent it off without much hope that the response would be positive.

Thank you for getting in touch with me Ms. Drake.

I am interesting in finding an artist who will paint a portrait of a deceased relative.

Of necessity, this portrait will have to be done using photographs. I realize this method may not be ideal but I am willing to help with the project as much as you will allow.

The person who is to be honoured in this way is very important to me and I hope you will consider meeting to discuss this further.

Anna Mason.

When no reply was forthcoming in the next week, Anna decided to start another search for a likely artist. She visited a downtown Artists' Cooperative Gallery and viewed the paintings there, looking for ideas. Strangely, there were no portraits on display. The majority of the work consisted of what she termed 'modern art' with angular forms and colours unsuited to a portrayal of the human body. She left without feeling she had accomplished anything at all and also feeling somewhat annoyed that the Drake woman, her most promising lead so far, had let her down.

As she drove into the driveway of the condo complex, Anna was surprised to see a young man with a bicycle standing near her front door. She quickly surmised he was not a Mormon or Jehovah's Witness as his clothes were very casual in style, but what he could be doing at her home was difficult to guess.

Perhaps it had something to do with Alina? She was always on the lookout for new skilled workers and this man may have mistaken their home address for the warehouse offices on the Wonderland Industrial Estate where interviews were usually held.

She turned off the engine and walked slowly around the car still watching the figure who did not turn toward her but waited patiently, holding his cycle.

An old instinct, born of the fear of stranger danger, made Anna observe his appearance more closely as she approached. A strong nose under sandy eyebrows; long hair tied back allowing his large ears to peek out from a dark baseball cap; a padded, black nylon jacket and faded jeans with a wet patch near the seat showing he had been cycling during a recent rain shower.

Confident she could now describe the man to the police, if required, Anna challenged his attention so she could see the expression in his eyes and determine if he had evildoing in mind.

Despite this precaution, her polite manners asserted themselves as she called out, "May I help you?"

"Uh, I am looking for Anna Mason? Do you know if she lives here?"

Anna was astonished to be caught in the gaze of a pair of extraordinary pale gold eyes. She stuttered in surprise. "I am she ... ... I mean I live here. Was I expecting you?"

"Probably not. I wasn't going to come but changed my mind at the last minute and now here I am on your doorstep."

Anna was feeling more confused by the minute. Who was this brash young man and why was he here?

Her tone revealed a growing anger as she responded with, "Well, now you *are* here, what is your name, and what is your business?"

"Drake Design is my business," he answered quietly.

Anna was no further forward after this information.

"But why are you here?" she insisted.

"You contacted me about some art work you wanted?"

The name suddenly clicked in Anna's memory. Drake was the last name of the woman painter. Her first name was Lawren. Was this some partner of hers? What was going on here?

"Look, we can't stand here all afternoon. You had better come inside till we sort this out. Leave your bicycle in the driveway. It will be safe there."

She quickly turned the key and opened the door leading the way inside and taking off her coat at the same time. She looked at herself in the mirror over the hall table that held keys and messages and saw a flush on her cheeks that had nothing to do with the temperature outside.

How frustrating this encounter was proving to be! The sooner she could work out the mistake and get rid of the man, the better she would feel. She stood by the open door as he came back to the front of the house.

He removed his cap and ran his fingers through the tousled front locks of his fairish hair. Without being asked, he bent down and removed his boots, placing them neatly under the hall table.

Anna hoped he would not be staying long enough to justify this gesture. She decided to take the offensive.

"I did contact an artist by the name of Lawren Drake for a commission but I have not heard from her. Is there some mistake here?"

"Not really. You are looking at Lawren Drake."

Anna's impatience vanished as she realized her error. She had assumed the name Lawren belonged to a female, not this incommunicative man standing before her in his stocking feet. The mistake was all hers.

"You had better come into the kitchen. I am in need of a cup of tea while I reset my brains. Can I offer you something *Mr*. Drake?"

"Just Lawren, please, but I will take some tea if you are making it."

The routine of making tea allowed Anna some time to gather her thoughts. She was wondering how to politely dispose of the man as she could not see him being sympathetic to her needs with regard to the tricky business of the portrait. She might, however, have insulted him with her assumptions and a chat over tea would compensate for that and allow her to bid him farewell as soon as possible. What Alina would say if she came home and found this strange man in her kitchen, did not bear thinking about. She would probably call the police before Anna had a chance to explain anything at all.

As Anna busied herself with cups and spoons and enquired as to his preferences for milk and sugar, she noticed the stranger's attention was not on his replies but rather on the kitchen and dining room which he seemed to be studying intently. The thought that he might be 'casing the joint' occurred briefly, but she banished that thought from her head. There was nothing immensely valuable visible in his view and should he pounce at her, heaven forbid, she had a selection of heavy cooking utensils immediately to hand.

Clearing her throat to summon back his attention, she placed the tea tray in the centre of the glass table and prepared to listen to the reason why this man had such a confusing name.

"My father was always interesting in art and artists. He was only a hobby painter who admired real artists, especially The Group of Seven. He named me after Lawren Harris in the hope that the name would influence me to paint the great Canadian landscape."

"Did it work?"

"Sadly, no!" He chuckled remorsefully. "He has never reconciled himself to the fact that I prefer the human landscape to the great outdoors."

"Your father must surely be pleased you did pursue art?"

"I doubt that. He hoped I would be more successful and, clearly, I am not."

Anna was beginning to find this personal conversation somewhat embarrassing so she moved on to the issue that concerned her.

"Are you at all interested in my project, Lawren?"

He turned his intent gaze from the depth of his tea cup onto Anna's face and she was startled to see the strange colour of his eyes darken to a deep gold hue as he considered the question. For a moment she wondered what age this fellow might be. There was something neither young nor old in his face.

"I am not sure. I need to get a better sense of your intention here. A portrait is a very subjective thing and a painting of a dead person can only show the surface and that is never satisfactory for an artist." Anna looked away from his penetrating eyes and responded reluctantly. "I am willing to try to provide some background for you, but I must confess that I have not ever met the relative whose portrait I wanted you to paint."

This information seemed to have settled the doubt in Lawren Drake's mind. He rose quickly and brushed his hands together as if discarding the entire prospect.

"I can't honestly take on this assignment when there is little hope of producing something either one of us would find adequate."

Anna saw all hope vanishing of ever completing the idea of honouring Helen Dunlop in this way. She stood to lead him out and simultaneously discarded the thought of protesting the artist's decision.

He appeared to have some integrity about his work and in a way it was too bad he was not interested. Anna got the sense he would have done a better-than-average job of it, if he had been willing to try.

"I am sorry to have wasted your time," she said, as she fetched his jacket from the closet.

He turned on his heel as soon as he thrust his feet back into his boots and, without replying, grasped the door handle as if to leave. Then, unexpectedly, he straightened up and became very still.

Anna drew breath and watched, curious to know what he might be thinking.

"Don't give up!" he declared, and quickly ran out into the rain without another word of explanation.

Anna closed the door and leaned against it for a moment.

"How strange!" she wondered aloud.

Dismissing the entire encounter, she walked back into the kitchen to clear away the dishes before Alina arrived home from the warehouse. There would be something unusual to discuss over their meal tonight she concluded with a rueful shrug of her shoulders.

Four

Alina arrived home with a video she had picked up from Rogers. As it was an Oscar winner, the two women decided to have a quick meal, make popcorn in the microwave, and settle down to enjoy the film.

By the end of it, both were pleasantly tired and after some desultory discussion about the movie's characters, they headed for their respective bedrooms. When Anna was almost asleep she remembered the conversation with Lawren Drake that she had meant to tell Alina about. She rolled over in bed and drew the covers up to her neck thinking she would try to find out more about the strange artist before she ventured to reveal to Alina what had been said and done in the house earlier that day.

In the light of day, Anna wondered what she had been thinking. The chance of ever seeing the man again was minimal at best. Why should she care to know more about him? She should be spending time on a new search for a more congenial artist.

She went about the daily household tasks and planned to check on the A Plus website later in the day to see if more orders had arrived from a store in the States that was taking a keen interest in their hand-crafted knitwear.

Alina was having a rest day. She rose late and shuffled around the kitchen in her robe and slippers while surveying a huge pile of recent magazines and newspaper supplements. It was her assigned task to keep up to date with fashion trends in knitwear and she had one of these catch-up days every two or three weeks. Her scissors, scrapbook and magnifying glass were set out on the dining room table and Anna knew not to interrupt until the job was done.

As silence settled over the house, Anna found herself drawn to the computer in the living room. She thought it would do no harm to investigate Drake Designs on Google. It would be one sure way to find out if such a person as Lawren Drake actually existed and might help to explain his remote attitude.

Two seconds after typing in the name of his business, Anna was startled to see a page of entries appear, including one for a website. Leaving the latter aside for now, she accessed the business logo and found the picture of a sign and an address in London. The location looked to be near the University in north London and the sign hung in front of a Victorian home. Beneath the Drake Designs lettering was a sketch of a mallard duck with a paintbrush in its mouth.

Anna was more surprised to see this illustration than anything else she had found. The whimsical nature seemed totally at odds with the man she had met. No evidence of humour had revealed itself to her during their brief encounter. Had she misinterpreted his nature? And if so, had she done something to discourage him from accepting the assignment?

As doubt flooded through her she decided to check out the website and see if any examples of his work were displayed there. This might give her an idea of the quality he produced and determine whether or not she would pursue the matter further.

The website revealed a brief biographical note and only three samples of work. There was a painting of a prominent London politician, a family portrait with two children and their parents, and a formal study of an older gentleman seated on an elaborate armchair. The caption under this painting caught Anna's attention. The name of the gentleman's company was familiar. It took a moment's concentration then Anna knew why she had recognized the name. This was the legal firm where her friend Susan had worked for many years.

Anna immediately called Susan to ask for more information. Fortunately, she was at home and answered on the second ring.

"Susan, it's Anna, I have a strange request for you. Do you remember seeing a painting in your old offices of an elderly gentleman sitting on an armchair?"

"Well, hello to you too, Anna!" she replied, with a touch of sarcasm.

"Oh, my apologies, Susan! You are quite right. That was not the most polite enquiry I ever made. May I start again?"

"Don't bother, my dear. I am only teasing. What has got you in such a rush? It must be something important surely?"

"Truth is I don't know if it is important yet. I am investigating a local artist who might be a candidate for an oil painting I have in mind for the Oban house and I noticed he had done some work for your legal firm. I need to see his work up close to get a better idea of his potential."

"Sounds serious, Anna!"

"Not really; just urgent. I need to get this started if it is to be completed before I return to Scotland."

"I see." There was a pause on the phone line and Anna could imagine her friend deliberating in her conscientious way. "Well, there used to be a series of portraits of the firm's partners in the boardroom upstairs. I can't tell which of them you are describing but if you send me the name and the artist's name, I can ask if it is still there. Would you like me to request a viewing when the room is unoccupied?"

"That would be perfect, Susan. Thank you so much."

"Don't thank me yet. I have to contact the right people first. Send me the names. Don't give up. I'll get back to you as soon as I can." Anna had put down the phone when she realized that Susan had used the exact same phrase as Lawren Drake.

Don't give up.

She was no closer to understanding what he had meant by it, but at least in Susan's case she knew there was a good chance that some information would be forthcoming.

How long would it take?

What could she do in the meantime to speed things along?

As soon as she had sent off an e mail to Susan with the two names she had requested, Anna took a deep breath and examined her feelings.

What was this urgency she was caught up in? Was it the mystery of the artist himself? He was certainly an unusual type. Perhaps that was because she had never had any previous contact with artists?

Was the anxiety to pursue more about Lawren Drake only a reflection of her need to complete the painting idea that had seemed such a perfect addition to Aunt Helen's house? Or was it something else entirely?

"I am just going around in circles, here," she mumbled angrily.

"What's that?"

Anna had not realized she had spoken aloud and disturbed Alina. "Sorry! It's nothing!"

And it should be nothing, she decided. She was just about to return to the computer when the phone rang.

"I'll get it!" she called out.

Susan's voice cut into Anna's negative thoughts and restored her interest in an instant.

"Look, Anna, I don't know how much time you have today but I think we are in luck. I just talked to the woman who took over my place as legal secretary and she says the lawyers are at a one-day conference in the courthouse and the place is empty. She says the portraits are still there and none has ever been removed from the boardroom as far as she knows. If you can come now, we can spend as much time there as you want. Margaret will let us in before she goes out for lunch and I can close up when we leave."

Anna was too stunned to reply at first.

"Well?" Susan insisted.

"Right! I am on my way, Susan. You really do work fast. I'll be at your door in 15 minutes."

The drive took only ten minutes. Anna tried to concentrate on the road but she barely remembered any of it, her head was in such a spin from the rapid speed of events. Was she rushing headlong into something or would the sight of this portrait settle the whole issue? Susan's car was waiting in her driveway with the engine running, so Anna automatically parked to one side and got out to see what Susan had planned.

"I'll drive," she announced succinctly. "I know where to park."

It was soon evident that Susan knew the shortcuts to her old office in the centre of town. She pulled into the parking lot and chose a spot close to the side entrance where Margaret was waiting. They exchanged hugs and greetings then Margaret left for a lunch date and Susan led the way upstairs to the boardroom.

"This is very good of you, Susan," Anna whispered. "I hope I haven't wasted your time with this."

"Not at all! Any excuse to get back here and see what has changed is a bonus for me!"

Susan grinned as she opened a double door with a flourish and revealed a large room with windows facing the street. It was furnished with an impressive polished wood table and matching chairs but Anna immediately looked at the paintings arranged on the left wall and between the windows.

"Which one is it?" she asked.

"He is one of the founding partners of the firm so it's over here on the left."

Anna followed Susan and they stopped in front of a large painting in an elaborate frame which matched those of the other portraits.

At first she could not distinguish anything remarkable about the elderly gentleman with his dark suit and tie over a white shirt, sitting at ease in the armchair which obviously was the same one Anna had just seen at the head of the table.

When she began to concentrate on the features, however, she was astonished to discover a wave of emotions welling up in her. What was happening? She had no connection to this man at all and yet she was feeling as if she knew him in some way. It must be the skill of the artist to evoke such a reaction.

It was all in the eyes, she thought. There was an expression there that drew the observer into a conspiracy of affection. There was a hint of laughter in these eyes and the sense that this man of power and prestige had, nonetheless, the ability to look at life in a more humorous way than his profession of   lawyer might lead one to expect.

Anna took a step back and noticed the signature on the right side, close to the portrait's frame.

It was the work of Lawren Drake all right, and it was remarkable. Susan had been sitting at the boardroom table watching Anna's reactions.

"Well, what do you think?"

"I think it is good work, as far as I can tell, of course."

"I can add something to your opinion, I believe, if you want to know more."

"Of course, I do. What do you mean, Susan?"

"When I started here, Mr. Tomlinson was the first lawyer to request my services. He was working on a computer program to codify the firm's client base and he was less than proficient with the technology. He wanted someone who could devote attention to the process and report back to him at regular intervals maintaining complete secrecy at all stages."

"So you had quite a lot of contact with the gentleman, Susan?"

"Yes, I did and gentleman is the correct term to describe him. He has retired now, of course, but he was the most charming and pleasant person I have ever worked for. He still sends me a Christmas card each year and reminds me of the hours I devoted to the project."

Anna had to ask. "Did he happen to have a good sense of humour?"

"So you caught that! I wondered if you would. Indeed, he was quite a joker at times. He would leave a cartoon on my desk some mornings and ask me about it later in the day. I kept an album of the cartoons as they were always about lawyers and politicians, the majority of our clients in those days."

Anna's opinion of Lawren Drake's skill was confirmed by Susan's comments. She thought to ask another question. "Did you see the artist while the painting was done?"

"No, I had left the firm by then."

Anna knew Susan had been retired for several years. She began to wonder at what age Lawren Drake had completed the commission. This drew her back to the portrait and a plaque on the wall which named the chairman, the dates and the artist. It appeared the portrait was done some ten years before.

"But, that can't be right!" she blurted out. "He couldn't have done this work so long ago."

"What do you mean?"

"It's just that there must be some mistake. The Lawren Drake I met would have been a very young man at the time this was done. The artistry I see here would require years of study to achieve this standard."

"Oh! Did his father paint perhaps?"

"No, no! Nothing, like artwork at this level, in any case. Lawren described him as 'a hobby painter'."

"Well then, what age is the man you met, Anna?"

She stopped to consider her answer. "I really don't know, Susan. He was hard to judge. He was dressed like a hippy, if you know what I mean; simple clothes, long hair and with very casual manners. I thought he was quite small until I took off my heeled boots and found we were the same height. I couldn't tell much from his conversation. We were together only a short time and he left without making a commitment to the project."

"But that doesn't tell me how old you thought he was. What did his face tell you about his age?"

Susan was becoming exasperated with Anna's lack of detail about this man she had gone to the trouble of pursuing further.

"I don't know! He had that smooth kind of look some men have. I suppose I thought he was much younger. Men don't seem to develop the wrinkles we get. Maybe his painting work gave him the satisfaction that makes a person look mellow."

"Well, let's see what we can derive from the plaque here. We'll presume an artist can't do work like this until his late forties at the earliest. Now add to the date and we can assume this Lawren must be close to sixty? Is that possible?"

"Good grief! I am so shocked! I never imagined he was that age!"

"Oh, I could be quite wrong. You can find out when you meet him again, Anna."

"*If* I meet him again. He didn't want to risk a commission when he had no hope of sitting with a live subject and now I can see why. Obviously, a great deal depends on the sense the artist gets about the personality of his subject. I can't provide that input. He would probably fear damaging his reputation by producing work of an inferior standard."

"Possibly! Only time will tell. Don't give up yet, Anna. Didn't your mother always say, 'If it's meant to be, it will be'?"

Anna laughed. "What she actually said was, 'If it's for ye, it'll no go by ye,' but you certainly have the meaning right, Susan."

With that, the two friends exited from the boardroom and descended the stairs. Susan had a good look around at the various offices she passed and stood by Margaret's desk for a minute.

"Huh! I told them this was a better position for the reception area desk. I'm glad to see someone paid attention, eventually."

Anna stopped for ten minutes or so at Susan's house on the way home. She greeted the two Labradors and spoke for a while with Jake who was finishing his daily exercises with a weighted medicine ball.

"It's great to see you looking so well, Jake," she enthused. "How are you feeling this spring?"

"Thanks to you, Anna, I have Angela to support me in my new routine. We talk often and she demonstrates technique for me on an internet link. I'm holding my own for now and glad to be able to say that."

He walked carefully over to Susan with only a stick for balance, and gave his wife a lopsided smile.

"What have you two been cooking up now?"

"Oh, Jake, you know us too well!" Anna said jokingly. "I'll let Susan explain it all to you. She's helped me out again as she always does."

"Yes," agreed Jake. "She does seem to have that helping gene firmly in her DNA, as I can attest."

Anna left them in the kitchen and let herself out of the front door. They hardly noticed her absence and Anna wondered for a moment what it must be like to be devoted to a partner in such a way that, no matter what life threw at either of you, one could always rely on the other.

Strangely, this thought made her think of Richard. Since their meeting in Egypt she had not had any contact with him. How had he coped with another round of chemo? Was he still with his Egyptian wife in Ottawa? She realized she had no way to answer these questions and wondered if she would ever find out. If Richard did not choose to get in touch with her she might never know.

On the drive home she decided to put aside all questions and concerns for now. She was not exactly giving up, it was just that she needed a break from the uncertainties.

"What's meant for me, will not pass me by," she repeated cheerfully, as she watched the streetlights come on, signalling the end of the eventful afternoon.

Five

"Mum, I've got your tickets ready. Dad asked me to tell you to collect them for him. He's got some meeting with the university administration tonight. Can you make it into town? We could have supper together if you want."

"Sarah, what a lovely idea! Could we go to The Peacock? I am longing for one of their steak and ale pies."

Sarah laughed at her mother's enthusiasm. "I don't see why not. Pick me up at six and we'll take one car."

"It's a deal!" replied Lynn. She put down the phone with a cheerful smile that made the rainy day seem a lot brighter than it had just a few minutes before when she was worrying over the imminent departure for Greece.

She decided this meal together would be an ideal time to talk things over with Sarah. Collecting the airline tickets would be the perfect excuse to discuss her misgivings about the whole topic of the Easter holiday that wasn't a holiday for her, and also Stavros' strange behaviour of late.

Perhaps I shouldn't burden Sarah about Stavros, she thought. That's hardly fair. But I do wish I had someone to talk to.

She deliberated about calling one of the women who worked with Stavros. Over the years of staff gatherings and department celebrations at the university, she had become friendly with a few of the less imposing members of staff. Most of the women professors were of the plain and earnest variety whose conversation was limited to weighty intellectual matters Lynn already heard too much about at home. But there were some, the part-time instructors, retired school teachers who made up a considerable portion of the work force, who were friendly to a professor's wife and of a similar age to herself.

Her thoughts turned inevitably to the remainder of the group she usually met at the end of term graduation parties. These women were the young and beautiful students whose very appearance demoralized Lynn. They fluttered around her husband and fell upon his every word in a way that Lynn found distressing and inappropriate. She felt invisible in their presence.

Years before, she and Stavros had had a series of arguments about the influence these young grad students had on his attitude to his wife. Stavros assured her, repeatedly, that she had nothing to worry about. He insisted the young women he taught were no match for the years of shared life experiences they had together as a couple. He admitted the attentions were flattering, but he also reminded Lynn that his work depended on maintaining a discrete distance between himself and his students. The least breath of scandal and his teaching career would be over.

This last argument convinced Lynn that she need not be concerned about the bevy of beauties who surrounded her husband for most of his teaching days. She knew only too well how hard and long he had fought for his present position as Head of Classics. Risking that, was not in his practical nature and discussing the topic with his colleagues, no matter how sympathetic, was also something she could not contemplate.

"Looks like I am on my own with this problem," she complained to her mirror, as she combed her silver hair into place and applied some lipstick and mascara. "No reason why I should look dowdy, or feel alone, when I am eating out with my darling daughter."

The 16th century Peacock Inn was not busy this early on a mid-week evening and Sarah found a table near the fire and away from the bar. They concentrated on the menu for a while then talked about the weather and Caroline and Mike's latest exploits until the delicious food arrived.

For several minutes they were too busy to talk but as soon as their appetites were satisfied by the hot food, Sarah looked up at her mother, wiped her mouth with a napkin and declared, "Now, Mum, what's on your mind?"

Lynn was startled by this declaration and immediately denied any concerns.

Sarah was not convinced.

"Look, Mum, I can see that little vein in your forehead that always pulses when you are worried about something. Fess up!"

"Oh, my dear, dear, Sarah! I *am* a bit worried. Nothing new, however, I am sure you are sick to death of listening to my complaints about the Kyriakos' clan in Greece."

Sarah reached over and patted her mother's trembling fingers. "I do know how hard it is for you to spend such a long time with Dad's people, but you must admit it is partly your own fault. You should have learned the language long ago. That alone would have endeared you to his brothers and sisters although I think you are right about the older generation's opinion. I can just hear them whispering to each other, 'She stole him away from us, the demon English woman!' "

Lynn had to laugh at her daughter's expression of mock horror. Sarah was right in many ways. Perhaps if she made more of an effort this year she could expunge some of the mistakes of the past. Then again, perhaps it really was too late now.

"Admit it, Mum! Things improved a few years back when Dad decided to shorten the holiday by taking you around to some of his favourite historical sites in Greece. Where are you both heading this year?"

Lynn knew Sarah was trying to distract her from the usual miserable complaints she endured around this time every spring. It was working to some degree and Lynn had to acknowledge it.

"Well, your father is hoping to take me back to Santorini for a few days. He wants to check on some ongoing work at Akrotiri."

"There you are!" exclaimed Sarah. "That's *your* favourite place in Greece, isn't it? Dad promised to take the whole family there one day soon."

"I know! I know! Why am I complaining when I get to tour such places with an expert archaeologist like your father at my command?"

Sarah dampened her enthusiasm when she saw her mother's true feelings in her eyes, despite those more positive words.

"Think of it this way, Mum. Things are bad in Greece this year as everyone knows. You might find the annual gathering is not so well attended as in the past and it may not last so long this time. It must be an expensive event for the family with all the accommodations and meals to arrange. "

"That's all true, Sarah," Lynn realized. "I suppose I could help out. I could contribute some spices and herbs for the feast. They often use saffron with the lamb and it is very expensive. Do you think that would be a good idea?"

"I am sure the family would be appreciative of your efforts, Mum. Attitude is everything, as Dad always says about his students. If you can think more positively about the situation, who knows what might develop? Give it a try at least. What do you say?"

Lynn responded by reaching across the dishes on their table and giving her daughter a great big hug that she hoped conveyed how much she had needed a pep talk. The worries were still there in the back of her mind, of course, but they seemed more easily dealt with now that Sarah had shared them.

Lynn gave herself a mental shake and changed the subject to more cheerful topics.

"Now, when did you say Caroline was coming back home?"

"Ah, I've been meaning to bring you up to date about that. There's exciting news. Caroline has been invited to attend the G(irls)20 Summit in Paris in June this year."

"Wait a minute, isn't that the conference for youth that takes place during the G20 when the world leaders meet? Stavros was talking about it being such a wonderful opportunity for young women.

How did she get chosen? Does her grandfather know about this?"

"She has been so active in women's rights this year at the London School of Economics. She did an entire study on the improvements that would be possible in rural areas of Africa if women farmers had access to mobile phone information about crop prices and weather conditions and things like that.

I don't pretend to understand all of it but David and I are so proud of our girl for caring for others the way she does.

As to your second question: Dad must have had some input into Caroline's decision to apply. He may have intervened for her in some way. I am not sure about that but it's just like him to do it without making a big fuss. That's not to distract in any way from Caroline's own achievements, of course."

"Indeed! I have a remarkable granddaughter and that did not happen by accident, Sarah. If you and David had not been such caring parents, Caroline would never have grown into the young woman she has become. I wish I had had such caring when I was a child. I might have been a stronger person myself. My home circumstances were quite different, as you know."

"I know you were looking after your mother at a very young age, Mum, instead of the other way around. You had no time to grow as a child before you were required to act like a grownup and then you were married and starting all over again with limited finances. I don't know how you did it!"

"I just did what I had to do, Sarah. I'm not sure all my choices were the best."

"Now, don't underestimate yourself, Mum. You were a wonderful mother to me; always there when I needed you to listen to my problems. Not like some of my friends' mothers who were working all the hours of the day while their kids ran rampant without supervision."

"Oh, I was there at home all right, Sarah, but it was because I lacked the confidence to pursue a career like Caroline will, and you have too."

"Who me? The travel industry is hardly a career to boast about. I chose to follow in your footsteps Mum, just because I knew how important it was to be available when my kids came home from school each day. You taught me that. I may not be a fancy doctor or a business expert but I will never regret the sacrifices I made for Mike and Caroline."

"Neither should you, my darling! Both of your children are a credit to you."

Lynn suddenly had an idea.

"Listen! What if you and David went to Paris in June to support Caroline and perhaps sit in on some of the debates and presentations? I would look after Mike and the house. Your father will be busy in June setting up his summer courses. He won't even notice I am gone."

"That's a brilliant idea! It's time we had a break together. It's been a tough year in many ways.

I'll look into it tomorrow and see what the possibilities are. Thank you, mother! Who else would have thought of something so unselfish?"

The meal ended on a positive note and Lynn drove home with a more optimistic attitude than she had experienced for months. It could be that this Easter would be a breakthrough for her and Stavros. She decided there and then to make a perceptible improvement in her attitude and watch for the results to come flooding in.

The Kyriakos' small house in the village of Horam was in darkness when Lynn drove along the leafy lane and into the short driveway. Stavros must be delayed at his meeting, she deduced. I'll turn on lights and fix something quick for his supper. He'll be tired and hungry when he gets home. These university meetings never seem to end happily.

Soon she was bustling around in the kitchen with the radio supplying local information interspersed with cheerful music. She started to hum along with a recording and realized it was unusual for her to do this.

"Aha!" she exclaimed, with a chuckle. "Evidence that my attitude adjustment is working, I think!"

Just then she heard the sound of her husband's car negotiating the limited space left in the driveway. Neither of them ever parked in the single garage. It was always crammed full of items that would not fit into the small closets in their two-bedroom home. That is, one bedroom and one office, home, she mentally corrected herself. Just as well we have no children living here nowadays. They would have to sleep in a tent outside, I imagine.

Stavros came straight into the kitchen and put his briefcase, laptop and coat onto the table top where Lynn had hoped to place his plate of western omelet stuffed with vegetables. She bit her tongue and stifled the complaint she would normally have delivered. This was one of her husband's thoughtless habits. No amount of house space would ever provide him with more tidy personal habits, it seemed, but she knew a complaint was no way to greet him if she wished to stay true to her resolutions.

Turning on a smile so that her voice would at least sound happier, she followed him into the lounge where he was already installed in his favourite chair with a newspaper opened up and his face obscured behind it.

"An omelet will be ready in a moment, dear," she suggested. "Would you like to have it in here tonight?"

Now this was definitely a concession. Lynn disapproved of sloppy customs such as eating in front of the television. She wondered if Stavros would notice the change. Apparently not. He simply nodded his head and continued reading.

So, the meeting did not go well, she concluded. I'll say nothing until he has eaten and had time to relax.

With this decision, Lynn fetched a bottle of red wine from the cupboard and pulled the cork very carefully. A glass of wine would smooth out the day for her husband and make the evening more sociable. She had a few announcements to make and a congenial atmosphere always helped such occasions flow more easily.

It took an hour, and the addition of his favourite apple tart with pouring custard, before Stavros appeared to relax enough to initiate conversation.

"Sorry, love! I know I've been a bit of a bear tonight."

"Usual reason?" Lynn inquired gently.

"Unfortunately! Things don't improve, and financial concerns outweigh everything these days. I wonder if it's time to call a halt to the whole teaching career?"

It was not the first time Lynn had heard this question. Previously, her husband had changed his mind when he returned to his students the next day. She knew he loved the teaching aspects of his job and felt the administration and negotiation responsibilities were a waste of his expertise. In the last decade, however, his complaints revealed that many more of what he termed 'secretarial tasks' were devolving onto his shoulders in the ever-expanding search for cost-cutting measures.

"Are you really ready for that change?" she asked, with some apprehension.

Stavros looked directly into his wife's eyes and replied in a serious tone of voice that alerted her immediately to the possibility of more than one announcement to be made this evening.

"I am closer to making the change a reality now, than I ever have been. How do you feel about that?"

Lynn was flustered. A thousand random thoughts flashed through her mind in a fraction of a second.

What would it be like to have her husband home all day, every day, when she was used to doing whatever she wanted, without interference? Where would all the books and papers from his university office go in their home?

Would he rearrange her tidy kitchen? This last male tendency was something dire she had been warned about by female neighbours whose husbands had retired.

She had to come up with a suitable response quickly. Stavros was probably already reading the uncertainty in her eyes.

"Well, it's up to you, of course. It would mean changes to our life here. What would you do with your time?"

"I would continue with my summer teaching in Greece, I think. I could write another book but this might be the chance to make a whole new life for us."

Fear coursed through Lynn's veins as she heard this pronouncement from her husband. Suddenly every small part of her daily routine acquired a rosy glow of sweet familiarity that she was in no way willing to relinquish.

"A new life…..? What do you mean?" her voice trembled but Stavros did not hesitate.

"I've been thinking about this lately. I think we should buy property in Greece and make it our permanent home."
Lynn could not stifle the sharp intake of breath that revealed how catastrophic this idea was to her.

"I…… I can't believe you have not bothered to discuss this with me first." She was relieved to hear the anger in her words. Inside she was devastated, and the trembling had transferred to her whole body.
At least through anger she could disguise the weakness she really felt as she contemplated her husband's true wishes and what they might mean for her.

"Well, I wasn't sure until recently that this is what I want to do." Stavros rushed to justify his choices.
He was shocked at his wife's reaction. Surely she could see how beneficial this move would be for him; for both of them.
Before he could begin, Lynn burst in with a cold statement even he recognized as something far removed from her usual calm manner.

"What do you mean when you say 'what *I* want to do'? I thought there were two of us in this marriage. When did you decide to make major decisions without consulting me? For heaven's sake, Stavros, you know how I feel about England and by now, even a blind man would be able to tell how uncomfortable I am in Greece!"
Lynn stood, knocking over the glass of wine in front of her, spilling the dregs which began to drip over the edge of the coffee table onto the cream rug. She stormed out of the lounge. Stavros heard her feet thumping up the stairs to their bedroom. He was aghast at his wife's extraordinary over-reaction to his news. Yet, it was clear by the way she had ignored the red wine on her new rug, that this was no storm in a teacup but a fully-fledged hurricane.
A weather system with which he feared he was unable to cope.

Six

Lynn tossed and turned all night in bed. She was alone and that was just as well, since one sight of her husband would have caused her to overflow with anger all over again.

The effects of that anger were still roiling around in her stomach. The much-anticipated steak and ale pie had congealed into a lump somewhere in her innards. She badly needed an indigestion tablet from the bathroom cabinet next door but nothing would make her risk encountering her husband in this state of mind.

She rinsed out her mouth in the washbasin of the small ensuite toilet then paced up and down from the window around the double bed and back. The movement helped her brain to organize thoughts instead of merely spraying panic around. She had to compose a rational case to dissuade Stavros from simply going ahead with his plan. If she could not impress him with the depth of her fears for the future, she could not see how they would be able to go on.

The thought of ending their marriage stopped her cold in her progress around the bedroom. What was she contemplating? Divorce? After a lifetime with this one man could she really be thinking of such a drastic step? And yet, the alternative was equally impossible for her. Give up her life here, her home and her family, for what? How could she endure an existence in what had always been, to her, a foreign land? Didn't Stavros like England after all these years here? England, where they had brought up their daughter Sarah; where their only grandchildren lived; the place where he had made a good life through the university work he loved. Why would he want to turn his back on all that and start again at their time of life?

Never had the contrast between their opposite views about life seemed so insurmountable. Lynn had often given in to Stavros' opinions when conflict arose. It was simply easier to do so. His ability to rationalize and his conviction that his ideas were much more potent than those of anyone else, had overwhelmed Lynn's wishes for years. She was the one who compromised to re-establish peace.

But this argument was different.

Into Lynn's mind came an image of herself as a warrior princess standing before the entrance to a treasure cave. In front of the princess stood a soldier in full armour but she was clad in a cloak of righteousness that could repel all invaders. She would prevail. She had to defend herself. Defeat was not an option.

"Oh, please!" she groaned. "That must have been a scene from a bad movie!"

And yet, there was a grain of truth in the medieval scenario. This time she would not give in to her husband's wishes. This time she would fight to defend her treasure; her family and her way of life.

A smirk twisted her lips. Stavros had no idea what he was about to encounter.

Stavros Kyriakos jerked suddenly and just prevented his body from falling to the floor. It was dark, and for a moment he could not remember where he was. The pain across his back soon reminded him that he had tried to sleep on the couch in the lounge. In no way was the furniture large enough to encompass his long legs and broad shoulders, as the uncomfortable aches throughout his body demonstrated. He tried to sit upright and discovered his leg was numb and something was twisted in his neck. The only solution was to roll slowly off the couch on to the rug and try to straighten out his frame.

By the time he had adjusted his body enough to sit leaning against the couch, he remembered why he was there.

"Damn it!" he murmured, as he massaged his neck muscles. "What is wrong with the woman? She never behaves like this. What did I do wrong? How could I have provoked this reaction by simply expressing a thought about our future? There must be something more going on."

He cast around in his mind for an answer. Nothing seemed to be appropriate for the situation he now faced.

He had been especially busy at work, although what he was doing was arranging things for their future; surely she could appreciate that. Perhaps he had been neglecting Lynn? It happened from time to time and often provoked strange reactions. He paused and thought back over the last month. After a minute or two, it came to him.

She's worried about Easter in Greece, of course!

With that realization Stavros felt relief. He had figured out the problem and now everything would, inevitably, return to normal. He flexed his toes and noticed the numbness had fled. He would pop into the kitchen and make a cup of tea for his wife. That would sort everything out.

When the tea was made, he arranged the cup and saucer neatly on a tray with a napkin and tea biscuits.

He considered if it was worthwhile to venture out to the garden and pick a daffodil for the tray but decided it was too early and, in any case, he had no idea where his wife kept such things as flower vases.

With a pleased smile, he tiptoed up the stairs, balancing the tray carefully so the tea would not slop over the side of the cup and spoil the effect.

He knew Lynn would not expect this treat. Their morning routines did not usually allow for such courtesies. Most often he headed off to the college early to get a start on preparations for the day ahead and frequently did not see Lynn until the evening.

Well, she would assuredly be suitably impressed by this gesture.

He gently tapped the door and waited for a response. None came.

He cleared his throat and called, "Lynn, dear, I have some tea for you."

"I'll get my own tea, thank you. That's a decision I *can* make on my own!"

Stavros pursed his lips. This was not going to be as easy as he had thought.

"Well, please come downstairs so we can talk about things. I am sorry I sprang this topic on you so suddenly. It's just that I have thought so much about the move that I assumed I had already mentioned it to you."

Lynn's feelings softened at the apologetic words. It was not often that her husband actually said 'sorry' out loud. She usually had to infer those words from his subsequent behavior.

She did not, however, bend enough to open the bedroom door. She spoke through it.

"I'll be down in five minutes. You can reheat the tea in the microwave. Remember not to put any of the good china in there!"

Her voice rose at the end of this request and Stavros took heart from the knowledge that she had been concerned about something other than his current mistakes. He turned and carefully negotiated the stairs. Everything will be all right now, he reassured himself.

Lynn took the time to dress carefully in an outfit she knew her husband admired. She brushed her silvery hair forward over the basin, to build some body, then smoother the top layer until it framed her brown eyes and disguised the network of laugh lines, as Caroline called them. Wetting her fingertips after she removed the loose hair from the basin, she whisked them over her brown eyebrows where she noticed some grey hairs had taken up residence. A new trick she had learned, was to make sure the ends of her brows pointed upwards. According to the TV makeover experts this lifted the face and gave a lighter look overall. She took another speculative look at her face and decided a better disguise was required for her blotchy complexion. She did not intend to let her husband see the effects of an hour or two of sobbing into her pillow. A quick application of a moisturizing foundation and a subtle new lipstick soon brought a fresher look. Her eyelashes just needed a layer of dark mascara then she was as ready as it was possible to be, under the circumstances. Men used to prepare for battle with helmet, armour and weapons, she thought. Women have more discrete ways of fighting their battles, perhaps, but I feel more empowered when I know I look my best.

Entering the kitchen as quietly as she could, Lynn noticed her husband's shoulders were hunched as he nursed the cup of tea he had re-heated for her.

Good, she thought. He looks vulnerable. I will need all the advantages I can muster.

"Oh, there you are! I was beginning to worry. I should heat this tea again for you."

"No, don't bother. I'll make a fresh pot later. We need to talk."

"Exactly!" Stavros responded, hopefully. "I am sure we can sort this out once you hear all my plans.

It's a beautiful site near the sea and you can be a part of every development of the house so it suits you completely."

Once again, Lynn was overwhelmed by the realization of how many decisions her husband had already made without consulting her. She felt the anger rising in her chest and took several deep breaths to quell the emotion that threatened to bring tears. She turned away and glanced out of the kitchen window until she had mastered her feelings.

"I am afraid you are just making the situation worse for me, Stavros. You have wasted both time and effort with all the plans you made that excluded me. Listen to me now!" She waited until she had his full attention.

"I have no intention of leaving England to live in Greece." Having dropped this bombshell, Lynn reverted to her customary wifely manner and pointed out that Stavros was going to be late for his morning grad session. She was gratified to observe that her husband's mouth had fallen open in shock and he could not summon a response to her abrupt and definitive statement.

Giving her a decidedly strange look, he left the kitchen and she could hear him collecting jacket, shoes and briefcase before exiting the house. Not another word was exchanged.

"That will give him something to think about today, besides teaching," she proclaimed to the couch in the lounge, where the rumpled blanket and twisted pillows attested to an uncomfortable night.

Just then she saw the wine stain on the rug and moved swiftly into action. She knew how to deal with a variety of stains and this housework activity would give her some respite from the worry swirling around in her brain.

She had thrown down the gauntlet in this battle of wills but what her husband's reaction would be was, as yet, an unknown quantity.

Stavros found the familiar drive to the Eastbourne motorway difficult for some reason. He usually completed the drive on automatic pilot and hardly noticed the weather or the other drivers. This morning he seemed to have difficulty matching speed on the fast lanes and was alarmed to be honked at by a car behind him. This cleared his mind a bit and he approached the traffic lights at Polegate with a better focus. As he waited for a green light, he had a moment to assemble his thoughts about the morning's disclosure. What had come over Lynn, was the predominant question. He was not accustomed to his wife debating his decisions in this way and the result was unsettling, to say the least.

Could she be serious? The implication in her final statement was that she would stay in England when he left for Greece. If she went through with the threat, and Stavros could hardly conceive of such a thing, the entire project would be futile. He could not spend his retirement pension on building a house for his wife if she was never going to share it with him. The vision he had of his happy future in his old homeland began to crumble at the edges. Something drastic would have to be done, and soon, if this disastrous situation was to be resolved. They were due to depart for Athens in a few days to meet the family on Paros. Another jolt passed through his body as he contemplated the possibility that Lynn might not join him for the Easter celebration this year.

What was he going to do about Lynn?

As the lights changed, the car surged forward and Stavros simultaneously stowed the issue, and all attending questions, in the back of his mind. It would have to wait until later. There was another disturbing item on his agenda which required his entire attention this morning.

What was he going to do about Pauline?

Seven

Anna Mason realized she was not having much success in her hunt for an artist to paint a portrait of Aunt Helen.

Had she not felt so strongly about it, she would long since have given up the search.

The trouble was, she could already visualize the finished effect, to the point where she could see the framed painting as it would appear, mounted on the fireplace wall in the big double bedroom upstairs where the morning light would illuminate the face of the woman she fervently wished she had met in life. The idea had seemed so perfect that she hated to let it go, but now weeks had gone by and no artist had emerged to satisfy her need.

Recent events had shortened the available time before the next trip to Oban. Fiona had sent an engraved invitation for Anna and Alina to attend her graduation ceremony in Inverness. The date was the beginning of June and there was no way Anna would miss this milestone in Fiona's career.

There were also two more pressing occasions to be marked in the same month. George and Jeanette's new baby daughter was to be christened and Jeanette had requested a Canadian presence in Oban since her own mother could not be there.

The other item was not really any of Anna's concern. Her brother, Philip, and her best friend and business partner, Alina, had been in contact through the winter. Phone calls, Skype and e mails were, no doubt, helpful in establishing some basis for a relationship but Alina felt the time had come for a face-to-face meeting on Philip's home ground.

As Alina had said, just the evening before, when this topic of conversation had occurred for the fifteenth time,

"Let's be frank about this, Anna, I hardly know the man. If, and it's a big IF, I want to take the connection further, I need to see how Philip lives and works in Manchester.

It is possible that we will discover we have little in common, other than you, Anna, and I am not about to make a mistake at this late stage in my life by getting involved with a man who does not suit me."

Anna was astounded to hear this amount of interest from her friend. From childhood on, Alina had expressed little inclination toward the opposite sex. There were a few dances when Richard and Anna made a foursome with Alina and some eligible young man of their acquaintance, but none of these dates had developed into a romance. Of course, Alina had been scared off men by a frightening attack when she was still a teenager. After that, she seemed content to stay home with her mother and only ventured out with Anna to places where she felt comfortable.

That was a long, long time ago, thought Anna. I truly believed Alina was a confirmed loner when it comes to romance. Yet, she might have said the same of her brother Philip. Not that she knew him that well, or for long enough to justify her opinion. It was just that he seemed ill-at-ease with women, in general. Perhaps, in his profession he dealt mainly with male clients.

Anna had met his sister, Lynn, when Anna and Philip had driven together from Oban in Scotland to Heathfield in East Sussex. Lynn had asked Philip to return to see their mother before she died.

In a brief conversation that day, Lynn confided a little about Philip's childhood. He had left home very early to apprentice to a construction company in Manchester. The shocking part of the story was that he had cut himself off entirely from his sister and his parents.

Anna now knew more about the reason for this estrangement. Philip was the illegitimate son of Anna's own father, Angus. Philip had been adopted by Kyle Purdy and never told about his origins. Lynn suspected that the shock of discovering his parents' deception had caused him to reject his mother and her husband, despite the fact that Kyle Purdy had been a true, caring father to him.

It was not difficult to see that Lynn resented the responsibilities Philip's decision had left for her to deal with.

Alina knew all this about Philip, of course, but she told Anna it was all water under the bridge by now and neither of them had reached their sixties without considerable baggage, including health problems.

"It could never be 'love's young dream' at this stage in our lives, Anna!" she asserted. "I am a lot more realistic than that. I don't need a man. My life is complete with you and our business and our Samba friends. Philip may be another friend in my life and I am happy if that is what happens. After all, he is in your life now, and forever. That makes him a part of my life too."

Anna had replied, "So, why would you want to take the step of travelling to England to see Philip?"

Alina took a moment to think about her response then smiled and said, "I guess I just want to be sure I am not missing out on something that could be beneficial for both of us….and Philip, too! He needs a female influence in his life, I suspect. In any case, he has agreed to meet me the next time we go to Scotland and I am pleased about it because you will be there in Oban if I should need to cut the visit short and flee back to Scotland."

"Aha! Hedging your bets, my dear!" laughed Anna.

"Well, certainly I am, and not ashamed to admit it! I may be old but I am not stupid. Living this long confers *some* wisdom. I don't wish to be trapped in a hotel in Manchester if things don't go well with Philip." Anna could only agree with her friend's caution and the conversation had turned to other topics.

Remembering this exchange, Anna felt increasing frustration. There was not much time between Easter and the beginning of June. Everything seemed to be falling into place for the desired trip to the U.K. except the business of the portrait.

Well, it looks like I will just have to abandon the whole idea, she sighed. Not the right time; and definitely not a suitable person on the horizon.

The phone message came a week after Anna had given up the whole idea of Helen's portrait. She had heard the phone ring when she was sending pictures to the A Plus' Oban knitting team. The process of attaching photos to a descriptive e mail was not yet so easy for her that she could afford to drop it in the middle of the operation, so she let the answer phone take a message.

Alina was at the warehouse doing the quarterly inventory with the business manager she was training to take over the complex job for her. Should her eyesight deteriorate, she wanted to be sure all aspects of the business were covered.

Anna admired this forethought and planned to help as much as possible. Hence, the e mail contact with Scotland. Alina had spotted a new trend towards knitted tuques on her last foray through the fashion magazines and she wanted to see if the Scottish knitters could do fairisle versions and devise other patterns to make the A Plus hats desirable to a new generation.

Anna's input to this idea was to suggest that the edge of the tuques, where the knitted border touched the wearer's forehead, should be lined with cashmere, or a soft cotton. She well remembered her childhood knitted caps causing skin irritation whenever she had worn them for a few hours.

Eventually, Anna had transferred all this information to e mail and she sat back with the contented sigh of a job well done. She stretched, then walked to the kitchen and contemplated which vegetables were available for a pasta supper dish. The flashing red button on the wall phone attracted her attention and she remembered the phone message she had missed.

Picking up the pen and writing pad by the phone, she pressed the button and prepared to take notes but she soon changed her mind when the strange message began to unroll.

"Look! I know this is a bit crazy, but I have been dreaming about out last conversation and I can't get on with my work until I settle this problem.

Would you mind coming to my studio this week? I have an idea that might work but it's kind of far out and you may not want to pursue it. I apologize if this is a bit disjointed.

You couldn't know this about me, of course, but I am slightly psychic.

Don't be alarmed, Miss Mason! I am sane most of the time! It's just that I got some weird vibes from your home and I can't seem to get it out of my mind.

Sorry if this sounds garbled. I am working on instinct here.

Please call my number. If you decide not to, I will totally understand."

The message ended and Anna immediately played it over again, hardly trusting her memory to grasp the details. What on earth did this mean? Did the caller realize he had not even given his name? Did he expect Anna to remember him from a brief encounter weeks before? And yet, she did recognize that quiet voice. It could only be

Lawren Drake. His phone message was similar to his face-to face speech, in as much as he gave little detail and expected the listener to follow along.

Anna did not know whether to be intrigued or annoyed by his presumption. What should she do, if anything? That was the strangest phone message she had ever received.

Alina's voice broke into Anna's confused thoughts at this juncture.

"Hello! I'm back, and there's lots to tell you, Anna. How did you get on with the e mails?"

Anna tried to bring her mind back to the present situation but when Alina entered the kitchen rubbing her hands together and complaining of a chill spring breeze outside, it took only a moment for her to assess the distracted look on her friend's face.

"What's happened, Anna? Who's hurt or in trouble?"

"It's nothing! Really! I just had a very strange phone message. Sit down and I'll play it for you. I have no idea what to do about it."

"Well. You have certainly got me interested already. I won't ask anything until I hear for myself."

By the time the message had replayed, Alina was giving every evidence of feeling just as confused as Anna.

"Who was that? What is he talking about?"

"Oh, I didn't remember that you never met the artist I interviewed here some weeks ago."

"So, it's that painter fellow? What was his name again; something about a bird?"

"Yes, it's Lawren Drake. I told you that Susan and I went to her former offices to see a sample of his portrait work but he was sure he could do nothing without a live subject to work with and I can't supply that of course. I have given up on the whole project."

"Do you mean this call came out of the blue?"

"Absolutely! I am stunned to hear from him again. Do you think I should do as he asked and go to his studio?"

"I have no idea, Anna. It's your decision, but I caution you about getting involved with someone who declares himself to be 'somewhat psychic'. What on earth does that mean? How did he behave while he was here?"

Anna had to stop and think about Lawren Drake's manner when he visited the house. He had stayed such a brief time. Was there anything weird in his behaviour?

"I didn't really notice anything. He spoke very little and only looked at me once or twice. He had eyes of a peculiar colour; almost golden, I would say, and they darkened when he was thinking."

Alina began to sense something unusual in her friend's description of this artist. "But what did he do, Anna? You are telling me how he looked while he was here. Did he do anything spooky?"

Anna laughed. "Spooky? No, I think I would have noticed that! He did look around the room quite intently. I remember wondering at one point if he was considering burglary."

"What? That's enough for me! It's best to ignore the entire thing, Anna. You don't want to get mixed up with some man who makes you feel unsafe in your own home."

Anna had to agree with Alina's sensible conclusion. She changed the subject by asking Alina to explain what had transpired at the warehouse and soon they were discussing the success of employing a female manager.

"She just multi tasks so much better than a man could," Alina said. "She has a good grasp of the need to keep a ready supply of inventory tied to seasonal demand. For example, if the knitted tuque idea works out, we need to have supplies in the warehouse before fall this year to meet anticipated demand in winter and for the Christmas market."

"Yes, I understand the principle, Alina, yet it always worries me that we might be left with piles of goods no one wants."

"That's the name of the game in retail, Anna. Our advantage is the wide range of customers we reach online. Anyone in the western hemisphere who remembers cosy knitted hats and wants to buy one for family or friends could make this idea a winner for us. So far we haven't lost money on new products and the site is growing in design and creativity thanks to James' skills."

"You are right, my dear. You are the expert in this area as your choices have proved.

Now, what idea do you have for supper? Shall we throw together a pasta or order out tonight?"

This weighty decision required consulting a folder full of take-out menus and discussing the virtues of vegetarian versus simply decadent choices.

The topic of Lawren Drake's phone message, slipped to the back of Anna's mind but it was not forgotten and much later in the night it returned with some force.

Anna awakened with a start and sat up in bed. Her heart was racing. Was there an intruder in the house? Had a noise woken her from a deep dream state?

She rubbed the sleep from her eyes and turned on a bedside lamp. Her ears were alert to any unusual sounds but she could detect only the dim hum of the heating system. False alarm, then.

She turned out the lamp and turned over in bed after a quick glance at the clock showed it was very early in the morning.

She soon discovered that not only her ears and eyes had been woken up, her brain also was firing on all cylinders.

"Drat!" she moaned with clenched teeth. It was clear she was not going back to sleep any time soon. Propping up her pillow and pulling the bedcovers up to her neck, Anna resigned herself to an hour or more of night thoughts. This was a familiar pattern. Too many things to think about always resulted in wakeful nights. The trouble was not the extra thinking time. In the quiet hours that was a bonus. The problem arose from the propensity of the mind to think only dark thoughts in the dark hours. It was rare to come to a positive conclusion from such musings but Anna knew she had to complete the cycle before blessed oblivion would be returned.

So what was on her mind? She cast aside all the domestic trivia that first presented themselves, leaving the trip to Scotland in the forefront. Certainly there were a few items to be done in preparation; gifts for Fiona and the new baby girl, for example. No problems there. Alina would find something exquisite for the baby and something suitable for her brother, Liam. It was always best to present two children's gifts at such times. Fiona would be given a substantial cheque along with a beautiful bouquet. Anna made a mental note to ensure a photographer was available to take pictures and video of the graduation ceremony. She would wear a new summer outfit from Maria's shop for the occasion.

There, now! She sighed deeply. Everything is in order. I can sleep. Minutes went by and again sleep eluded her. What next?

The phone message from Lawren Drake popped into her mind.

"Of course! I should have known *that* was going to haunt me. What do I do about it? I need to make a decision if I want to get any more sleep tonight.

Go to his studio and see what happens? Forget the whole thing and admit the idea was hopeless right from the start?

Once again the vision of the fine portrait of Helen Dunlop, hanging over the mantle in the McCaig Estate Farmhouse, rose before Anna's eyes. Deep down she was unwilling to give up on the idea. It had seemed such an appropriate thing to do. It was meant to be something to honour not only Aunt Helen, but also Anna's own mother.

Was it possible to take a chance on the strange young man? What if Alina was right and he was more than strange and less than sensible? Anna gave herself a mental shake. She was no giddy girl. She could take a chance if she wished, and if it did not work out she could withdraw. After all, a little psychic ability was probably a good thing in a creative person and if the portrait was ever to be completed it would require more than a little creativity on the part of the artist, and on her own part, if she was to provide any clear idea of who Helen was.

A surge of fatigue washed over Anna when she made this decision. I will go ahead, she promised herself, as sweet darkness filled her mind and slumber overcame her.

Eight

Lawren Drake received the phone call from Anna Mason and made an appointment to see her at his studio on the same day. He had nothing pressing on his agenda with a small commission almost finished and a couple of commercial projects to start as soon as he worked out the ideas. These were merely bread-and butter assignments that paid the rent on his studio and living quarters in the attic apartment. His true art was in portraits but who wanted a formal portrait these days?

His father's words returned unbidden. "You will never make any money with portraits, Lawren. You were meant to follow in the footsteps of your namesake and capture the grandeur of the Canadian wilderness."

Lawren smiled ruefully whenever he thought of these words. Unfortunately for his father's ambitions, Lawren hated camping, hiking and all forms of outdoor wandering in places inaccessible by bicycle.

His father had once admitted, in a moment of weakness, that there was a genetic link to a family ancestor in England who had been a famous painter of his wealthy patrons generations ago.

Lawren felt this information justified his own choices and he had refused to listen to his father's complaints thereafter.

Looking around the studio, he realized it might not be the most impressive place in which to receive possible clients. There were canvasses against the walls and tubes of paint on every surface competing for space with jars of water sprouting brushes in a variety of sizes.

Not much I can do about this, he summarized. My tiny, private quarters are in a worse state; unlikely to provide a good first impression on a lady like Anna Mason.

At the thought of his visitor, he scratched his head with the end of a brush and wondered again what it was about her that had made him unable to concentrate on the tasks he had already committed to.

She was pleasant enough and attractive in her own way, he supposed. Older, of course, but interesting in that serious manner, and certainly issuing a challenge to his abilities with the unheard-of-idea to paint a portrait of someone she had never even met.

It was the challenge that excited him. He really needed the stimulus of attempting the impossible once in a while and if this lady could pay the costs, which seemed likely from his visit to her home in the Rosecliffe Estate, it would be a worthwhile exercise to stretch his imagination.

He selected one of his own canvases to place on the easel. The florid scene of a city in the tropics was not for sale. He dabbled in extemporaneous flamboyance in the middle of the night when sleep eluded him and this was one of the results. Might as well show the lady he was not all about careful reproduction of that which the camera could capture.

He was just wiping paint off his hands when the buzzer sounded to signal the arrival of someone at the front entrance to the house.

He ran down the two flights of stairs at top speed, fearing Anna

Mason would take fright and leave before he had a chance to talk to her. Through the stained glass window in the door he saw a rainbow figure nervously smoothing her auburn hair and shuffling her feet. She was, in fact, turning around as if to leave when he opened the door.

"Oh, I wasn't sure which bell to ring. It seems there are several businesses in this lovely old house."

Lawren had caught his breath and managed to say, "Please come in. I have a studio apartment on the top floor. It's a bit of a climb but the light from the skylight windows makes it worthwhile for me.

Nothing else was said between them as he led the way, pointing out the lawyers' and insurance offices on the other floors as they ascended.

Finally they reached the attic level and the open door led right into the messy studio. Lawren suspected his visitor had never actually seen a working artist's studio before, so he stayed back and let her absorb the scene. This was the first test of her intention. If she fled now, it was not a project for him.

He watched as she was drawn to his colourful canvas on the easel. Test number two. She looked surprised, but not shocked by the purple shadows and the trailing blossoms against stark buildings and enormous overhanging trees. He waited for her comments but she merely turned to him and began her rehearsed statement.

Test number two passed: she had refrained from facile observations about the painting that would demonstrate her ignorance of art.

"I don't want to waste your time, Mr. Drake. The portrait I had in mind would require some weeks for you to complete, if, indeed, you chose to take the commission. The problem is that I am leaving for Scotland in a few weeks and I wanted to take the portrait with me. That now seems impossible given the time frame. I came today to explain this to you and to apologize for misleading you. The project is probably not viable. I have had a chance to consider the difficulties it presents and I am on the verge of discarding the entire idea."

Anna Mason had left no space in her declaration for Lawren to speak and she had not intended for him to comment. She moved to exit and was surprised to hear a low chuckle emerge from the man in front of her.

"Hold on a minute! Don't I get any say in this decision?"

"Oh, of course you do! I just didn't want to ...."

"I know, 'waste my time' is what you said before. Well, it's *my* time and you are here now, so please can we sit down and discuss it for a minute?"

She seemed flustered by this unexpected turn of events but sat down on a stool which he had previously covered with a clean towel. He propped himself on a trestle with a good view of his client's face.

"What do you want to discuss?" she said tentatively.

"Tell me about the person. What was her name?"

"Helen!" they said in unison and the vocal duet broke the tension. She visibly relaxed and began to talk with an enthusiasm that transformed her face, bringing a blush to her cheeks and a liveliness to her blue eyes that made her seem like a young girl.

"This is a long story but the essence of it is that I inherited a house in Scotland from a relative who was unknown to me. Helen Dunlop gave me the gift of property but also the gift of independence, and she was the catalyst that changed my life. As far as I can gather, Helen was a shy person who kept herself to herself, as they say in Scotland. She had a tragic childhood and an unhappy marriage and when she found the estate house outside Oban she knew peace in her life for the first time. I owe her a great deal and from what I know of her, she deserved better."

"But if you never met, how do you know about her life?"

"I had some background research done, and I talked to the few people she trusted. I also found some photographs of her, but more recently I discovered a diary of sorts that revealed her innermost thoughts."

"Where is that diary now?"

"Ah! That's another long tale! It's gone, but I know it by heart." Lawren was intrigued, despite his inner reservations. "Tell me about the house," he asked quietly.

"It's in the most beautiful glen. The wind blows from the sea in the west, but the house is of weathered stone with a slate roof and it has withstood storms and assaults for a century or more. Behind the house is a high hill with a tarn at its summit that reflects the passing clouds like a mirror. From up there you can see for miles and the air is like wine yet it is so peaceful that birds fly silently beneath the hill and sheep are like tiny white dots far below. I love it there and I can't wait to return."

Anna Mason had spoken with such feeling that Lawren felt a catch in his throat. His artist's imagination began to conjure up the scene his visitor was describing.

"Go on," he said softly. "I'll just make some notes." He picked up a nearby sketch pad and began to draw a quick outline of Anna's face, holding the paper in such a way that she would not be able to tell he was not, in fact, writing anything.

"Well, I had a few alterations done to bring the house into the present century but I think it retains that old-world feel. The rooms are generous in size and the furnishings are updated versions of the style Helen preferred. I now let the property to guests but it's mostly family and friends who use it when Alina and I are not there. I have good friends in the Oban area who keep an eye on the house and make sure it is in peak condition. I have some plans for the garden one of these days." She broke off with an embarrassed frown between her eyebrows. "Look! I didn't mean to ramble on like this. As I said, there's no time to do justice to the picture I had in mind. Perhaps we might try at another more suitable time in the future?"

She stood up and smoothed down the coat she had unbuttoned when she began to speak.

"Wait a minute, Anna! May I call you Anna?"

"Oh, of course!"

"I had an idea for this portrait but it requires further input from you. I need to know how you are related to Helen and I will need to see any family photographs in addition to the ones of Helen you mentioned."

"I can give you that information, Lawren, but is it worthwhile right now? I understand your reluctance to work without a live subject." Lawren put the sketch pad down so that the drawing of Anna's head was concealed. The action gave him a moment to compose a reply.

"I don't want to give you a false impression of my work. I have done very formal portraits in the past but there is little demand for that kind of thing these days. If I show you something I have done more recently, it might help you to see what could be achieved with your project." Anna looked confused at this turn of events. It was clear that she thought the discussion was over. Lawren walked quickly to the wall and selected a canvas from the stack there. He turned it around and substituted it for the vibrant scene he had placed on the easel.

"Take a look at this."

He watched as Anna tried to come to grips with the modern take on portraiture that he was showing her. A minute went by. He could not tell from her stillness how she was reacting. Finally, she spoke.

"This is amazing, Lawren. Obviously, I don't know the man in your painting but the way you have incorporated natural elements in the background and placed subtle hints around his figure, it is as if I can tell who he really is. This is so much more effective than the formal portraits you mentioned. Would it be possible to create something like this for my Scottish house?"

She turned to face him and he was conscious that she had passed the third test: she was able to recognize and appreciate creativity.

"Let me give it some thought. We should meet again soon to exchange information. What about Williams Coffee Pub next to Victoria Park?"

"Yes, fine! But before I go, there's something you need to explain to me, Lawren Drake.
What did you mean when you said there were 'weird vibes' in my home? "

He laughed out loud. She had effectively turned the tables on him and now he needed to answer her questions.

"Oh, that! It's true, I do sometimes get a sense of people from their surroundings but perhaps 'weird' was not the accurate word to use. I sent that e mail in the middle of the night and I may have exaggerated somewhat."

"No, no, sir! You don't escape that easily. I want to know what you sensed."

Lawren accepted the inevitable and hoped his answer would not cause this lady to back down from the project. He was aware of a growing interest in the challenge of producing work from such difficult circumstances and also, surprisingly, a growing interest in this most unusual woman.

"I confess I felt a strong feminine factor in the décor and in the atmosphere of your home. There was a palpable air of energy and ambition. Yet, I felt a hint of something tragic in the background. I saw photographs indicating travel but everything was pristine so I guessed you had not lived there for long. That in itself was remarkable. I generally get vibes from buildings where people have resided for long periods of time."

"I am astonished that you absorbed so much from a short visit, Lawren. You really are psychic!"

"Well, my skills depend on good observation. It's my stock in trade, I suppose. So, we'll meet again soon?"

"Definitely!"

General chit chat accompanied them down the stairs to the front door. Anna Mason got into her car and waved as she drove off. Lawren Drake went slowly back into the house and realized he had a great deal of thinking to do before their next meeting and not all of it was related to a work project.

Alina was waiting when Anna returned home.

"How did it go? Was he weird after all?"

Anna had been trying to identify how she felt about the unusual encounter with Lawren Drake all the way from the downtown to their west end housing estate, and she was no closer to a conclusion.

"I honestly, don't know how to describe it, Alina. It was one of the most amazing hours I have ever spent. So much happened, it's hard to know where to start."

"Well, start with what you thought about him."

"You were right! He's not as young as I had first presumed. In his own place he looked more mature and even with paint smeared on one cheek he is a consummate professional who has worked for many years to get to his level of expertise."

"So, you saw some of his work?"

"I have never seen anything like the paintings he showed me. Two entirely different types of work and the portrait of a man was outstanding in its composition and execution. I am no expert on art, as you know, Alina, but I was stunned by the work. If Lawren Drake could create something similar, and equally remarkable, for the Oban house, I would be utterly delighted."

"Wait one minute! I thought you said the project was a no go. There wasn't a hope, you said, of getting the work done before we have to be in Scotland at the beginning of June. How did all that change?"

"I can't tell you! I must have been mesmerized the whole hour I was in his studio. I went in there with one mind set and came out in a completely different frame of mind. We will be meeting soon to discuss the portrait further and I think he believes it can be done."

"Oh!" said Alina, and there was a wealth of meaning in the syllable.

Anna caught the emphasis and the raised eyebrows that went with it. "Don't make something out of nothing. It's a business arrangement, that's all. He's way too young for me."

Alina decided there and then to find out the exact age, and any other relevant information, about Lawren Drake before Anna's next meeting with him.

She was not worried that Anna would fall for the man. She was far too sensible for that kind of thing.

She was more concerned that this artist might take advantage of her friend's generosity and leave her poorer and with no fine portrait to show for her trust in him. That she would not tolerate.

Nine

It had been a disturbed, and disturbing, night but Professor Stavros Kyriakos assumed his mantle of educational responsibility as soon as he stepped inside the university building where his classroom and office were housed.

There were a number of papers awaiting his attention in the IN box and several items that needed to be taken to the secretary for inter-college mail. He brushed these aside, regretting the changes that had deprived him of a department secretary who used to take care of these details for him.

While the students were assembling in their classes for the morning lectures, he had a few minutes when he could count on being undisturbed. In these minutes he accessed a private folder on his computer. This folder was transported in his inner jacket pocket via a memory stick that never left his possession. It was labelled simply, 'Pauline'.

Inside the folder were a series of e mails dating from two years previously. He read these from the beginning as he often did, in an attempt to understand how he had ended up in this dangerous relationship.

It had started very innocently. Pauline was a star student, easily identified as soon as she entered the graduate program. Her undergraduate degree was in classical art history and she demonstrated her interpretive skills on one of the first field trip digs she had ever experienced.

The small, select group of students had permission to excavate a field adjacent to the privately-owned Bignor Roman Villa site in a remote location deep in the West Sussex hills along single-track lanes and far from the usual tourist routes. It lay close to the old Roman Road, Stane Street, remnants of which could be seen on the high ridge above the excavated remains of the Roman Villa.

This site was a favourite of Stavros' because it was the only Roman site he knew where visitors could actually walk on pathways where tesserae remained in their original positions. Nothing else could give students that thrill of being so close to the legions who lived in Britain for over three centuries.

Pauline grasped immediately, the necessity to work with excruciating care in order to plot the position of each tiny piece of stone, or other matter, the earth could reveal. It was, however, her vision of the overall plan of the partly-excavated site itself, which was extraordinary for a beginning student.

She made a link, instinctively, between the tiny pieces of tesserae she uncovered in the field and concluded these remnants must be a sign of the continuance of the mosaic pathway in the interior of the house. Her hunch was correct. Subsequent investigations revealed the pavement was one of the longest ever discovered in Britain's many Roman ruins.

The other students were as astonished as was Stavros himself. The men crowded around Pauline in the hopes that they could inhale some of her skill from just a small contact with her breath. But she was not interested in their advances. Her eyes were for the professor only, and his approval was the only one she sought from that time onwards.

He admitted she was easy to like. It was not just her stunning good looks and vibrant youth. He was immune to these usually. It was her willingness to learn and grow that caught his attention.

Many students enrolled in the archaeology masters program in an attempt to postpone their entry to adult life and responsibilities. Others thought of the program as a 'bird course', a sinecure that permitted them to do field work and breathe the fresh outdoor air instead of the stale air of academia.

Pauline was never destined to fall into either of these categories.

Stavros recognized his tendency to favour her with special smiles and shared jokes, based on their common knowledge of Latin and Greek languages. He also recognized the danger in this favouritism and worked all the harder to include the rest of the group, but there was always that special feeling between him and Pauline from the start.

Now she was enrolled in the summer session in Greece. He could not avoid her there. They would be in close contact all through the month of July and he knew from previous experience just how powerful the influence of sun and classic sculpture could be, when away from the confines of the university and the uncertainty of English summer weather.

He dared not challenge her admission to the course. All the plans were made and the accommodations had been paid for. The latest e mail underscored her desire to meet up with him again and, although he had been circumspect in his online correspondence with her, he feared there might be mobile phone messages which could be misinterpreted by someone who had mischief in mind.

Not that he had singled Pauline out for special advice. It was commonplace to talk frequently with his students whenever projects or papers were to be submitted. Yet, he knew his voice mail must reveal his affection for the dedicated young woman. He so wanted to encourage her in her studies. It had crossed his mind more than once that she would make a perfect candidate to succeed him in a few years and with that objective he had actively encouraged her to reach her highest potential.

This thought reminded him that the final draft of Pauline's graduate thesis presentation should be in his secure e mail site by now. A few clicks brought him to the site and he scanned the list. Good! The work was there. The quality was not in question as he had been involved in her presentation preparation from the outset. Nevertheless, he thought it advisable to scan quickly through the pages to confirm that all was in order. Occasionally a student forgot to include the summary or all the required references.

He was about to resume his folder reading when an appendix, addressed to him personally, popped up at the end of Pauline's work. A chill brought gooseflesh to his arms as he realized there could be something incriminating in the short note. He read it at speed, anxious to delete the message as soon as possible but stopped in horror when he saw the contents.

The test confirmed that I am definitely pregnant. I have not yet decided what to do about this news but I am determined it will not prevent me from completing my thesis presentation or from joining you in Greece this summer. You know how ambitious I am and your encouragement has always been of the greatest importance to me.

Please keep this information secret for now. I will be in touch before my scheduled presentation date.

Yours,

Pauline.

His head was in a whirl as he saw the future he had planned for this amazing young woman vanish, like a raindrop in a stream. How could she be so stupid as to risk everything in this way?

What was she thinking? Pregnancy at this stage in her education would be fatal.

He re-read the message then eliminated it. The second reading had brought his attention to the sentence 'I have not yet decided what to do about this news.' Perhaps there was a chance she might abort the foetus. He could not bring himself to use the word *child*. If so, all might be saved. It would be up to him to persuade her when they worked together in Greece. He dared not discuss the topic in the environs of the university. There were always listening ears.

He tried several deep breaths to calm his nerves but this only increased his heart rate. What was happening to his life all of a sudden? Had contemplating retirement, and the changes this would involve, caused his entire life to veer off the rails?

His mind jumped back unexpectedly to his home life. The problems with Lynn were still to be resolved and now this issue with Pauline had become a million times more complex. The timing was so wrong.

He had serious decisions to make and their departure for Greece was imminent.

The situation with Pauline would have to wait until the summer course, but he must settle things with Lynn as soon as possible. The last thing he wanted was to go to the family Easter celebration with a wife who was aggrieved and unwilling to contribute even the minimum participation she usually managed to summon up. Family members would notice and questions would be asked for which he had no satisfactory answers.

He must do something today. It couldn't wait. He opened the desk drawer and pulled out a file where he had been storing papers related to the purchase of land on Paros. It crossed his mind that he should probably have shared this step with his wife, but he dismissed the thought quickly. It was too late to fix that particular oversight. What could be done now, to make the new home more acceptable to Lynn? He pored over the papers in the hopes that inspiration would strike. He had already mentioned to her that she would be consulted on every aspect of the design. What more could he add? How could he make the move to Greece more palatable to her?

Think!

It was difficult for him to put himself in Lynn's shoes. It was not something he had normally to consider. His wife usually fell in with his plans without any debate, yet, on this issue, she was obdurate. He had to take her objections seriously or his plans would come to nothing. There was no chance of supporting two residences on his pension, even if he used all their savings. The question of what this would do to his marriage was not yet something he could contemplate.

A photograph of the site on the small bay near the ocean was attached to the offer of purchase.

He would not show this photograph to Lynn as the building was derelict nowadays. As a boy, he had often swum on the beach with his brothers and sisters then bought food from the restaurant where sandy feet and damp swimsuits were welcomed on the wide patio. It was a sad relic now and typical of the changes the economic disaster that was Greece had brought to small businesses. At the same time, he had to acknowledge that the financial downturn had given him the opportunity to fulfil a dream he never expected to be able to bring to fruition.

What could be done with the site? The building restrictions required that a new structure should fit within the footprint of the original restaurant. This would mean some clever plan to utilize the space while providing an attractive and appealing home. Height could be a factor to impress Lynn. There would need to be sufficient space for bedrooms to accommodate Sarah and the grandchildren. This would be a major factor in his wife's satisfaction with the move.

As he thought about the structure, Stavros realized he would need the services of an experienced architect. Suddenly, an idea struck him. If he could employ Lynn's brother Philip to do this work, it might be possible to kill two birds with one stone, as it were. He had not yet met Philip, but the conversation about this brother had increased lately as Lynn puzzled about how to reconnect with him before it was too late. By all accounts, Philip Purdy was an esteemed architect. He might be persuaded to reduce his usual fees for a family member and also take this chance to learn more about his sister and her husband.

Stavros felt a weight lift from his mind. He stood and walked over to the window. The familiar view calmed him. All was not lost. Working with her brother on the house design would be an offer Lynn could hardly refuse. This one idea could turn the tide.

A quiet knock at his office door interrupted his ruminations.

He returned to his desk and shoved the file back in the drawer while inviting the students to enter.

By the time the two men and the girl had found seats at the conference table and opened their laptops. Stavros had switched to his professional mode and was ready to listen and respond. At the back of his mind, however, he retained a satisfied glow. Tonight he would sort everything out with his wife.

Normal life would resume.

As darkness fell, and Lynn closed the curtains in the lounge, she was aware that she had spent the entire day wandering through her home picking up one thing after another without accomplishing a single useful task. The tickets for Greece were lying on the kitchen table and she realized she had been staring at them for fifteen minutes without a cohesive thought in her mind.

Could she really allow her husband to leave for the Easter celebration without her? The very thought struck panic in her chest. This estrangement between them was something she had never known before and she was responsible for it. Guilt swept through her. The image of the role of a good wife, to which she had always clung, did not include setting her will against that of her husband. And yet, the alternative of capitulating to his wishes was inconceivable to her. What, if anything, could be done about this impasse?

Glancing at the clock she saw that Stavros could be heading home soon. The fact that she had not prepared anything for their evening meal was swept aside as irrelevant under the circumstances.

She could not concentrate on the domestic when matters of such vital importance to their marriage remained undecided.

In all the long years of their marriage, Lynn had never thought to deliver an ultimatum to her husband. When Stavros first came to England to visit her, the year following their meeting as student workers in a Greek island tourist hotel, he had proved his worth by instantly offering to help her out at home.

At this point of crisis, her beloved father was becoming severely depressed and sinking into a passive stage where he rarely left his bed. Her mother's condition of mild dementia went into overdrive when she realized what was happening to Lynn's father and she understood that he no longer wanted help from his wife.

Lynn was left alone to deal with this dire situation. Her older brother, Philip, had already fled to parts unknown so she was a teenager with responsibilities far beyond her capacity. Her mother required monitoring to ensure she took her prescribed medication and her father was too heavy for her to lift when he was comatose, or when his bed needed changing. Her mother had always impressed upon the girl how important it was that no social services should be involved in their family affairs. Isobel Purdy had a long-standing fear of authorities and passed this fear on to her daughter.

Lynn's absences from school were becoming an issue and she was at the end of her tether with no family around to advise or assist her. Stavros rode into this chaos like a knight on a white horse, taking charge of her father's care and leaving Lynn more time to deal with her mother. She would never forget the gratitude she felt for this strong, handsome, foreigner who turned an innocent summer romance into a lifetime commitment.

They married at a registry office in the town hall and Stavros moved into the big old house permanently.

At first, it was a marriage of convenience, but before too long Lynn's feelings of gratitude transformed into a deep and abiding appreciation for the unselfish qualities her husband had brought to her life.

Since then, no matter the trials they had encountered in the years when Stavros was applying for university admission, and when he struggled to attain his advanced qualifications, she had always known him as a tower of strength. Her own ambitions never rose above the level of ensuring her parents were cared for, her husband was supported, and their home was run as efficiently as possible. She had never worked outside the home and preferred to stay in the background while Stavros steadily made his way up the academic ladder.

When Sarah was born he proved to be a loving father. Lynn knew then their bond was complete.

That bond was further cemented when Lynn had a series of miscarriages that devastated her confidence and reinforced her desire for a quiet life. Despite his own sorrow, Stavros stayed by her side, even in the darkest nights until their little girl's needs overcame his wife's grief. Sarah was to be her 'one chick' and the thought of being separated from her was insupportable.

No wonder she felt guilty. Although she recognized her own contribution to their marriage, there was no question in her mind that Stavros was responsible in great part for the purchase of their comfortable little home in the leafy suburb of Horam and for her contented life there.

Until now.

Her thoughts had been circling around in this way all day without a sensible idea presenting itself. She had to come up with a solution to the dilemma, and fast, or her marriage, and therefore her whole life, would be in jeopardy.

Stay in this house and deny Stavros his opportunity to build a house in Paros?

This could lead to separation and divorce and she would be alone.

Sell their home in England and move to Greece, far away from Sarah, David and the grandchildren?

This was not an option she could endure.

Move in with Sarah and family and let Stavros go?

There was no extra space in Sarah's home and Lynn had always promised herself that she would not impose on her daughter in the way her mother had imposed her illness and dependence onto Lynn.

Which alternative was the most painful? Losing her home, her daughter or her husband? This thought stopped Lynn in her tracks. Did it come down to this, then? If so, which choice would be the most painful? She knew in her heart that she loved all three, but two of the choices were people rather than an object.

So, two choices, then: Stavros or Sarah? England or Greece?

"This is impossible!" she yelled out in anguish. "I can't choose!" Tears flooded down her cheeks and raw emotion drove her head onto her bent arms as sobs tore through her chest.

It was in this condition that Stavros found his wife when he came quietly through the front door.

The unexpected sound of her sobs struck him in the heart in a way that her anger never could.

In a rush came the memory of the only other times he had heard her cry like this. Each time she lost a much-desired baby through miscarriage, her sobs had wrung his very soul.

He knew this was a moment of vulnerability for Lynn. He acknowledged that, had he been a better man, he would have left her to weep until she recovered and opened the discussion about their future at a more opportune time for her. But, her very weakness gave him a huge advantage at this moment.

He had a plan to propose and, if the Gods were willing, he could at least delay the major decisions that threatened to divide their lives across a chasm that could never be bridged.

He breathed her name and crossed the kitchen floor in two steps, taking his wife into his arms and cradling her there with the rocking motions that reached deep into her insecurities and soothed her to the depth of her emotions.

When she had calmed a little, he began to whisper his plan in her ear.

Ten

Alina's investigations of Lawren Drake revealed nothing new. His online profile gave every evidence of being accurate and authentic. His studio and residence were long-standing rentals and a number of worthies in London spoke highly on his website about his work ethic and skills as an artist.

Although his birth date was not supplied, she calculated his age must be around fifty-five, judging from the work quoted.

In spite of all this information she was not satisfied about his intentions.

She considered spying on him when Anna went to their next meeting. She could hide among the coffee drinkers and watch his face from a distance. She always believed a lot could be learned from just observing a person's expressions and an objective observer could probably discover more than Anna would, while she was involved in conversation.

The fact that she was seriously considering this action proved to Alina how worried she was about this interloper in their calm lives. Yes, she had to admit she was concerned about herself, but she was more anxious about the effect it would have on Anna if he turned out to be some trickster who just wanted her time and money and had no intention of delivering on his promises. She knew Anna was generally a good judge of character, yet this portrait project had obviously taken hold of her imagination and from the way she spoke about it, she was determined to go ahead with the idea, no matter what it might cost.

The financial cost was not a concern. Other than travel expenses, such as their recent adventures in Egypt, Anna rarely spent any money on herself. Both cars they owned were older models. Their condo was paid for, after the sale of property and the combination of legacies and investments they owned, and the A Plus business more than covered their living expenses and also assisted in any business-related costs, such as James' salary and yearly trips to Scotland to seek out new products and materials.

What really concerned her was the possible emotional cost to Anna. Despite her friend's practical and controlled exterior appearance, Alina knew the tender heart that exterior concealed from the world. In many ways they were, both of them, damaged goods as far as men were involved. Richard's betrayal had affected Anna so deeply that she had sunk into a depression that lasted years.

The entire fiasco in Luxor when they met Richard so unexpectedly had brought about a softening in Anna's attitude to her former husband that surprised Alina as much as it did Anna herself. She did not want to see the barriers against men rise again if this artist fellow turned out to be a charlatan.

Out of respect for Anna, she could not just barge into this touchy arena with guns blazing. That, she suspected, would send Anna zooming off in the opposite direction. Subtlety would have to be employed, and soon. If a direct attack was not viable and spying was a bit outrageous, what could a friend do to prevent a possible disaster?

Anna sat in Williams Coffee Pub and watched customers drive into the adjacent parking lot. She had been scanning every car and its passengers before she realized Lawren would be much more likely to arrive by bicycle since his home was only a few blocks north of Victoria Park. She fiddled with the items she had brought to show him and wished she had not set out so early, leaving herself enough time to get nervous about this meeting.

Turning her attention to Victoria Park, she saw old men seated on benches feeding squirrels, and children skipping along ahead of their mothers in the spring sunlight. She felt she had not experienced many carefree moments lately since this idea of a portrait had entered her thoughts so forcibly. She made up her mind to decide one way or the other after this meeting. Either the project could be completed satisfactorily or she would be done with the entire thing and give herself some peace.

Alina, at least, would be pleased if the latter was her decision. Anna knew she had monopolized their conversation at home with speculation about what Lawren Drake might be able to achieve with his painting. Once or twice she had caught an expression on Alina's face that announced her impatience with the entire topic but she could not seem to divert her mind from the work she had seen in his studio and the possibilities he had indicated might be achievable.

And here she was clutching a selection of old photographs and even odder objects, and, for all she knew, he might not even turn up.

A tap on her shoulder brought her head around and away from the outside view. Lawren Drake was standing there having entered the restaurant by a door on the street side, opposite to where she sat. She immediately wondered how long he had been watching her and what that might have told him.

"Hope I haven't kept you waiting Anna. I see you have brought some things to show me?"

"Yes. I mean, I haven't been waiting long, and I do have the photographs and stuff although I can't imagine what help they will be to you. I warned you some of the photos are far from professional standard."

"Don't worry about that! The photos are just a backup. I am more interested in what you can tell me.

I'll order coffee and we can talk for a bit."

Anna managed to nod her head in agreement and watched as he strode off through the rush of customers towards the order counter. What was it about this man that threw her off guard? He always seemed to be more in control of a situation than she was. This was an unusual feeling for her. Knowing what to expect was a hallmark of her existence and probably came from years of teaching. She thought she was prepared for this meeting but as she saw him approach with a tray and a confident air that he had chosen the right coffee in spite of not having asked her preferences, she wondered again just what kind of person he really was.

"Okay! I ordered a latte for you and brought a selection of sugars, creams and milks. Did I get it right?

I confess I hedged my bets a bit by choosing a regular coffee also. I can drink either kind."

"The latte is fine for me, thank you." Anna fussed around with a packet of brown sugar she really didn't need, just to gather herself while Lawren shrugged out of his dark blue pea coat or donkey jacket, as they used to be called. He was wearing a stylish paisley-patterned shirt and the colours made his peculiar gold eyes pop. She made a mental note not to fixate on those eyes while he was seated opposite her. Staring would not be polite.

"Start any time you want to."

"Uh, what do you want to know?"

"Let's begin with your mother. You said before that she was related to this Helen person in some way?"

Anna was relieved to talk about someone other than herself and launched into an account of her mother's sad tale of family misunderstandings which led to her brother Simon's tale about her father's regrets late in life, and so to the marriage of her parents.

"Truly, my mother never suspected she had an aunt who was the child of my grandmother. Whether it was kept secret or just something to be swept under the rug because of guilty feelings on my grandmother's part, I can't tell. I never met my Scottish grandmother. My parents left Glasgow very quickly after they married because of a scandal that was brewing. Their departure, and, I suspect, their marriage, caused a rift between mother and daughter. In any case, I grew up with no idea of my family connections in Scotland."

Anna suddenly realized that what she was talking about might be overheard by people in nearby booths. A long-held fear of private information causing public difficulties, that came from her teaching years, made her feel uncomfortable.

"Oh, please stop me, Lawren. I am babbling away here about ancient history and I'm sure that isn't what you want to know."

"On the contrary, Anna, I am very interested and not just because of the portrait you want, but also because my own family is riddled with secrets and problems related to 'the old country' as my father used to call it."

"Are you kidding me?"

"No! Seriously! My father's family were landed gentry with a mansion and estate somewhere; in Kent, I think. My father fought with his parents over his choice of a bride and the result was that he and my mother fled the country and emigrated to Canada with little more than the clothes on their backs."

"Goodness me! Did *they* ever reconcile with the family in England?"

"Unfortunately, no! My grandfather's will gave everything to my father's younger brother. My father was reluctant to contest the will after such a long absence of contact. I think he was happy to get away from the expectations of the upper classes and make his own life in the colonies, as it were."

"Isn't that strange? Our parents started out in the same way once they emigrated. It must have been hard for them."

"I am sure it was. Building up finances with no family support is difficult at any time. Why do you think our parents' generation never attempted to repair the relationships that were severed?"

"I am not sure." She stopped to think; then continued in a low voice. "It may have been the distances between the different parts of the family, but it could also have been about forgiveness. When there is no forgiveness the pain and sorrow linger on and much damage is done."

"It sounds as if you have given this a lot of thought, Anna."

"Not until I discovered the whole mess with my mother's family. Now I regret not knowing sooner and being able to ask questions. I might have been better prepared for the surprises that came later when I learned about my half-brother Philip."

"What kind of person was your mother, Anna?"

"She was a hard-working nurse who took on night shifts to get a foot in the door of one of the large teaching hospitals in London. For a time when Simon and I were young, she must have worked two jobs. My dad had to re-qualify as an engineer and there would not have been much money coming into the house, and a mortgage to pay, I suppose. There were long spells when I saw her for only short periods in the day and that was when I began to spend after-school hours with my friend, Alina."

"Oh, I misheard the name before. I thought you mentioned an Al."

"Oh, yes! It's an unusual name but she has been a true, lifelong friend to me."

Lawren tucked away that piece of information and encouraged Anna to go on with her story.

"I never saw the resemblance until recently, but I was looking in the mirror and I thought for the first time that I now look like my mother in her later years. She took ill with some vile bug she probably picked up in the hospital and I had to have a leave of absence from teaching to care for her. I think it was the closest we were in our whole lives. Those final months showed me her true nature and I am sad I waited so long before I found out what a strong, brave woman she was."

Anna stopped, sipped her coffee and tried to prevent a tear from forming.

Lawren politely fiddled with his paper napkin until she had recovered her equilibrium, and then asked quietly if she had a photo of her mother.

"I do, although it was quite a search to uncover it. I think digging around in past memories is the reason I am feeling emotional today."

"Don't apologize! It's a fine and rare quality in a woman these days."

Anna hid her blushes by opening the folder she had brought and withdrawing two photographs. One was a candid snapshot of Simon and herself on a beach with their mother. They were all three laughing at the photographer who was more than likely Anna's dad, Angus. The other was of a much older Marion sitting in the garden of their family home.

"I am sorry there isn't much more to show you, Lawren. I had to dig around for these. Our family was not given to displaying photographs. Perhaps they never had much leisure time to think of such things."

Lawren took hold of the photographs and searched for the resemblance Anna had mentioned.

He saw a younger version of Anna in the beach photo. The same fine bone structure, long legs and arms and straight shoulders were there. The hair colour could have been a lighter brown than the bronzed colour Anna now favoured, and the style was much shorter these days, but much seemed the same.

As for the older Marion, Lawren thought Anna was much younger and the comparison was false. He knew how different the face one saw in a mirror was from that seen by an observer and he chose to say nothing in response.

"What did you bring with you that you associate with your mother?"

Anna stretched out her hands on the table top and waited.

He saw her narrow fingers and the white skin, lightly freckled, with the faintest hint of blue veins running through them.

He was admiring the shape and colour of her nails. They were devoid of polish and buffed to a healthy natural shine. It took another moment before he registered the fact that she wore a delicate ring on the third finger of her right hand.

"This was my mother's engagement ring. She gave it to me during her last illness and insisted I sell it for whatever value it might have. It was not something she wore all the time. When she was nursing, she said the raised setting caught on rubber gloves and she was afraid of losing the tiny stones that make up the flower shape. I never had it valued and disobeyed her wishes. I wear it on my right hand so as not to confuse my many suitors." Anna chuckled at this statement but her companion was not smiling.

He reached across the table and gently removed the ring from her finger. Anna was too shocked at such an intimate gesture to protest. He turned the ring around between his hands and looked for an inscription, then, finding none, he placed the ring tenderly on his pinky finger and covered it with his other hand.

When Anna looked at his face in surprise, she found he had closed his eyes. This gave her the chance to examine his clasped hands. They were the hands of a workman with short nails and blunt fingers. She could see a rim of paint under one or two of the nails and the cuticles were ragged. His hands were strong and very masculine.

She hardly dared breathe as she waited for him to speak. It was as if a bubble of silence surrounded them. The chatter and clatter of the coffee shop disappeared in the intensity of her concentration. What was he doing?

At last his eyes opened. Anna noticed at once that deep golden tint. Then the bubble broke and normal life resumed with his next words.

"Forgive me. I just had to do that. Sometimes I can understand better when a beloved object is in my hands."

"What did the ring tell you?" Anna's curiosity overcame her natural skepticism at a stranger claiming to learn something from an inanimate object. She waited.

"It tells me you are more like your mother than you know, Anna. The ring has elements of both of you, woven together by love. She loved you dearly."

Anna could not hold back the tears that came with these statements from such an unexpected source.

"I.........I don't know what to say. To hear that after all these years. Your words touch me deeply."

"God, I didn't mean to make you cry! I apologize for going off like that. I should be more careful when I get these impulses. Please don't think I am crazy. I don't behave like this with everyone I meet, I assure you. I hope I haven't scared you away."

"No, no! You surprised me, that's all. I have never known anyone who could sense feelings like this.

Do you mean you can use this information when you compose a portrait?"

"Sometimes. I think the urgency you feel about the portrait you want is affecting my responses. Can you tell me about Helen now? What did you bring?"

Anna reclaimed her ring from Lawren's hands and removed the last items from her folder.

"These are the best photographs I have of Helen. I like this one because she is smiling and most of what I know about her is so sad. The other is taken on top of the high hill at the rear of the house in Oban that I inherited from Helen. It is a magical place and I sat in exactly this spot myself before I knew Helen loved it too."

Lawren looked steadily at each photo in turn. He saw a faint resemblance to Anna's mother's older photo but none to Anna herself. This woman was marked by grief. Even in the photo where she was smiling, the expression seemed forced, as if happiness was a foreign concept to her.

Anna placed the last item in front of him with the explanation, "This is a letter I received from Helen when I first went to Oban. It is the only portable thing I have from her that was meant specifically for me."

Lawren picked up the page of handwriting but did not turn it over to read the words. He shuddered once and returned the folded letter to Anna, saying quickly, "This was written by someone who anticipated her own death. I can feel the sadness from it. "

Anna gasped. There was no way this man could have known what the letter announced. If she had doubted his abilities before, she no longer did.

"I must ask you, Lawren. Can you paint this portrait for me or not? I don't know how much influence these things I brought today have on your decision, but I really must ask you to tell me now, one way or the other.

Lawren Drake looked straight at Anna with eyes that darkened as he spoke.

"I very much want to accept this commission for you and I will do my utmost to complete it in the time frame you have given me. I must advise you, however, that such work has a life of its own and I am not always able to force the pace. I will be in touch soon to let you know of my progress. If you agree to these restrictions, Anna, let's shake on it."

Anna reached out her hand realizing she was committing to a project that had an unknown price tag attached. At this moment she cared little about that. If this extraordinary man could produce a work approaching the quality of the examples she had seen in his studio, she knew she would be more than satisfied.

As their hands connected, a familiar voice interrupted the moment.

"Well! Look who's here!"

Anna found two figures standing beside her table. Alina and Susan held cups of coffee but Anna was not deceived by that. These two were here to spy on Lawren Drake. She knew it.

Before she could summon up a word of disapproval, Lawren was on his feet and pulling on his jacket.

"Excuse me ladies but I have work to do. Goodbye, Anna. It was a pleasure."

With that, he picked up Anna's folder and left the restaurant.

 Anna confronted an eager Alina and a shamefaced Susan.

"It's not my fault, Anna. Alina got me here under false pretences, I swear. She tells me that is the mysterious painter fellow. I was right. He's not much younger than you and quite attractive in a sort of hippy way. He has a good head of hair."

"You two schoolgirls had better sit down right now and explain yourselves. Alina, I am shocked at such underhanded behavior."

"I told you she wouldn't take this well. That's her strict teacher tone. We're in trouble now!"

Lawren Drake's fingers were itching to get paper and pencils so he could capture his first ideas about the portrait. He hopped onto his bicycle and sped through the traffic on Richmond Street. This work was going to be something special. As special, he hoped, as his client.

Eleven

Lynn found herself on a ferry to Paros before she had time to catch her breath.

Her doubts and stresses had calmed as soon as Stavros made peace with her confusion and outlined his plan for the possible new home. He had no longer insisted that his ideas were the only way forward. On the contrary, he left the final decision to his wife. This, in itself, was reassuring to her. As long as she was not forced to make an immediate choice between her life in England and a problematic existence on a remote Greek island, she could retain some semblance of control over the entire enterprise.

The sense of restored peace had lasted long enough for her to survive the plane trip to Athens and the landing on the runway. After that, the ferry to Paros was an anticlimax. She deliberately did not think beyond the next hour. Stavros had promised to make the Easter trip less troublesome for her.

As soon as the weekend festivities were over, they would head for Santorini for a day or two, and then a ferry trip back to Paros where they would stay in a hotel in the town and travel by bus out to the site Stavros had described as "a piece of unspoiled paradise by the Aegean".

Lynn reserved her opinion on that description until she saw it for herself. She was determined not to be swayed by her husband, despite his well-honed skills as a passionate orator. She would try her best to remain neutral while keeping a firm hold on the promises Stavros had made.

First, he was employing her brother Philip as architect.

Second, Lynn had a free hand to confer with Philip about all aspects of the house design, including ample space for visiting family.

She was not so naive that she did not fully realize the implications of these promises. Asking Philip to be involved was a clever move to meet a stated objective of her own to get closer to her long-lost brother.

The idea that she could insure the house met her need to provide a holiday home for Sarah and her family, was a subtle way to get her to agree to sell up in England. The house of a size that would be required could never be financed without the sale of their home in Horam.

As she stood alone by the railing of the ship with the sea breeze blowing through her hair, she committed these conclusions to memory. Stavros was guarding their luggage in the upper deck lounge.

He had left her to "blow away the cobwebs" in the hope that his new reserve would work in his favour. He knew the results of this trip would be the most crucial of their whole lives and affect their future, if there was to be one, in every way possible.

He intended to restrain his natural impulses to persuade Lynn further. Now was the time to let her decide for herself. He was confident that she would see the reason in his arguments, given a little time.

In his mind was a clearly defined picture of their future life in retirement and that picture could not have been more different from their decades in England and his work situation in the university.

He tamped down the excitement the very thought that future created in him.

Just a little longer. Take it easy and wait for the results.

Time would tell. Time was on his side.

Kyriakos family members were waiting at the dockside in Parikia when the Blue Star ferry arrived. Lynn stood back, as she always did, while Stavros was engulfed in a flood of excited Greek language and the welcoming arms of his sisters and brothers. By now, Lynn knew them by name but it had taken years before she could distinguish one from another, so alike were the siblings. As one of the younger members, Stavros stood out with his head of thick, black hair. His brothers, Dimitri, Costas and Yiorgos showed various stages of greying hair but it was all similarly abundant. They seemed to retain dark moustaches and eyebrows whatever their ages. The trio of sisters who approached Lynn, and welcomed her, were fashionable women from Athens and their hair, makeup and clothes demonstrated that amply. Among the little old ladies of Paros on the dockside, dressed in black from head to toe, these women looked like colourful peacocks.

Lynn knew the senior members of the family waited at the old home in the centre of town. There were fewer of the old ones each year as lifetimes of hard work in the Kyriakos' grocery store took their toll. In fact, as Lynn cast her eye over the assembled group she wondered where Stefanos and Daphne were. These two usually never missed the chance to cover their big brother in kisses as soon as possible.

She linked arms with Alexa, the sister nearest in age to herself, and followed the large and voluble group as they pushed through the crowd waiting to board the ferryboat and headed for the old house behind the store.

Stavros no longer elected to stay at his parents' crowded home, preferring the comparative peace of a room in the nearby small hotel where Lynn could get a break from the constant chatter and late night noise of a family reunion. Their first hours on the island would always be spent on folding chairs set up on the yard between the house and the back of the store while the paschal lamb slowly revolved on the spit above the huge barbecue and the family news was shouted from one to the other over copious bottles of Athos beer and the fumes of the ever-present cigarettes. Children and grandchildren milled around contributing to the chaos and added volume to the general noise.

Lynn, in her new mind set, refused to be upset by any of this and contented herself with deep breaths of the warm air and the calming sea sounds. Even the cries of insistent seagulls hovering over the fishing boats in the harbour could not disturb her mood.

This was Stavros' special time and she would do nothing to spoil it for him.

Alexa fetched Lynn a cool drink of lemon water and settled down beside her to keep her company while Stavros brought the family up to date with his latest career developments. His work in England was admired by the rest of his siblings, none of whom had made such a drastic move away from their beloved Greece. Lynn knew he was keeping his plans for retirement under wraps at the moment until final decisions had been made, so she contented herself with small talk about Sarah and the grandchildren, sharing similar stories with Alexa who had five grandchildren of her own.

Lynn asked Alexa if Stefanos and Daphne were arriving later and was surprised to discover they would not be attending the annual feast this year as they had both recently moved their families to Malta where they had business connections.

"You must have heard about riots in the streets of Athens?" she asked Lynn. "The economic situation is so bad, many fear they will lose their jobs and others know they will never be able to pay the extreme high taxes that are coming for all of us. Our new prime minister has vowed we must tighten our belts to stay within the European Union. It is a very bad time."

Lynn nodded sympathetically as Alexa continued in a whisper, "As you can see the parents are getting older. It is too difficult for them to manage the store nowadays. Dimitri lost his job with the port authority and now he has taken over the family business. We are all helping out one way or another but it is not clear how long this can continue."

In a much louder voice, but one in which even Lynn could tell there was forced cheerfulness, she called out, "We are going to enjoy this Easter season here at home, no matter what is happening outside Paros. Am I right?"

Everyone responded with enthusiastic cheers to this positive declaration and Lynn thought to herself that the changes happening throughout this large Greek family were no less devastating than the ones she was facing in England. We have this much in common, she concluded. I will try to be sympathetic even if I can't yet explain the situation Stavros and I are in.

Well before sunset, the women of the family disappeared inside the house in their turn and emerged with their hands full of platters and bowls. The lamb continued to revolve on the spit. It would take twenty-four hours to reach perfection and that Easter delicacy would be shared after the church service in the morning.

A long trestle table was set up in the yard and it soon began to fill with fresh salads liberally topped with the finest feta cheese, tomato, shrimp and zucchini appetizers and delicious local sardines baked in special sauces. Lynn looked for the traditional moussaka in individual dishes and knew she would enjoy that with room left for baklava. She gave the chilled ouzo a miss as it had a bad effect on her digestion, despite its reputation, electing instead to enjoy a *cafefredo,* the iced cappuccino which was Costas' specialty. She needed the caffeine to keep her awake until the festivities drew to a close.

It was close to midnight before Stavros could drag himself away from the arms of his family. Lynn had waited patiently with a warm wrap over her shoulders but she was glad to walk with him along the shore road towards the small hotel. From past experience she knew he would be somewhat unsteady on his feet so she held tight to his arm and steered away from the grass verge. The outdoor tables at the tavernas were still occupied at this late hour but the customers were wearing heavy jackets to ward off the chill evening air. Nevertheless, it was more pleasant than Lynn had remembered to breathe the scented air of the evening stroll beneath palm trees strung with tiny lights.

She finally felt herself relax. Today had not been as bad as she had feared. In spite of herself, she was viewing everything through a different lens, now that the idea of living here permanently had been broached.

The entire town converged on the small Greek Orthodox Church on the highest point of the island, early in the morning for the Easter service. Lynn accompanied her husband as a mark of respect to his family although she understood little of the ceremony. It was a time for her to admire the perfect white building against the purity of the blue sky and to appreciate the sincerity of the worshippers as they welcomed their risen Lord with faith and joy. It was a mark of the importance of religion to Greeks that every island she had visited had dozens of gleaming white chapels with bells suspended from an arch.

Everyone walked down the hill and through the labyrinth of narrow alleys in the town, greeting friends and neighbours and wishing them a happy Easter. When they reached the Kyriakos' house, the women went inside to change out of their church clothes into something more comfortable while the men merely loosened ties and waistcoats then assembled around the lamb whose fragrant smell they had followed eagerly all the way home, commenting loudly on the skill of the chief barbecue expert and the quality of the lamb as chosen by his brothers.

Lynn's gift of herbs and spices had been accepted gladly and now appeared in another parade of superb dishes emanating from the tiny kitchen inside the house. It soon became apparent that a kitchen in the grocery store was also called into service to prepare the feast.

By the time the lamb had been carefully sliced into mouth-watering, tender portions, Lynn and Stavros were, like everyone else, suffering pangs of hunger. Silence descended for a full ten minutes while due appreciation was given to the delicious lamb. Soon 'ooohs' and 'aaahs' of delight spread through the family as the complementary flavours of meat, vegetables and wine flowed together in the mouth.

The entire group ate their fill and the rest of the afternoon saw smaller groups break off to chat and smoke cigars and cigarettes while the grandchildren played with new toys and chased around the courtyard at top speed in pursuit of any local cats or dogs foolish enough to be attracted by the cooking smells.

Lynn saw her husband approaching with a plate of fresh fruit and some honey-drenched treats. She told him she could not manage even a mouthful after two plates of lamb with all the side dishes, and he smiled in acceptance as he put the plate down on the ground for the younger family members to enjoy.

"How are you doing?" he asked.

"I am doing very well thank you. It has been a beautiful day and I have enjoyed it more than I expected to. I can't deny how warm and close your family is, Stavros. I have never experienced a family gathering to compare to this in England and I can see how selfish I have been to insist on keeping you distant from them for so long."

"Don't say that, darling! I have been happy in our home with our family. Our lives have been in England by choice."

"Perhaps, but you must regret the missed opportunities to enjoy a large family. I wish we could have had more children."

"Hush, Lynn! Our Sarah is a treasure beyond compare. I regret nothing. Let's not think about the past. We have a wonderful future ahead of us."

Lynn was aware of what he meant. But, her husband's arms were warm around her, someone was softly playing a bouzouki guitar and the stars were beginning to sparkle in the night sky. She decided to put the hard decisions aside for now and to let the next few days point her in the direction she should go.

Tomorrow she would be on Santorini with her husband.

The ferry arrives at the island of Saint Irene across the caldera, approaching the sheared-off cliffs topped with a thick icing of white houses that melts down the cliff top in perilous drips. It was a view that never failed to astonish Lynn. To build a town on the top of the remains of a gigantic volcanic eruption seemed to be either extremely foolish or a testament to the abiding optimism of the Greeks.

Lynn was never able to take the zigzag tourist route to the top of Thira. She felt sorry for the donkeys and mules laden with travellers in all shapes and sizes who lurched up the steep stairs winding up the rock face. She had once tried to walk up the route but the steps were slick with donkey droppings and she soon discovered how fast one had to move when the donkey train arrived at the same corner as the walkers.

Stavros approved, and they took the bus along the less spectacular road to their hotel on the heights overlooking the other side of the island where the gently sloping fields led to black sand beaches.

Lynn stood on the walled balcony outside their simple room and breathed the air of her favourite island.

Although it would be wonderful if Stavros had decided to settle on Santorini she knew the summer months when tourists overran the place would be impossibly crowded and busy. Not to mention the cost of buying any of the limited suitable land would be outrageous. Stavros often visited the Akrotiri site to inspect the latest archaeological findings so she reckoned Santorini would likely be available to her whenever she wished, *if* she lived on Paros, of course.

The bus to Akrotiri wandered through several villages and eventually stopped at the beach area to disgorge tourists. Lynn had once tried sunbathing there, only to find out that black volcanic sand retained such heat that sunburn was an inevitable result.

Akrotiri, itself, was right at the southwestern edge of Santorini and the parking was limited to local and tour buses with stands for a few taxi cabs. Stavros had the public bus schedule with him so they could enjoy the area without the need to rush back to join a tour.

They walked briskly down the stony path toward the sea and Lynn allowed her husband to draw ahead of her. It happened every time they visited the site. Stavros could not wait to consult his colleagues and see what had been unearthed since his last visit. She smiled at his receding back and advanced more slowly watching the placement of her feet in their beige slip-ons on the rough path. She had learned on prior visits to wear sand-coloured clothing as the excavation area was dusty and darker colours suffered the most from the fine particles floating in the air.

The metal superstructure came into view first. It looked like a partially-constructed warehouse but it was designed to shelter the exceptional ruins from the effects of wind and weather. Beneath the metal superstructure lies a small percentage of what was the largest Minoan city outside of Crete itself. Stavros claimed, less than five percent of the amazing site has been excavated and wonders will still be revealed. As far as Lynn was concerned, the fact that a 3000-year–old place, buried under thirty to forty feet of solid pumice, had ever been discovered at all, was just as astonishing as the finds inside it. Stavros spoke in hushed tones of Professor Marinatos who first dug tunnels through the volcanic ash and found signs of an advanced civilization there by the sea. Lynn thought his descriptions rivalled the unearthing of the tomb of Tutankhamen in the Valley of the Kings in Thebes.

She was always glad to walk along the streets of Akrotiri between two and three-story houses and imagine she trod in the steps of the 30,000 inhabitants who must have rushed to their boats just before the ash cloud from the gigantic volcano's explosion reached them. No bodies had ever been found on the site so she was pleased to envisage the men, women and children escaping the rest of the disaster and re-establishing themselves somewhere safe. She had seen murals of the boats the Minoans used for trade and travel and although no trace of the residents or their transport had ever been found, she preferred to think some at least had found safe harbor somewhere. This was an infinitely better prospect than that of the bodies found in Pompeii where the agonies of their last moments could be seen clearly on their remains.

The murals and frescoes were no longer situated in their original Akrotiri locations, being considered too rare and valuable to be left in the open site. Lynn had seen the originals and some expert replicas in various museums in Greece and the impact had been staggering. It was immediately obvious that the Minoans enjoyed a very high standard of living to have time and leisure to produce such fine art to decorate walls in the inner chambers of their homes.

The scenes of the saffron pickers were the ones that impressed her the most. Stavros had a poster of just one of the women from the wall paintings found in Akrotiri. Whenever she passed the poster at home she drew breath at the sheer beauty of the woman at her work. From the top of her head where a blue cap covered her skull, (or could it be a shaved head painted blue?), leaving a wisp of hair over her forehead and a long, high ponytail at the back, to the detail on the pantaloons that covered her legs, she was a picture of style and decoration in every part of her costume. Lynn loved the tiny tassels that swung from her short-sleeved and embroidered, golden over-vest and dangled in larger version from the layers of her costume as if to keep the various materials in place. The sleeves, in a very light fabric, were edged in a blue bobbled circle. The detail was incredible and her large gold hoop earrings combined with what looked like make-up on her exquisite face, gave the unknown woman a modern look that belied her century.

Lynn knew that even today, women in Afghanistan were employed to pick the precious spice from crocus plants because their fingers are smaller and would be less likely to damage the delicate flowers, but to think of these Minoan beauties in their individual fantastic costumes working amidst the wild plants in a rocky field where swallow-like birds frolicked and exotic flowers bloomed, was to be filled with wonder at an age lost in the far reaches of time.

She stood on the paved streets, looking up at the two and three-story houses where she knew sophisticated drainage systems had been found amid stores of pithi jars containing oil and wine. There, where everyday kitchen utensils lay abandoned when the earth roared, Lynn could imagine again the splendor that once adorned the walls of these homes.

She could see Stavros further up the street that wound between the houses. He was deep in consultation with two dust-covered young men. Often, one or both of the resident archaeologists was a graduate of her husband's courses. No doubt they were discussing progress on the latest excavations.

It was a painstaking endeavour to extract the rock-solid pumice without destroying what might lie beneath.

Lynn left them to their deliberations. She knew that Stavros would regale her with all the important news when they relaxed over dinner later. In the meantime she would conduct her own leisurely exploration looking for signs of daily life 3500 years ago. Then she would wander out to the shoreline and sit by the sea thinking of the past and the future and trying to decide what was best for herself and for her family.

She knew Stavros would find her there eventually.

Twelve

"I have never been so embarrassed in my whole life, Alina. How could you do that to me?"

"I apologize, Anna. It was a bad idea but I really wanted to get a look at him."

"Well, you certainly did *that* and did you notice how fast you chased him away? I doubt I will hear from him again after that fiasco."

"But you looked like you were getting along so well together. Susan and I thought you were quite a nice couple, gazing across the table at each other."

"That's another thing. How could you inveigle Susan into this mess? I'll bet it wasn't her idea!"

"Well, no, I kind of forced her into it, but, in my defense, she was just as curious as I was. We don't want you to be duped into anything by some unscrupulous fellow who will just take your money and run."

"Thank you very much for your confidence in my ability to take care of myself!"

"Now, don't get defensive, Anna. We were only looking after your best interests. You hardly know the guy and there you were enjoying long looks across the coffee cups like a couple of teenagers."

"I beg your pardon! That was a *business* meeting and I was beginning to get to grips with exactly what I wanted from him before you two barged in with your feeble excuses and scared him off."

Anna thought it advisable to keep secret the incredible insights Lawren had revealed to her. Now was not the time to give her friend any more ammunition against the artist. After all, it was true that she would not likely hear from him again. She turned away so that Alina would not read on her face the disappointment this thought created.

"Look, my dear, I am so sorry for upsetting you. Perhaps it's best that he ran off so fast. We may have saved you from a terrible disappointment."

"If there is any disappointment, it will be because a special project I really wanted to complete is now impossible before we leave for Scotland."

With this final word, Anna stormed out of the kitchen and headed for her bedroom leaving a stricken Alina wondering if she had misinterpreted the entire situation.

Lawren Drake had not slept all night. Since rushing back to his studio he had devoted his attention to sketching Anna's face, and also that of Helen Dunlop, and trying a variety of positions for the two heads. Slightly overlapping looked too much like a ceremonial coin and head to head was too aggressive.

For an hour or two during the night when the building was all but vacant and the stillness of the night sharpened his inner focus, he turned to the background of the painting. What elements could capture the personalities of these two women? Each tiny item would be highly significant as an indicator of their lives and times. It came to him that books were a common connection. Anna had been a teacher and librarian and Helen had revealed her story through diaries and letters. He quickly added a book which he placed in

Anna's hands, or where her hands would be in a finished portrait. He stepped back and considered the effect. No, the book was a link between the women so it needed to be passed from one to the other as their stories were passed from one generation to another.

This made him wonder if three women were involved in the story. He sketched, very lightly, a ghost-like figure of Anna's mother fading into the background. That seemed more interesting but he was not sure. The background was becoming more insistent. He needed to solve the problem of what lay behind the figures.

The obvious thing was the house in Scotland. The portrait would hang on the wall of that house so it made sense to incorporate the very thing that had brought Anna from Canada to Scotland in the first place. The only problem with this idea was that he had no clear vision of the house and Anna had not supplied a picture. If there was to be a house in the background, it had to be the authentic building not one made up out of his head. That would be essential to the integrity of the painting.

He stopped for a moment and rubbed his tired eyes. He was creating more problems, not finding any solutions. He had only himself to blame for this dilemma. Once he had broken his rule to work only with live subjects, he had wandered off a path where he knew his way. Yet, he was now committed.

There was something about Anna Mason that captured his interest and he knew from long experience that this was the sign of something good to come. In all the successful portraits he had ever completed, this very feeling of deep interest had been a prime factor in his perseverance and eventual artistic satisfaction.

He threw down his pencils in frustration and was about to rip the cartridge paper from its place on his easel, when he decided to re-evaluate what he had done in the light of morning, after he had achieved a few hours of sleep.

His bedroom was hidden in an alcove behind a curtain and consisted of a futon liberally piled with blankets and pillows. A small television sat on a three-drawer chest and this served as a table to hold a bedside lamp. Neither the television nor the lamp, were much used. By the time he gave up working in the early morning it was his practice to flop into the nest of pillows, adjust the covers and sink immediately into sleep. His final thought as he pulled blankets over his working clothes was that he was glad Anna Mason had not caught even a glimpse of his spartan sleeping conditions. Her pity was not something he ever wished to confront.

When he opened his eyes it was close to noon. The light flooding into his studio from the skylight in the roof indicated the time of day was perfect for painting. He dragged himself out of the tangle of bedcovers and yawned hugely as he filled an electric kettle at the tap in the stone sink, liberally decorated with paint splashes, and emptied the last of his instant coffee into a metal mug which he favoured because it held the heat inside even when he forgot to drink.

Holding this mug he positioned himself in front of the easel and angled it so as to catch the northern light perfectly.

Now what?

As sometimes happened, the sketches of the previous night held a germ of an idea that just might be workable. He retrieved a pencil and began to rough in a foreground where the figures of Anna and Helen would take predominance. Behind them, in the middle ground, would be the house, and here he drew a featureless box. In the distant background a hill rising to the sky would complete the scene.

Once again the lack of detail about the house and the hill Anna referred to as Helen's Hill, brought his frustration alive. There was nothing else for it. He would have to contact Anna again and plead for any photographs she had in her possession. Until then, he could work on the faces of the two women.

As soon as he felt he had captured Anna's spirit he would invite her back to see an initial painting. This would take a few days to accomplish to his satisfaction but would be, he admitted to himself, by far the most pleasant and easy section of the work. Yes, he said aloud. I will enjoy this part.

Working mostly from memory he began to deepen the light pencil lines of his original sketch. He found her face came quickly and he reached for coloured pencils to try to capture the colour of her hair and the blue eyes that crinkled at the corners when she laughed.

The coffee mug stood abandoned on his stool as he brought Anna Mason to life with a few dexterous strokes. This was what he lived for; the power that flowed through his fingers and transformed blank white paper into a living, breathing being.

The sun slid down the sky and Lawren Drake gently nudged his easel across the floor to capture every last ray of its light. He did this unconsciously. He was immersed in another world where nothing mattered at all compared to the creativity that commanded him. Occasionally, he closed his eyes briefly, but the pencil continued to move inexorably as if it had a life of its own.

When the light had all but faded, he stepped back and without looking at his efforts, took a washroom break which involved leaving the studio and walking across the landing to a facility shared with the tenant in the other studio apartment. As usual, the washroom was vacant. The other tenant was an older man who appeared rarely. Lawren had spoken to him only a couple of times and it had occurred to him to wonder what his purpose was for a studio apartment which he seldom used. This suited Lawren, however, as he had almost exclusive use of the top floor.

Washing and shaving occupied a few minutes. By the time he had finished his ablutions, hunger was making itself felt. He returned to his studio, grabbed wallet and keys then ran down the stairs to retrieve his bicycle from a locked shed at the rear of the property.

A ride to the university would clear his head and he could eat at one of the student cafeterias where the prices suited his income. He fit in perfectly with the varied student population and often used the library facilities for research or browsing through their vast collection of art works, looking for inspiration.

Tonight the community centre cafeteria was noisy and bubbling with the energy of evening class students. Lawren chose a meal from the daily specials board and decided to eat his food in one of the secluded courtyards he had discovered at the rear of nearby college buildings. A stone bench served as table and seat. A convenient, and, he noted, well-designed, garbage/recycling receptacle, soon received his meal's plastic cover, paper plate and napkin. He stowed the disposable plastic utensils in his jacket pocket for later use. Dishwashing was not one of his few domestic activities.

With hunger satisfied, he waited for a sense of relaxation to enter his mind but instead he felt more revved up than before. The moonlit night was calm, the air cool, the paper coffee cup comforting and the surrounding under-lit plant beds soothing to the eyes, yet he could not rest. He needed to see the results of his day's work on the easel in his studio. Once the thought had entered his mind there was nothing for it but to return home immediately.

As soon as he unlocked the studio door and clicked on the overhead light, he knew what was disturbing his peace of mind. The initial portrait of Anna on cartridge paper was there in front of him and even through the prism of his high standards he knew it was superb. A few deft touches and the application of custom-mixed oil paint colours that he instinctively combined in his mind as he looked at the sketch, would ensure the compelling figure was captured accurately as the centre of the work.

Her head was turned slightly so that she would gaze out at the person viewing the painting but she was firmly embedded in the background also. He had caught that quizzical expression that he had first noticed when they met at her London home. It seemed perfect to imbue the feeling of the mystery she had undertaken when Helen Dunlop came into Anna's life. He was surprised to see that his attempt at the less distinct figure of Helen, drawn just behind Anna, was more successful than he had hoped.

His fingers itched to pull out a canvas, stretch it onto the easel and begin the oil portrait, but something stopped him. The atmosphere of the piece depended on the background. He knew this element could subtly affect everything in the foreground, particularly the figures.

Without further thought he dialed Anna's number on his cell phone. When he heard it ringing he realized he had no idea of the hour and it was too late to wonder if he was disturbing her household. After three rings he almost cancelled the call when a female voice responded.

"Hello!"

"Yes, this is Lawren Drake. Could I speak to Anna Mason please?" A silence met this request. Lawren had a sudden image of his rapid exit from the coffee pub and the expression on the face of one of the women who had interrupted his meeting with Anna. The person on the line must be Anna's friend Alina and her first impression of him could not have been positive.

"Just a minute. I'll get her for you."

No polite conversation then. He waited, scarcely breathing.

Alina found Anna watching television and informed her, "That artist guy is on the phone for you." She could not resist a cautionary comment as Anna jumped up from the sofa. "Now, don't be tricked into anything until you've seen his work."

Ignoring this unwanted advice, Anna walked quickly into the small office so she could close the door and have privacy during her conversation.

"Anna here. Can you hold on a moment?" Without waiting for an answer she listened until she heard the other phone click into its base. "Sorry! I wanted to be sure we could talk freely."

"Does that mean your friend dislikes me?"

"No! I wouldn't say that, but she is protective of me and she doesn't really know you yet."

Encouraged by the sound of that word, 'yet', Lawren felt emboldened to jump right into the reason for his late call.

"I've been working full out on your portrait, Anna, but I've come up against a problem."

"Really? I gave you the photographs just yesterday. Surely you haven't finished the project?"

"Not a chance!"

Anna detected the chuckle in his words and felt embarrassed that she had said such a foolish thing. "But, the good news is that I am remarkably pleased with my progress!"

"That's wonderful! Then what is the problem you mentioned?"

"Well, I need a good photograph of the house and the site. It is going to be an essential element in the background and I want it to be accurate."

Anna's heart sank when she heard this. She was no photographer. She cast around in her memory to see if she had actually taken any photographs of the house. She knew there were photos taken from the top of Helen's Hill but that would not suit his purpose. There were interior photos taken after the renovations were completed, but again, not what he was looking for.

"I………. I'm afraid I don't have anything here, but you could check out the web site where they advertise the property for rental. I think there are some shots there that might be useful. Oh, and my young friend Fiona is an expert photographer, I could ask her to take some for you and send them online. Oh, no, on second thoughts, she's in Inverness at the moment. That won't work. I'm so sorry! Is this going to hold up your progress?"

"It could do. I am conscious of your deadline of the end of May. I'll look at the source you suggested and see if it is what I need. Don't worry! We'll sort something out. Bye."

In spite of his hopeful words, Anna could tell that Lawren was disappointed. She quickly turned on the desk computer and called up the website for holiday rentals in Scotland. There were, indeed, several photographs of the property but they were taken at a distance in order to display the superb setting rather than the house itself. Interior photographs were the main feature of the mini video. People needed to see the accommodations they would be acquiring.

Anna realized Lawren would not be satisfied with the site photos. She waited for another call from him to tell her so, but the phone was silent.

As the minutes passed, she grew more and more annoyed with the way things were developing with the portrait project. She had had such high hopes initially, but now everything was falling apart and she would not be able to take the finished work to Scotland for the June visit. It looked as if Alina was right about the futility of it all and Anna hated the thought of admitting it to her.

Her annoyance was mainly with herself and not with the artist. He had made every effort to meet her unrealistic demands and now she was adding another difficulty. It all seemed to stem from the choice he had agreed to, when he said he would take on the job even although it was impossible to work with a live model of Helen.

Anna felt guilt flood through her. She had insulted this man's expertise by demanding one compromise after another. How could he be proud of the finished portrait if he could not work with the authentic setting?

An idea came to Anna. It was impulsive and irrational, perhaps. Alina was not likely to agree but it felt right in the moment and Anna hit redial on her phone before she could change her mind.

"Lawren? I think I have a solution to the problem. What do you think of coming to Scotland with Alina and me?"

"I beg your pardon? Repeat that please. I'm sure I heard you wrong."

"No, you did not. I feel so guilty for all the difficulties you are dealing with. Why not come to Scotland and complete the work there. You can see the spectacular scenery for yourself and possibly get a better sense of Helen Dunlop from her house. What do you say?"

"I don't know *what* to say. It is a very generous offer, of course, but I couldn't afford the plane fare, I'm afraid."

"Oh, no! You would come as my guest. I insist! It's the least I can do to make up for the difficulties I have saddled you with. Please say you will come."

Anna heard an intake of breath on the other end of the phone. She automatically crossed her fingers as she waited for his answer. Seconds ticked by until she heard his solemn voice.

"If you are really sure about this, I would be grateful to accept your amazing offer, Anna, but I want you to think it over tonight. I'll talk to you about this tomorrow. Don't hesitate to change your mind if you wish to. I think this is the most surprising and generous thing that has ever happened to me and I thank you sincerely."

Anna could detect a catch in his voice on the last words. She said goodbye and put down the phone before he could say more.

Impulsive conduct was all very well, but now she would have to explain it to Alina.

Thirteen

"You did *what?* Why would you do such a thing? You hardly know this man and we have no idea what he might do at close quarters. He could rob us blind and disappear, or worse! Honestly, Anna, this behaviour is quite out of line for you. Is this blessed portrait of Helen so important to you that you would risk so much for it?"

Anna had known that Alina was unlikely to welcome her suggestion that Lawren accompany them to Scotland but she had not expected the outrage she heard in her friend's tone of voice.

Rather than escalate the argument by commenting in a similar vein she kept her shock under control and replied in a quieter voice.

"I can't imagine why you should be this disturbed by the idea, Alina. He may not accept my offer and, in any case he would be working in the house and not getting in our way at all. You need not see him. He would sleep downstairs and once the portrait was finished he would return to Canada."

Anna did not mention the fact that she was sponsoring Lawren's travel. With any luck, Alina need not know about this little nugget of information.

Before Alina could marshal another objection, Anna went on calmly, "After all, you will be in Manchester with Philip for some of the time. Lawren would be company for me."

"What makes you think I would be reassured by that?" Alina threw her hands in the air in exasperation then decided to change tactics. "You still haven't answered my question about Helen's portrait. What's the urgency about it?"

"I really don't know. I do feel that now is the right time for this. It's as if I have received so much from Aunt Helen and given nothing back. I just want to honour her in some way and this idea felt right to me. I am sorry it doesn't meet with your approval, Alina. I would prefer to have you on my side."

Anna's heartfelt appeal to her friend's better nature seemed to have the desired effect. Alina moved from the chair by the fireside where the confrontation had begun even before breakfast was over, and sat down beside Anna on the couch. She reached behind her and squeezed her shoulders in a gesture of affection and support.

"You are right, of course! I am a fool for overreacting that way. I think I must be jealous of the trust you have in this artist fellow. I'll agree to back down right away. But, if he does decide to go with us, I will not leave for Manchester before I am sure we won't be murdered in our beds!"

Both women burst out in spontaneous laughter at the absurdity of this statement and the tension between them evaporated.

Still gasping for breath, Anna managed to blurt out her final assurance.

"I promise you, if I see any signs of murder weapons when I go to his studio today, I will call off the whole project."

"I will hold you to that promise Anna Mason, and don't you forget it!"

Anna approached the elegant old Victorian house with its gables and fretwork and could not resist straightening her yellow spring jacket and smoothing down her hair again before she rang the bell labelled neatly; 'L. Drake'.

A clatter of feet on the wooden stairs announced his imminent arrival and with a last tug of her navy skirt and a welcoming smile, she prepared to encounter Lawren Drake for the third time.

A thought passed through her mind that perhaps Alina had a point. What did she really know about this man? Before the thought could take root she was following him up the stairs and into the studio apartment where a covered easel held pride of place beneath the skylight.

"Now, I need to warn you that this is only a preliminary version of the finished work," he began.

"I wanted to give you some idea of what I am trying to achieve, before I hear your decision on how we progress from here."

Anna noted some trepidation in his manner. He had not asked what her final decision was on whether she meant to invite him to work on the portrait in Scotland and she had to admire his restraint.

Suddenly the material to be revealed on the easel assumed enormous importance.

Sweat began to form on her palms.

What would she say if the work in progress did not match the ideas she had already? She cautioned herself to control her first reaction. After all she was not the expert in this field. She must not jump to conclusions.

These thoughts were no sooner in her mind than they were tested in the extreme. Lawren's portrait emerged from its dust cloth shroud and Anna was shocked to see her own face, or a version of it, front and centre. She hardly noticed the other details, so surprised was she by this turn of events.

With rigid control to prevent herself from exclaiming her distress, she stood silently, aware of Lawren's eyes on her and calculating that close scrutiny of his work was something he would expect at this point. She prayed he might not be aware of the reason for her silence.

After what seemed like an age, she stepped back and attempted a half-smile. He took that as an invitation to speak up.

"As I said, Anna, this is only a glimpse at what I intend to achieve. I don't usually allow clients to see this stage of my work but the circumstances are different in this case. I couldn't let you commit to the expense of sending me across the Atlantic if you were not happy with my progress."

She cleared her throat and ventured a reply. "I see. Well, I must admit I was not expecting to see myself in the portrait. I thought Helen Dunlop was the subject."

"That's a natural assumption, I guess. My thinking was that neither of us can see the real Helen and you are the obvious link to her. As a live subject, you are much easier to capture."

He stopped and waited for a reaction.

"You have certainly shown me in a flattering light, Lawren. I don't see myself looking like this."

"Ah! Well, none of us sees what the observer does. When we look in a mirror we see a reversed image so a painting looks unfamiliar at first. I can assure you that what I have done so far represents the real you very well."

Anna looked again at the figure in the centre of the sketch. She was seated with a book in her hands and shown from the waist up. Her face was lit from the side and her bronze cap of hair shone in the light as if every strand had been drawn separately. There was something blue wound around her shoulders and it picked up the colour of her eyes. There was a glow on her cheeks that she had never noticed in her own mirror and she truly felt some embarrassment at the overall effect of seeing a younger, more attractive version of herself; a version that Lawren Drake had never seen in reality.

"How did you manage to do this when we have scarcely been in each other's company for a couple of hours in total?"

"I am trained to observe closely and to retain the visual image in my mind. You may not think so, Anna, but you are an interesting subject. There is experience and sadness in your eyes and yet a great sense of optimism in the lift of your chin and in the way you hold your head."

He paused and stepped forward to look into her eyes.

"Are you displeased with the work so far?"

Anna caught the hint of concern in his enquiry and rushed to assure him that she was flattered more than anything. "It's hard for me to look away from the amazing person I see here, but now that you have explained it, I am noticing much more about the sketchier parts of the work."

"When I transfer the finished ideas to oil on canvas everything has a greater intensity and there will be some changes to this initial plan. What do you think about the idea of your benefactress appearing just behind you with her hand in view and a journal or letter being passed to you?"

"Now that I think of it, it is a brilliant way to tell the story of our connection. I can see the resemblance to my mother and Helen's figure seeming less pronounced, indicates that she is no longer present in real life."

She dragged her eye away from the foreground and saw the tentative attempts at pencil outlines where presumably he wished to use the Scottish scenes. The time was right to announce her conviction aloud.

"I think we should agree that it is necessary for you to travel to Scotland to complete this work, Lawren. It is the only way to do justice to the setting. What do you say?"

"I can say nothing other than a most heartfelt thank you, Anna. It is a remarkably kind gesture. I look forward to it immensely. I must confess I was bold enough to think about this last night and I figured that I could transport these sketches easily on the plane and take my canvas, paints and brushes with me. You would have to commit some time to sit for me at first and I could look for the perfect frame for the portrait in the country where it belongs."

"An excellent idea! I know just the person to help you search. My friend Jeanette knows every antique store and auction house in the area."

Enthusiasm added a higher pitch to her voice and a warm smile to her face. "You will love, Scotland! Oban is quite the most beautiful place you can imagine. I will work out the details and get in touch with you soon. Do you mind travelling on your own? I doubt we could get you on the same plane at this late date."

"Not at all! I don't want to interrupt your plans more than necessary. I have one or two small jobs to finish up and then I am free to go."

"Wonderful!" She reached out to clasp his hand in the traditional sealing of a deal and found his strong hand ready to grip her own. He really has the most amazing eyes, she thought, as she bid him farewell and almost skipped down the stairs.

I will introduce this carefully to Alina, she planned. Lawren's arrival at the McCaig farmhouse need not interfere with our attendance at Fiona's graduation. Alina should be leaving for Manchester shortly after that and Lawren can concentrate on his work.

The day seemed brighter than before as she drove out of the city. She chuckled to herself when she imagined the effect of the finished portrait on the wall above the mantel in the big double bedroom.

It will be spectacular, she thought. Perhaps I will have a gathering to introduce Lawren to the friends I have made in Oban. Wouldn't it be fine if he found more work when people see an example of his talent? She quietly hummed a Scottish folk song she had heard and loved. It will be so good to be back there again, she decided with a pleased smile.

Alina met her at the door as soon as she had parked the car.

"There's a registered letter for you, Anna. I had to sign for it. It looks important."

"Probably just a request for some of our new A Plus goods to be mailed somewhere," insisted Anna.

She refused to echo her friend's anxious tone of voice. The day had gone too well to be spoiled at this point, but when she saw the legal firm's letter head, she had a sensation of déjà vu. It was a lawyer's letter that had started the whole business of Helen Dunlop's legacy and everything that had emerged from then.

Tearing open the stiff brown envelope, she found a letter typed on cream bond paper and as soon as she recognized the Ottawa address, she shivered. This could not be good news.

"What is it? You have gone quite pale Anna."

"I'm afraid it's about Richard."

"Oh, dear! I'll leave you to read it on your own."

Anna did not notice her friend's departure to brew a large pot of tea. At moments like this, tea was always the drink of choice in their household. She grabbed her reading glasses from the desk and put them on with a shaking hand.

> Mr. Richard Mason asked us to inform you of his death after a valiant fight against cancer.
>
> A cremation took place three weeks ago in Ottawa. The delay in this communication is at our client's request.
>
> Please find, enclosed, a private letter from Mr. Mason. We await your further instructions.
>
> Sincerely,
> Aaron Schuyler
> *Brooks, Winston and Schuyler.*

Anna sat down on the nearest chair with a thump. Although she had half-expected this news she had always retained a hope that Richard would contact her before the end. The memory of his nasty wife had stopped her from making any enquiries in Ottawa and now it was too late to have that last conversation with him.

The letter from Richard was closed with a wax seal. She slowly unfolded the letter, breaking the seal apart and began to read. Tears formed as soon as she saw the first words.

My Dear Anna,

As you will now know, my final battle with cancer has been a losing one. The truth is, I am beyond exhaustion and ready to go.

I wanted to tell you how glad I am that we met in Egypt. Despite the difficult circumstances, I feel we resolved some issues and parted as friends. This gives me considerable peace of mind.

One more thing needs to be settled between us. After the divorce, I made sure that my mother never contacted you. As you know, she was very fond of you and I did a disservice to both by keeping you apart when you might have consoled each other.

My mother's diabetes finally took her life five years ago. She left something in her will, specifically for you and I have withheld it until now, to my shame.

If you can forgive me, and accept her small tribute, it will allow me to draw a line under another of my life regrets.

Be happy.
Richard.

A flood of emotions overwhelmed Anna and her sobs drew Alina back with a tray of tea things which she promptly set down on the coffee table. "What is it Anna? What's happened?"

"Richard has died." When she heard the words spoken aloud it brought on another bout of weeping and for a time all Alina could do was to gently pat her friend's back.

When the storm had abated somewhat and a box of tissues offered, Anna found her voice again.

"It's not just that. He sent a letter to solve a mystery about his mother."

"What kind of mystery? I thought she cut you off because you divorced her son."

"That's what I believed all these years and it hurt me so much. We were good friends during the marriage and I couldn't understand why she would take Richard's side and let me flounder on my own with so many unanswered questions."

"I remember you saying how you shared many a laugh with Rose about her fixation on everything red or pink."

"That's right! She had rose-themed wallpaper and bedspreads and her wardrobe was full of delicate flower prints. She was quite an eccentric character and totally different from her son."

"Is Rose still alive?"

"No. Richard tells me in the letter that she passed away five years ago. I wish I had known. I would have gone to see her, if I had known the truth."

"What truth?"

"He says he deliberately kept his mother from contacting me after the divorce and that's why I never heard from her again. She must have moved to Ottawa with Richard because her old address was taken over by a new family."

"This is sad, Anna, but you must have suspected Richard would not survive the winter. When we saw him in Luxor, he was not at all well."

"I know, but I hoped his latest round of chemo might have bought him some more time."

Alina poured tea for both of them and placed the hot cup in Anna's hands. There was always comfort in tea, especially at a time like this.

They talked over the old days when Richard and Anna were happy and gradually Anna began to put the past back where it belonged. She felt a sense of closure. It was finally over. No more vain hopes or thoughts of restoring what had been lost. It was a surprise to realize she had still held such wishes at the back of her mind.

The future was a clear path before her now and into that future jumped an image of Lawren. She was shocked to the core at this unseemly juxtaposition. What was she thinking? She was not consciously looking for a replacement for Richard. He had been gone from her life for so long and she had never noticed the lack of a male partner. She and Alina were content and happy together. Good work partners and good friends. The last thing she wanted was to venture into the minefield of a new relationship and most certainly not a relationship with a younger man.

Clarity came to her mind with the shock of this discovery. Perhaps it was the influence of Alina's new interest in Philip, or possibly the fact that she had spent time with Lawren in the last little while and his strong personality had affected her. Whichever it was, she would have to guard her actions and words very carefully from now on. She was clearly vulnerable at the moment.

"Have you heard one word I've said in the last five minutes, Anna?"

"Uh, sorry! My mind is all over the place. I think I'll go and lie down for an hour. There's been a lot to think about lately." Silently, she thought, this thinking includes whether or not I will contact Richard's lawyer to find out about Rose's bequest.

Alina stood aside and watched her friend close the door to her bedroom. She was thinking Anna's behavior was definitely unusual.

This business with Richard must have affected her much more deeply than I would have guessed, she concluded. I'll leave her to it. No doubt she'll tell me when she is ready.

As she picked up the tray and headed for the kitchen a stray thought drifted into her mind and was quickly pushed out again. Accompanying the phrase; 'Time heals all wounds', came the counterpoint, 'Time wounds all heels'.

"Lord above!" she exclaimed, "I did not know I still held these deep feelings of anger at Richard. Thank God Anna did not hear that said aloud! What would she think of me?"

Fourteen

Two days after their trip to Santorini, Stavros judged the time was right to show his wife the site of their proposed new home. Lynn was visibly more relaxed and she had acquired the light tan that made her skin glow and brought her silver hair into sharp and attractive contrast with the dark eyes and eyebrows that gave her face distinction.

She wore a new peach dress he had bought for her, with broad straps, a flowing skirt and a gold belt around her neat waist. She looked like the young girl he had first met on the Greek islands so many years before and his heart accelerated to see her so content.

He had waited for the perfect moment; a brilliant day with just a light breeze and fresh green dappling the stony hillsides. Borrowing a ramshackle old car from one of his many cousins, they drove out of town after a particularly good lunch shared on the patio of a tavern. He had ordered one of Lynn's favourite dishes; fresh lobster thermidor with green salad and feta cheese washed down with a delightful semi-dry white wine that even he realized was worth every penny it cost.

A recent rain had damped down the dusty road and after a drive of a few pleasant miles, he turned off the main road and down a bumpy track towards the Aegean, slowing deliberately so that the incredible view would come into sight gradually, unrolling slowly before them for the greatest effect.

Lynn was aware that she was getting the full treatment. Not only lunch, gifts and a country drive, but, more importantly, her husband's complete attention. Despite this awareness, she could not but respond to the influence of the day and the occasion.

She held her breath as the car slowly advanced onto soft sand, and stopped. The windows were down and the first thing she noticed was the sea-scented air blowing her hair gently back from her face. The small bay before her was enclosed by two low and curving headlands, like the fingers of a lover caressing a beloved face. Between them was the brilliant blue of the sea and in the sheltered bay the waves creamed on the shore with scarcely a murmur.

At first Lynn could not speak, or even tear her eyes away from the combination of sight, scent and sound. In the back of her head she knew this occasion had been choreographed by Stavros for maximum impact. Her own impressions were what mattered most now and she would be true to herself and still give this amazing place a fair chance to work its enchantment on her.

She sensed her husband's impatience to speak, but she held up a warning hand and opened the car door so she could see and experience everything.

The sand was soft and warm through her sandals. She walked parallel to the shore line until she came to the ruins of a wooden shack situated right in the centre of the bay but about 200 yards from the sea. Behind the shack a hummock of scrub and bushes acted as a windbreak and sheltered a hidden flock of small birds twittering in alarm at her approach.

She stood on the concrete pad that was all that was left of the terrace Stavros had told her of, where he and his brothers and sisters had dried off after swimming and enjoyed calamari with Pepsi cola.

The time had come to seriously consider if a house on this site could possibly translate to a home in which she could happily spend the rest of her life.

Looking out again at the constantly changing azure shades of the sea she noticed for the first time that there were two or three small homes tucked into the hillside closer to the waves. Neighbours, perhaps? That would be a good thing when Stavros was off teaching his courses. How would these people feel about a foreigner invading their pristine paradise? Would she feel isolated here? What would it be like to live here in the winter when stormy waters pounded the shoreline?

As if he had heard her unspoken questions, Stavros appeared at her side and placed a warm arm around her shoulders.

"What do you think, Lynn? Isn't it a magical place?"

Without taking her eyes away from the stunning view she said, "No one could deny that Stavros, as you very well know."

"I wanted you to see it at its best so we could discuss the house together. I think it should be tall enough to capture all the views. The original small footprint of the restaurant does not allow us to expand too far forward so I thought three levels would be appropriate with a deck area on the roof for days when you prefer not to get sand between your toes."

Lynn let him ramble on. She scarcely listened to his enthusiastic plans. As far as she was concerned it was far too early to be discussing how many rooms there would be or what type of windows would work best. These were decisions for a future time when, and if, she had committed to the entire move to Greece. There was a lot more than square footage at risk here. Her entire life would have to be reset like a clock when the seasons change. She would not, could not, be swayed by the importuning of the master persuader at her side. For once in their life, she would have to make up her own mind. The consequences of a mistake at this point were too awful to consider.

She hated to burst the fantasy bubble he was expanding to encompass them both but it was time to bring some harsh realities to bear on the issue.

"Stavros, please sit down here beside me and please listen to me. You know I love you. I can see how much this plan means to you and I know what you have said about the opportunity this gives us to capitalize on our savings. I can't deny any of that and I know I am behaving out of character in questioning your decisions about our future."

She stopped and swallowed, but could not look at her husband's face in case she saw disappointment there. She had rehearsed this speech many times in the middle of the night and if she failed to deliver it now, in this place, she would never have the courage again.

"I wish I could throw myself into your arms and agree to every wonderful thing you have planned but the truth is, I am afraid.

No, don't stop me. Just listen.

My little life in England may not be as interesting or as stimulating as yours, my dear, but it is my security. It is where I belong. My family, my friends and my routines are my anchor when you are far away or involved in your work. They define me.

Who will I be when all that is gone?

You know very well, Stavros, what my greatest fear is. You watched as both my parents descended into their separate hells. My self-confidence is all that keeps me from being overwhelmed by the fear of dementia. I dare not risk such a disorienting change in my life at this point. Perhaps I am too old, but I am definitely too afraid."

Lynn stopped and tried to still her shaking by breathing deeply of the briny air. A seabird called out raucously and she heard it as strident ridicule of her fears. She dreaded what her husband would say next. She could almost hear the wheels of his fine mind whirling and clicking as he selected and rejected a hundred reasons why her protests were invalid. To his credit, he did not express anger or try to change her opinion.

After a minute he did the unexpected; the one thing that could actually help her situation. He asked a question.

"Tell me what else is bothering you?"

A rush of air escaped from her lungs. The relief was palpable. She had done it. She had said her piece and the world did not dissolve away. She leaned into his shoulder and began again.

"Well, it's really part of the same problem but on a more practical level I suppose. If we leave England, I will have my old age pension but it will be frozen at the current rate and never benefit from any subsequent cost of living increases."

"But, my dear, my pensions are sufficient to keep us comfortably here in Greece where we can definitely live more cheaply."

"I realize that, but the more serious implication is that our access to the National Health System will expire after a period out of the country."

He hesitated and then continued in a more subdued tone of voice. "Oh! Are you thinking that if the worst happened, you would not be able to rely on health care, similar to what your mother had in the nursing home in Heathfield?"

"Exactly! You know how I feel about being a burden on Sarah and you also know how we had to sell my parents' home in order to qualify for the care she received in the English nursing home towards the end of her life. Neither one of us was capable of looking after her by then, Stavros. I could not bear for you to lose your home to fund my final years in either country."

"But, Lynn, why would I not look after you here? We could plan a ground floor bedroom suite that could be converted to nursing care if it ever became necessary. That would work for either one of us. Who knows what the future will bring."

"Oh, my dearest! I am so moved by your generosity but I could never allow you to sacrifice your life for me in that way. I know what it means and I would hate it if you tried. We know each other very well and you would, no doubt, endure to the limits of your patience but it would kill me to see you fail, as you inevitably would."

Silence met this dire prediction. Cruel reality seemed out of place here in this lovely bay, but Lynn knew it was a reality that had to be dealt with. Strangely, she was not depressed by stating her fears. She felt warmed through by the understanding Stavros had shown. He had not denied the truth of her concerns and this gave her hope that he might turn his creative mind to solving their current problems in the same way that he solved teaching and archaeology challenges in the other areas of his life.

He was a brilliant man. She hardly knew how she had managed to hold on to him for all these years and now she was threatening a precious plan for his well-deserved retirement in this place where his roots lay so deeply.

She had no idea what would happen. It seemed to be a dilemma with no obvious solution.

Stavros returned to the car and brought back a knitted wrap for his wife's shoulders.

Without a word, they sat with clasped hands and watched the sun slowly descend toward the sea. A glorious sunset would soon be unfolding before them as if to display the finest, most appealing views the location could offer.

Lynn saw the splendour but felt drained of sufficient energy to respond.

Her husband's brain, however, was humming with layered plans and strategies.

Yes, this was a setback.

Plan A might not proceed but there was always a plan B. Always.

Lynn seemed emptied of emotion in the days following her confession about her fears. She was content to sit in the sun reading or sleeping. They had a meal or two with Stavros' relatives and took leisurely drives to visit familiar land marks on Paros, but Lynn was glad to rest for most of the time. They did not discuss the dilemma any further and this suited Stavros very well. His plans progressed without interruption.

First he contacted Sarah at home in Uckfield and swore her to secrecy. His enquiry was related to the possibility that her mother could spend several months of the year living in Sarah and David's house in England.

Sarah was startled to get this request from her father and answered swiftly. "Of course, dad! You don't have to ask. We will shortly have two spare bedrooms the way things are going over here. Does this mean that you intend to go ahead with the move to Greece? What does mum say about it?"

"Your mother has concerns, naturally, but I am trying to work out solutions for her. Please say nothing until I have more information."

"All right, if you insist. When will you two be home again?"

"Your mother will be back soon but I am going to stay on for a while. I have work to do for my summer course as well as all the other stuff here on Paros. Give my love to Caroline and Mike and thank David for me."

"I will do, dad. What am I thanking David for?"

"Oh, just for marrying such an amazing wife!"

He closed off his mobile phone while Sarah's laughter still rang in his ears.

That was the easy part done. Now he had to tackle something much more delicate. He had to renew his previous contacts with Lynn's brother Philip. This arrangement, also, had to be kept secret for now so he waited till his wife was dozing on the hotel terrace in the afternoon sun and snuck off down one of the town lanes where he would be overheard only by pots of geraniums and sleepy cats.

*"Philip, it's Lynn's husband Stavros again. Do you have
any more information about your schedule this summer?"*
Stavros knew how busy the architect was and got straight to the
point. Philip was not a person who enjoyed small talk.

*"Ah, I was about to contact you Stavros. I have been
thinking about your ideas for the beach property. As you
know our firm specializes in solar and green technologies
and your building in Greece seems a good candidate to
try out some new ideas. I want to experiment with a
technique for a movable solar panel that tracks the sun
and collects much more energy. We could install several
on the roof and still have room for the upper deck area
you mentioned."*

Stavros was elated. He had expected to have to persuade Philip to
get involved in the project and instead, he was running with it
beyond any of Stavros' expectations.

*"I am delighted with these ideas Philip. Does this mean
you do have time to work with me this summer?"*

*"I can come down and see the site and draw up plans
subsequent to that but I can't commit a team of on-site
people. We are too busy with the London Olympics here.
Once I know the technologies we can use on Paros, I will
send a tech expert. Can you furnish a builder and
construction workers at your end?"*

*"Absolutely! I have brothers and cousins in the business
and I will supervise when you are not available."*

*"That should work then. Let my sister know when I will
be there; probably in July for a few days. In my experience,
a woman needs to be involved in the planning for her new
home, or there will be hell to pay."*

Stavros thought that was quite likely, if everything in his elaborate
scheme did not go according to plan.

He thanked Philip and insisted on bills being forwarded to his university office as soon as possible, then he returned to the hotel with a satisfied grin on his face. There was one thing to be said about having to deal with a brother-in-law who was an unknown quantity. Matters could be kept on a business level without family issues intervening. Short and focused communications were always more productive in the end.

His mind moved to the next part of the plan; contacting an estate agent in Uckfield or Heathfield who could obtain the best price for the Horam house and do it swiftly.

Fifteen

Anna debated for three days, then eventually gave in to her curiosity and called the Ottawa legal firm whose address was on the envelope. Their conversation was short and a promise was made to forward a small parcel to Anna in London, Ontario, forthwith.

"That's that then," she surmised. "They seemed glad to get the matter settled, as will I, when the contents of the parcel are revealed."

"What's to be revealed, Anna?"

She had forgotten that Alina was nearby, packing a case for their trip to Scotland and her visit to Philip in England.

"Oh, it's nothing important! How are you getting on in there?"

"Well, the only problem seems to be predicting the weather conditions. It could be rain all the way or scorching sunshine which makes it difficult to know *what* to pack."

"I agree! They say dressing in layers is the answer. You can always add or subtract something for comfort as the temperature changes. What did you decide to wear to Fiona's graduation?"

Alina abandoned her packing and moved closer to where Anna was sitting at the office desk.

"I thought a summer dress and jacket might suit the occasion. What do you think about this one I am trying out?"
She twirled around so Anna could inspect the violet outfit with pearl grey accents on collar and pockets.

"I have always liked that colour on you, Alina. The grey belt is a toning shade and you can wear navy shoes or black. If Philip invites you out to dinner you would look smart but not too formal."

"That's what I was thinking. What about you? You are practically standing in for Fiona's mother at the big event, you know."

"Yes, I thought about that aspect. She's such a dear girl and I am proud to be invited to her special occasion. I don't want to seem too parental, however. Could I get away with a stylish pant suit, do you think?"

"I don't see why not. You have that new lightweight caramel-coloured number Maria picked out for you and if you change your mind there are several items stored in the locked, cedar-lined room in the Oban house."

"Mmm ….. that's true, although those are mostly winter clothes. Still, it can be chilly in Scotland even in June or July so I might well need the heavier stuff."

"By the way, what are you planning to wear for the portrait?"
Anna had eventually confessed to Alina the details about the new portrait with herself as front and centre. There had been some fireworks until Anna convinced her that she trusted Lawren completely, as evidenced by the fact that he would be staying in the house with them for part of the time. More explosions had erupted at this news but finally, Alina decided to 'zip her lip' for the sake of peace and let Anna find out for herself if this painter guy was all that he purported to be.

"I won't stress about the portrait. Lawren will know what he wants me to wear when we get there. He says the light makes all the difference to colour."

"I'm sure he does," said Alina under her breath. She was not reconciled to the situation in any way and relieved that she would be on hand to watch what the artist was up to. Anna did not seem to realize how foolish it was to invite a virtual stranger into her life this way.

"What did he say when you sent the plane ticket?"

"Oh, he's delighted of course. He's never been to Scotland although his family came from England originally. Lawren will be arriving three days after us. I've given him directions on how to get to the Oban house as we will be in Inverness at the graduation. Bev knows about him and she will give him a key and help him out if he needs anything."

Alina nodded in mock agreement. Inside, however, she was thinking Lawren might just help himself to everything he needed and be gone before they returned. She almost figured it might be worth the loss to get rid of him altogether, then she bit her tongue as the jealous words echoed in her mind.

The surest way to drive Anna into this guy's arms was to require her to defend him. She had seen enough of this during their previous arguments about the situation and she need to guard her tongue to prevent the worst from happening. Although she had heard about his artistic skills from Susan's description of the founder's portrait in her old law offices, she still doubted the new portrait would come up to that standard. There was always the chance that he would fail to meet Anna's expectations and the entire project would fail dismally. This was a more reassuring thought and, comforted for the moment, she went back to her packing.

The parcel from Ottawa arrived on the second day by courier mail delivery. Anna was relieved that Alina was in the warehouse and not on hand to criticize this latest secret endeavour. Alina had finally found a use for the plethora of fine, coloured cotton threads she had brought home from their Egyptian trip. There was a new multi-coloured fashion scarf in vogue that consisted of complex twisted knit or crochet. Alina had been experimenting at home with the style but found it taxed her eyes to pick out the tiny stitches.

Now she wanted to see if it could possibly be manufactured by machines. If not she would be transferring the process to the hand-knitters in the Oban area. She suspected the process could work equally well for woolen scarves.

Anna took the parcel into the dining room and sat down to open it. Obviously it was something small but she had no clue as to what it might be. The outer wrappings came apart quickly and revealed a black gift box with the name of a well-respected jeweller inscribed in gold on the lid.

Without speculating one more second, she lifted the lid and saw at once what lay inside. A turmoil of memories and emotions caused her to catch her breath. The ruby solitaire gleamed up at her, seeming to draw into itself all the light from the large windows. How many times had she seen and admired this very ring on the chubby hands of Richard's mother? It was something Rose wore all the time and so was closely identified with her. It was a large stone and must have cost a great deal of money once upon a time when Rose was a new bride. She always took great care of it, removing the ring when she washed dishes and wearing rubber gloves whenever she did housework. There were several ring-holders around the kitchen and bathrooms in her home to safely guard the ring when it was not on her left hand. Anna had searched for attractive china and wooden ring holders and given them to her mother-in-law over the years. Memories absorbed her for several moments.

Anna finally picked the ring out of its cushioned base and held it between her fingers. Rose had wanted her to have this. The wound that was caused by her abrupt parting from Rose healed over in an instant.

The fault was Richard's and it was good to know that the affection between Anna and her mother-in-law had not been false. With this belated gift, the last pain related to her divorce dissipated. She felt completely free of all of it for the first time. A deep sigh escaped from her at this realization.

Free.

She would never choose to wear this ring on her wedding finger, so she went to place it on her right hand and found that it would not fit over any knuckle other than that of her ring finger where her mother's old ring was firmly in place.

What to do? Remove her mother's ring and substitute this much more flamboyant and expensive solitaire? That seemed inappropriate in more than one way. Her mother's dainty ring was a part of her daily life for many years now. She rarely removed it. Rose's ruby was a far more precious item, in monetary value at least, and would require careful maintenance to preserve its appearance. She did not really wish to adopt Rose's solution and litter the place with ring holders. At once she decided that this ring would remain in her jewellery box for now. Perhaps it might be worn on special occasions or even sold for charity in the future. A Heart and Stroke campaign sprang to mind but the decision was made and Anna happily popped the ring back in its box. Knowing it was out of sight would certainly avoid explanations and she needed time to let the right idea present itself.

The ruby ring was forgotten in the usual last minute scramble to finish up the business arrangements, clear the fridge, alert the condo committee that their property would be vacant and say goodbye to Susan, Jake and the dogs. Maria and Paul's farewell visit involved the transfer of a very expensive, digital single lens reflex camera which Paul had recommended for Fiona's graduation gift. Anna was delighted with this selection as she knew how important it would be in Fiona's future job as a Scottish Wildlife Officer. The opportunity to take outstanding photographs while trekking through the glens and mountain tops of Scotland would be an added benefit for the talented girl, as well as an additional way to make money.

Over a quick meal at the mall with Maria and Paul, the conversation ranged over a variety of topics from Egypt to A Plus and this year's strangely-mild winter and spring weather.

Anna asked how Lucy's fashion ventures were developing. She had noticed a larger presence of teen fashion displays in the window of the new store adjacent to Maria's in the mall .

"She's certainly bringing in the younger set," Maria agreed, with a hint of pride in her voice. "But I'm not sure how much longer that will be possible."

"Why, what's wrong?"

Paul replied while reaching out to touch his wife's shoulder briefly. "It's going to be fine, honey. She won't be far away. Toronto isn't the moon, you know. You can keep in touch and her grandparents are right there if needed."

Turning to Anna he explained, "Lucy has nabbed an apprentice position with a film company in the new Harbourfront Studios complex. She's young, but they were very impressed with her interview and her portfolio of designs. It's a great opportunity for her and she will have the chance to explore a number of related areas where her style and creativity will shine."

"That's wonderful for her!" exclaimed Anna, but she could see Maria had doubts about letting her last chick flee the nest.

"Wasn't it your mother who passed on the fashion and clothing design genes in your family, Maria? You must all be very proud that a third generation has kept up those skills."

"I know! I am pleased for Lucy. I made her promise to keep up her studies online, if necessary. She will be sharing a flat with two other women who work for the studios so I trust they will keep her feet on the ground."

"Who will take over at the store?"

"Nova is wonderful, of course, and Theresa has been a great asset there. She looks after many day-to-day details to release me to keep up with the fashion show trends. We were thinking of trying a Baby Boutique section in the new store if Lucy is too busy to keep up with the constant changes the teen crowd demands. I want to feature Alina's beautiful hand-knits and your fairisle patterns that are coming back into style."

"Seems like you have everything in hand, as usual," laughed Anna.

"Well, I need something to keep me from worrying. Paul is off to the far north again for Canadian Geographic to shoot the final photos on the Arctic global warming series."

"Now, you know how well they look after me, Maria! They can't risk anything happening to one of their key photographers." Paul laughed at his hubris but it was clear that he was delighted to be included in a select group of top professionals.

Anna had to rush off, but her last glimpse of the couple as she left the restaurant showed how close and contented they were together. Glad that her friend's life had settled down and that even the troublesome Lucy had found an outlet for her energies, she turned her thoughts to Scotland.

A familiar lift in her spirits occurred. They would be breathing that glorious sea-tinted air in a matter of hours now. There was much to look forward to; Fiona's graduation, Jeanette and George's new daughter's christening, the garden at the farmhouse, and, of course, the portrait painting.

Her steps quickened to the rhythm of her heartbeats. Life was good.

The flight to Glasgow was accomplished without delays. Emerging into the daylight from the airport, Anna and Alina were surprised to see Grant, Fiona's old driving partner, waiting by the roadside to collect them in the large car.

"Ach, it's Fiona who should be thanked. Not me, at all. She insisted I should pick you up and take you to Oban. She said you would be worn out after that long overnight trip."

"She was right, Grant! I can't tell you how glad I am to see you. I should have realized you were taking over the car business while Fiona was in Inverness. I was still thinking you only drove the car on overnight trips as before."

"No, I am the man in charge now, Mrs. Mason. We've cut back on the overnight jobs, which suits my wife fine now that we have two bairns to look after. Fiona keeps an eye on things, though."

"I imagine so, Grant. Let's get on our way. I can hardly wait to see those hills again."

Both women fell asleep shortly after they left the outskirts of Glasgow and they woke to see the red front door of the McCaig Estate Farmhouse with Grant piling up their luggage there and Bev opening the door to let him inside.

"Welcome home, you two! It's so good to see you, and just look at the summer weather you brought from Canada! We are promised three or four more days like this.

Come away in, there's a pot of tea on the hob and coffee waiting. Jeanette sent fresh-baked shortbread and cookies, though how she has the time to bake with a new babe in the house, I don't know."

Anna and Alina exchanged a glance as they heard the Scottish lilt in Bev's speech. Alan's accent seemed to be rubbing off on her. They had never seen her look so happy.

"Oh, and there's someone waiting for you inside." Bev picked up the last case and held the door to the kitchen so the travellers could enter.

There, on the padded bench under the window was the visitor. Morag looked up and gave Anna a happy miaow, then curled up again in the afternoon sun.

"Well, she looks right at home!" proclaimed Anna, as she plopped herself down on the nearest kitchen chair. "She doesn't seem to mind being shuttled between two houses, by the looks of it."

"Not at all! She's a good wee thing and company for me when Alan's out on the hills with Prince."

"How is your husband, and where's Eric currently?"

"Alan will be along later with Eric. He's picking him up from secondary school. You won't believe how tall Eric is now. This good Scottish air agrees with him or maybe it's the appetite it gives him. He eats like a horse!"

The conversation continued for the next hour. Despite frequent e mails and phone calls there were always parts of life on both sides of the Atlantic for the old friends to catch up on.

When the tea pot was emptied and the coffee poured for Alina's second cup, Anna wiped the cookie crumbs from her mouth and, with a satisfied sigh, began to relax into the holiday mood the old house always created in her.

As the others chatted on, she mentally tested the atmosphere. Although she had never actually felt the presence of her Aunt Helen Dunlop in this house, she now knew even more about the lady and the unhappy aspects of her life. She could not help wondering if Helen's spirit was more at ease now that her final wish to have her private journal destroyed had been accomplished on the last day of their trip to Egypt. Anna smiled to think of the journal's ashes flying in the wind towards the Nile to sink forever in that eternal river.

"You secrets are safe now," she whispered. "Only Alina and I know what was written there and we will never reveal them."

Morag lifted her head and looked steadily at Anna as if she had heard the faint words. Anna quickly checked to see if Bev or Alina had noticed, but they were still immersed in conversation.

"So when is the christening service?" asked Alina.

"It's tomorrow and we are all invited to attend. Wait till you see the new baby! She's the most beautiful creature I have ever seen and that includes my two boys, although don't you dare tell them I said so!"

"Oh, I may hold that over your head if I ever need a favour," joked Alina, and she elbowed Bev to emphasize her intent.

"Right, then! You two have to unpack and inspect the property and get ready for the service tomorrow. We meet at George and Jeanette's before the ceremony. They have something to say to you, Anna, but I am sworn to secrecy."

With this enigmatic statement, Bev was gone from the kitchen and the front door closing was the last they heard of her.

"Wonder what that means?" stated Alina with a yawn. Look, I think we'd better get settled in before I fall asleep again. Bev said she had left a fish casserole and vegetables in the fridge for an evening meal.

Shall we unpack and reassemble here later to eat?"

"A perfect plan!" Anna agreed." Isn't it great to have caring friends on hand wherever we go? I can't help thinking of Helen and how solitary her life was here."

"That's true! But think how satisfied she would be to see this house full of happy people now. She wanted to you to transform this place and that is exactly what you have done, my dear!"

"Still, it all started with Helen and that is one of the reasons why I want to have her portrait here in the house so others will know it is because of her that my life has been changed for the better."

Alina refrained from adding a sour note to what had been a delightful hour or two. She merely murmured something non-committal and led the way up the stairs carrying her suitcase.

Anna remained in the kitchen for a moment or two watching Morag stir and stretch then reassemble herself into a new position as the sun moved toward the horizon.

Tomorrow's dawn will awaken me in the main bedroom, she thought. In a few days, Lawren will be here. What will he think of it all? There will be so much to show him and tell him before he begins to work.

She recognized that the thought excited her and with renewed energy she, too, grabbed a suitcase and climbed the stairs.

Sixteen

"Here! Can you hold her for me, please? She's fed and dressed which is more than I can say for me.

I'll be just a minute. Bev's going to give me a hand upstairs. Now don't move from there, Anna, I have something to ask you before we leave for the church. Don't you say a word, George! Remember!"

With this admonition, Jeanette rushed up the stairs leaving Anna holding a warm baby body in her arms.

Alina was entertaining Liam with a storybook and George was loading the dishwasher in the kitchen. There was no one to see the impact on Anna of the little girl who gazed trustingly up into her face with eyes the colour of summer cornflowers.

Bev had spoken the truth when she proclaimed the child's beauty. She was dressed in a traditional white robe with a lace- trimmed bonnet and matching jacket in the palest shell pink that Anna knew had come from Alina's hands. A wisp of wavy fair hair, the colour of her father's, peeked out from the bonnet and she had, from her mother, the beautiful, long dark eyelashes, most often seen on boys. The total effect combined with perfect rosy skin was remarkable.

Anna had not been familiar with many babies but even she could tell that this was an exceptional child.

The two were encased in a silent bubble of mutual admiration. Anna's arms cradled the solid weight of the baby as if they had been waiting for this all of her life. She gazed at the perfect face and felt the promise of a brand new life, untouched by sorrow and failure.

Still holding that clear-eyed gaze, Anna spoke in her mind the thoughts that filled her heart.

> *Oh, little one, how pure and innocent you are. I wish with all my heart that you will be as safe and happy all your life as you are right this minute.*
>
> *I hope that those who fall under your spell will treat you with kindness and love and guard your peaceful spirit.*
>
> *Be open to the adventures life may offer you, little girl. Have courage to dare; be a giver, but beware of life's takers. Don't let them steal your soul.*
>
> *Be all that you can be. Trust in yourself and your instincts.*
>
> *Above all, be happy, as you were meant to be.*

"Now, there's a peaceful scene! She has really taken to you Anna and that makes my request much easier."

Anna dragged her eyes away from the baby and tried to focus on what Jeanette was saying about a request. She could not think of anything she could refuse this most fortunate mother at this time.

"George and I want you to be the baby's godmother. Please say you will! I know it's very last minute but I really wanted you to meet her first."

"But .... but I don't even live here! Surely there are others closer to you both; family members and such. I am enormously flattered of course, but I don't want to horn in on something so personal."

"I knew you would say that, Anna! I'd explain better. You are my only Canadian contact who comes here to Oban regularly. I want her to hear the accent so she is happy in both countries. My mother will travel to Scotland whenever she can, but she is tied to the BC coast with my father's illness."

As he heard his wife's pleading falter a little, George jumped in with additional reasons.

"Anna, we do have a Scottish couple as godparents also, but Jeanette wanted especially for you to be included. It's a kind of tribute for everything you have done for us and for others in this community."

Anna was having a hard time keeping tears from overflowing. She was deeply touched at this gesture.

She replied with the only possible answer.

"Of course I'll be a godparent. Thank you both. It's wonderful!" She hugged the baby gently.

"Oh, what's this little beauty's name to be?"

"Well, that's the really special part. Her middle name is Rosemary, which is my mother's name. She's to be christened Annette after George's mother, but we want to call her Anne for now. When she's older she can choose which name she prefers. What do you think?"

Anna took a sharp intake of breath. She was immensely affected by this kindness and the tears she had been suppressing simply rolled down her cheeks unchecked.

A baby girl named for her. It was a lost dream now coming true.

Fortunately, Jeanette rescued her child before she was swamped by tears and everyone, including Anna, chuckled to see the baby's expression of amazement when she was lifted away from Anna's warm arms.

"Just give me a minute to mop myself up," asked Anna, and she fled to the powder room in the hallway to gather her dignity, emerging in a moment or two to join the party as they left to walk to the nearby church whose bells could be heard ringing out the fifteen-minute summons.

Anna floated on cloud nine for the rest of the day. She smiled all through the service in the ancient stone church and cradled her namesake when the baptism ceremony began. Listening to the minister's questions as if for the very first time, she felt the import of the responsibility she was taking on and knew that she would take her pledges seriously for as long as she lived.

The other godparents who stood with her were a younger couple and the parents of three children of their own. Anna could see that this child would never lack for caring adults.

Little Annette Rosemary McLennan did not cry out when the minister let a few drops of water from the baptism font drip onto her forehead. Although ancient tradition insisted that the cry chased the devil from the newborn child, Anna was pleased to see nary a frown on the perfect little face and she watched as the baby's arms lifted toward her mother as soon as the ceremony was over.

A tableful of treats awaited the family and friends when they returned to the Victorian villa on the hillside above Oban town. Jeanette disappeared to feed the baby and put her down for a nap while Anna and Alina renewed acquaintance with several local people who were interested in what had been happening lately to the 'Canadian Contingent' who had brought a North American energy, and welcome jobs, into their economy.

Much of the conversation concerned Fiona. Callum Moir, the town's vet, knew Fiona well as an occasional veterinary assistant, and he kept track of her progress.

"Ach, she won't tell you herself, but she's won a prize at the college for a study of the Scottish wildcat. She must have been taking pictures of that wee beastie you two rescued. Her theory was, that reared carefully and without too much human contact, the wildcat can be raised safely in animal sanctuaries and gradually reintroduced into wild areas of the country, under protected status, of course."

Anna was not at all surprised to hear this. She knew exactly how and why that study had been initiated, right in the kitchen of the McCaig farmhouse. Callum Moir had never known all the details of the story and it was unlikely he ever would know.

"She's quite an amazing person, our Fiona," agreed Anna. "I have a special present for her, so make space in your surgery for more of those startling wildlife pictures she shoots."

"I'll be happy to do that. In fact, several of my regular patrons have purchased her photographs lately. I need a new batch, for certain sure." Callum fixed his companion in his steady gaze and continued quickly.

"Now, on a different topic, what's happening with you, Anna? Any new men in your life?"

She was not shocked by the vet's abrupt change of topic and the very personal question he asked. She had spent a date evening or two in his company and sensed that she was someone he was interested in for the position of the second Mrs. Moir. She replied calmly that she was far too busy to worry about that and realized at once that the better answer would have been to claim a beau and discourage the acquisitive gleam she saw in the vet's eyes.

Her mind flashed to the one prospect she could think of for that role. Lawren Drake was the only man she had met, and connected to, in years. If she had mentioned him, it could have led to speculation and, since he would soon be in the vicinity, it would probably have given rise to comments when his age was seen to be so much younger than her own. Oban was a small enough town that gossip swept around the place like wildfire.

She dismissed this line of thought with a mental shake of her head. Best to say nothing, but she wondered who she could confide in about the entire portrait project. Jeanette was an obvious choice as she had been suggested as the one who would seek out a suitable frame for the finished work. Clearly, Jeanette was too busy on this day to take time for Anna's confidences. She looked around the room full of chattering, happy people. Alina was talking animatedly to one of the Oban hand-knitting team. Alina had not, however, shown any interest in discussing the project further. Her opinion about the artist in question was not in any doubt.

Who then? Fiona might have had an objective view of the matter but Fiona was likely to be far too involved in her new career to be around when Lawren arrived.

Anna sighed. She would just have to soldier on alone for now, following her own instincts. Had she not recently recommended this same path to a certain very young lady?

The elderly gentleman who volunteered at the local library approached Anna to inquire about new book titles in Canada and the question of the portrait vanished from her mind.

The Monday following the christening could not have been a greater contrast in weather. Rain poured endlessly out of a grey clouded sky. Anna searched the farmhouse for umbrellas and found one large golfing specimen in the old wood shed in the garden and another hiding in the back of the barn that served as the garage,

Unfortunately, by the time she had uncovered these, she was soaked to the skin and had to start the process of styling her hair and applying make-up all over again from the beginning. Her dressy outfit for the graduation ceremony had escaped the drenching and was still hanging safely in the wardrobe.

Alina was very thankful that Grant had agreed to drive them to Inverness for Fiona's graduation. Checking her watch, she saw that this dressing delay would have cost them dearly if they had stayed with their initial plan of taking the train.

While she waited for Anna, she inspected the lounge where Lawren was going to sleep when he arrived in a day or two. She wanted to make sure that nothing too personal was left in full view. She checked that the door to Anna's office was still firmly locked and then re-checked that the key was in Anna's possession and not on the hook in the outer kitchen storage area where house and barn keys resided.

Alina had to admit to herself that she was overly suspicious of the artist although she had no real evidence for this feeling. The next few days before she travelled down to Manchester to meet Philip would tell the tale of his true intentions. She meant to keep a close watch on the fellow and also to see what Bev and Jeanette thought about him. Bev, particularly, would have a clear idea of whether he was likely to be an imposter of some kind; a man who wanted more than artistic benefits from his patron.

Alina recognized that she was not a good judge when it came to Anna's affairs of the heart. She had been too close to the whole Richard fiasco and it had coloured her feelings about any man who was interested in Anna.

For the first time, she acknowledged to herself that Anna was actually interested in Lawren in more than a professional way. The trouble with this was that Anna was in a particularly emotional place right now because of Richard's death. It made her vulnerable and Alina was determined to protect her friend from any impulsive moves that might threaten her peace of mind.

"All right! I'm ready again. Is Grant here with the car?"

"Not yet. Do you have the camera bag?"

"Heavens! What's wrong with my brain? I left it upstairs."

Anna clattered back up the stairs in her platform sandals leaving Alina with both raincoats, the umbrellas, and the job of watching out of the window for the large black car.

"He's here!" she sang out, as Grant drew up to the side of the house where the new driveway led to the barn. A paved path from the front door now allowed them to walk along the house, past the big kitchen windows and straight into the car instead of trying to rush down the long gravel pathway and through the gate. Alina was glad her high heels would be spared the inevitable scrapes and scratches the gravel would cause.

They were soon shaking rain off the umbrellas and greeting Grant with delight.

"So glad you suggested this, Grant. We should have known you would want to celebrate Fiona's success also."

"I'm happy to be of service, ladies. Now sit back and enjoy the journey. The weather chappies say it will clear in an hour or so and there's some splendid scenery on the way."

Anna and Alina exchanged a smile. Although both of them were proficient drivers, it was certainly pleasant to be chauffeured around when they were in Scotland.

"I could get used to this," chuckled Alina.

"Agreed!" stated Anna, as she settled the camera in its large gift bag safely beside her.

Graduation Day at Inverness University was all about waiting and watching. The excited crowds were huge, jostling and chatting in every nook and cranny as they waited to be admitted to the Great Hall.

Alina regretted immediately that she had not procured a summer hat for the occasion. A varied collection of headgear from tiny fascinators attached to plastic headbands, to full-brimmed cartwheels, that she always termed "Scarlett O'Hara hats', seemed to be the order of the day for women.

The graduates were nowhere in sight and Anna worried that Fiona would never be able to pick them out from the large assembly.

Grant had wisely obtained a parking permit and he found a convenient spot for the car. When he returned to the crowd in front of the Great Hall he managed to track down his passengers and informed them that he knew where to see the graduates as they entered the side doors to the hall. He had spotted the line-up from the parking lot and watched for a moment as the candidates were arranged in alphabetical order.

Anna and Alina were delighted to steal this opportunity. They might even get a glimpse of Fiona and let her know they had arrived. Following Grant, they left the forecourt and slipped around the side of the massive building. Sure enough a long line of gowned figures shuffled along slowly on a level below them, with a guard of gowned and caped professors carrying clip boards and checking names assiduously.

They scanned the line from end to end and were about to conclude that they had missed Fiona when Grant spotted her. Fiona's head was down as she was grappling with her robes which were somewhat too long for her and threatened to trip her up if she did not pull them firmly into place. Alina let out a piercing whistle and among the heads that turned to see where the sound came from was Fiona's dark one with her distinctive neat ponytail.

A frantic amount of waving and jumping up and down then ensued and the three figures were delighted to get the desired response from Fiona. Frantic signalling commenced on both sides which translated roughly to, 'Wait here after the ceremony and I'll find you. Wonderful to see you!'

Shortly after this exchange Fiona reached the head of the line and hiked up her robes as she entered the side doors.

The atmosphere inside the hall was unexpectedly warm. Part of this was because of the packed rows of seats and the remainder was because of the lack of air conditioning. Alina folded her program into an impromptu fan and applied it to her face with some vigour.

"You realize this country is backward in some respects?" she whispered to Anna.

"Hush! The cost of cooling this huge place would be astronomical," Anna commented. "Just be grateful you are not freezing in here in the winter!"

The entire area in front of the stage was filled with eager students. Fiona's dark head had disappeared in the throng and Alina was calculating there would be a long wait before they could finally emerge into the forecourt again. She noticed Grant had nodded off almost as soon as he sat down and wished she, too, had the ability to cat nap on demand.

After about thirty minutes, a procession of dignitaries accompanied the university provost onto the stage. The chatter and noise of the auditorium dropped down to a muted shuffling of feet as heads turned to the stage and conversation ceased.

The welcome greetings and praise for the graduates occupied the next forty minutes until even Grant woke up and started to gaze around him.

"Has Fiona had her turn yet?" he asked hoarsely.

"Don't you worry Grant," replied Anna in a low voice. "They haven't even started to call the names, I'm afraid."

"Oh, I see! Ah've nivver been to one of these things afore. Does it aye take this long?"

"I'm afraid so, Grant. But there are many students graduating today."

"I jist hope they all get jobs, then!"

Anna noticed one or two heads in the vicinity nodding in agreement as this pithy comment travelled along the rows of parents and friends.

Fortunately, the pace of processing the graduates was fairly speedy. After watching brave parents try to make it down to the stage in time to film their progeny at the moment when the appropriate mortar board was passed over their heads, Anna decided to stay seated and get her pictures in the comparative sanity of the outdoors.

Their hands were sore with constant clapping when, finally, Fiona made her way across the stage and shook hands with her biology and zoology profs. Anna noted how quickly Fiona adjusted her robe before descending the steps and returning to her seat. Smart move, she thought. Tripping on these steps would not be the kind of attention Fiona would relish. Her colouring was more florid than usual but Anna imagined the girl was used to the great outdoors with cooling winds blowing around her, rather than this exciting and superheated venue.

Finally, and with great relief, the crowd exited the hall following the graduates. All the doors were flung open and everyone rushed to the cooler air to find their special person, take pictures, and escape to a town restaurant to celebrate.

The Oban party caught up with Fiona in the place she had designated, and were relieved to find she had kept her bothersome robes for a while longer. Grant kindly took pictures while Alina surreptitiously lifted the robes at the back so they would seem a better length for the photographs.

Fiona was radiant with delight to see her friends again. She had been so intent on final exams and projects that she had felt like a cloistered nun in the last few months. There was much news to share including her apprentice position with the Highland and Islands Wildlife Service where she would be monitoring hunting and fishing practices on some of Scotland's large estates and mapping the territories of osprey and other endangered species.

"Oh, Fi, I am so happy for you!" rejoiced Anna, enfolding the girl in her warm embrace. "You have worked so hard for this and you deserve every bit of your success."

"I have you to thank for a large portion of that, Anna Mason, and I will never forget it," she responded solemnly.

"Och, away with you!" said Anna, in her best imitation of a Scottish accent.

All four dissolved in laughter and Fiona was shooed off to return her robes and rejoin them at the car.

The evening was a triumph.

Grant drove them to a small Italian restaurant off the beaten track where they had a splendid meal toasting Fiona in champagne then quaffing red wine with their meals. Anna whispered to Grant that she would make sure he had a bottle of the red to take home and enjoy, since he was staying sober in order to drive the women safely home .

Fiona was thrilled with her new digital camera and the dozen red roses from the women that Grant had placed in the rear of the car for her. Alina had brought a selection of A Plus knitwear for Fiona including their new Fairisle knitted cap with the pompom on top and side panels that would ensure her ears were warm whatever the weather.

"Let me know if the colours don't suit you," she said. "We have a wide range to choose from."

Fiona thanked Alina and did not mention that she would most likely be proudly wearing the headgear of her new profession when on duty from now on.

Fiona was driven back to the university residences and stood at the entrance blowing kisses and smiling from ear to ear with her hands full of gifts as the car set off for Oban where Grant would eventually enjoy the wine with his patiently-waiting wife.

The Scottish summer nights were long and light and the two women were able to sit back in comfort and watching the twilight shade the land as they thought over the eventful day.

"So, what's next on the agenda, Anna?" asked Alina in a sleepy voice.

"Lawren arrives some time tomorrow," she replied. "You will be travelling south in another day or two, I think. How do you feel about that?"

"Well, it's merely a trial run, of course. I don't hold out much hope for a relationship but I will give it a try, if only for your sake, Anna."

"Now, don't feel obliged to do this for me! Philip is my half-brother but we are virtually strangers and you don't owe me anything in that department. Take it day by day, Alina. You will know what to do."

"I hope you are right."

At this point all conversation ceased until they had reached Oban again. Each woman had much to think about.

"It has been a grand day, ladies," was Grant's parting comment. They waved until the car disappeared down the lane and arm in arm the two friends walked the paved path to the front door and soon headed for bed, tired but pleased.

For Anna, a deep feeling of contentment swept through her. She had acquired a goddaughter and sent a young woman out into the world who was like a daughter to her. Life is strange, she thought. The things we long for do not always appear when we need them most but sometimes, if we are patient, they do arrive when we can appreciate them most.

Seventeen

Sarah Fenton was worried. She had been concerned since her father's strange phone call from Greece a week ago. When he asked her to keep a secret from her mother she had agreed, but on reflection she wondered if that was the right thing to do. She had always been especially close to her mother and keeping any secret from her did not feel natural.

It was not that she mistrusted her father. She knew well how intelligent he was and how forward thinking in everything he undertook. His determination was legendary. She remembered how he had fought to persuade his only daughter not to leave school and go out to work after secondary school. It had been a fierce contest of wills in which Stavros had battled with every force he could command, and he could command many.

Nonetheless, Sarah was adamant. She was determined to join the working world. She had already met her future husband, David, although her father did not know this. She wanted a family life without the stresses and strains her mother had endured and she wanted to start soon.

Sarah was well aware of the sacrifices it took to attend university and earn a sufficiently useful degree to guarantee a decent position in life. After all, she had watched her father go through that very process and despite his obvious talents it had been a difficult road at times. She had no desire to follow him into the world of academia. Indeed she had disdain for the faculty members who occasionally arrived at their home in Horam for wine, and intellectual conversation that ranged far above the heads of mere mortals.

She had enormous respect for her father's accomplishments but she still harboured a grudge about the way her mother had been sidelined in the rush to the top position he had obtained.

Sarah had fought her battle bravely and held her ground against all attacks until her father gave in. There seemed no point in pursuing it further. He finally recognized a personality as powerful as his own. His only child was not going to follow in his footsteps and that was that. In time he recovered from the disappointment. He did not allow it to diminish his love for Sarah. That could never happen.

Sarah had spent a day with her mother after she returned from the Easter trip to Greece and carefully quizzed her about the situation regarding their living arrangements once Stavros retired. To her surprise the answers she received were fuzzy at best. Her mother did not seem to have a clear idea of what was about to happen. Indeed, she seemed relieved to be back in England and happy to settle into her normal routines without much concern about the future.

Sarah worried even more. She knew her father was always one step, at least, ahead of the pack. He had the skill of planning out a range of clever moves so as to be prepared for any eventuality. He had the mind of an expert chess player; a game at which he excelled.

Much as she loved her mother, she knew this kind of planning was just not in her nature. Lynn Kyriakos was, if anything, too trusting, and Sarah feared the changes that were coming in her parents' marriage if her father's requests were any indication.

What did it mean if her mother spent months at a time in England while her husband was living in Greece? Was this the preamble to a divorce? Heaven forbid! Sarah felt her world rock on its foundation at the very thought.

Lynn bustled around the house happily. She usually spent hours arranging her home to suit herself when Stavros was teaching his summer courses. This included placing the TV remote on her side of the couch, organizing the kitchen cupboards so everything she needed when cooking was exactly where she wanted it and spending as much time as she wished outdoors in the garden just pottering around with seedlings and new plants. She took deep breaths of the air and felt as if she herself was a plant in exactly the right soil and the right location for full growth.

"This is my place," she often murmured to herself.

Two things occurred to disturb her contentment.

The first was a simple request from her husband to retrieve an e mail from his home computer.

"I need the details about the number of students currently on the class list for the summer course, darling. Would you look it up for me? I am trying to arrange accommodations on Aegina and I need to know how many separate males and females I have to house."

Lynn had done this kind of thing for Stavros before, so she followed his phone directions as she sat at the computer and soon tracked down the folder titled 'Aegina Course 2012 '. There was some debate about one adult student who Stavros remembered as 'Joan' while the class list stated 'John' but other than that, the task was soon completed.

"Thank you, my dear. How is England?"

"As glorious as ever, I am glad to say. When will you be coming home?"

"Not sure. I'll be in touch. Must run. Lots to do here."

Lynn was about to start the shut down procedure when she caught sight of an e mail folder headed 'Students Aegina'. Thinking there might be a more recent e mail from students that Stavros had missed, she quickly opened it to scan the names. The list was similar to the one she had just studied although there were several from a Pauline Jeffries. This was probably the same Pauline who Stavros talked about with huge admiration. She was one of his best and most able students.

Without realizing it, Lynn had pressed the cursor on the line of Pauline Jeffries' last e mail and it opened up to show a brief paragraph of text. Her eyes skimmed through it before the content had struck her brain.

At first the words did not make sense then she read it over again and tried to reject the sense she did make.

> *As I told you, the pregnancy is going well. The morning sickness has gone and I feel fit for future decisions, although the summer course may not work for me.*
>
> *Don't worry about us. I have so much to discuss with you, dear sir. This is an important point in both (all) our lives. Can't wait to join you on Aegina.*
>
> *Till then,*
>
> *Your Pauline.*

How odd for a student to send such a personal e mail, she thought. She must be in dire straits to involve a professor this way but she certainly seems concerned about the summer course in the heat of summer in Greece. She must be desperate to talk to Stavros. I wonder why?

Suddenly the thought struck Lynn that this Pauline could be involved with Stavros in more than a teacher-to-student relationship. God forbid that Stavros was the father of this child! Surely not!

Her mind could scarcely grasp the implications of this conclusion. Her husband had been carrying on an affair in secret? He had deceived both his wife and this young girl whose career he had proclaimed as so promising?

Lynn sat back with a thump as errant thoughts invaded her mind. It would, of course be simple for Stavros to conduct an affair without her knowledge. Evening meetings, marking, and research demands at his college office, the summer courses in Greece; all of these provided ample opportunity.

Could she have been so blind as to miss the signs?

Could he have been so devious as to pull the wool over her eyes?

How long had this been going on? Who else knew?

Once the poison had entered her brain everything she knew began to be tainted. So this is why Stavros was so anxious to retire from his beloved job at the university. He could not risk being found out and losing his tenured position and all the attendant pension privileges.

The proposed move to Greece also became part of a self-preserving plan. Once established far from England he could choose to continue his affair or drop the girl and her child, safe from prying eyes.

Stavros' reaction to her own refusal to fall in with his retirement plans now took on the mark of desperation. Of course he was shocked when she failed to meekly accept his ideas. His entire carefully-laid scheme was in danger of falling apart.

A red rage consumed her emotions. How dare he betray her trust in this way? After all she had sacrificed for this marriage, how could he turn her world upside down at the point when they should be enjoying the prospect of a leisurely life together with their family? Anger drove her out of doors. She could not sit still as thoughts crowded her mind and her heart began to feel the pain of these revelations. A tiny voice whispered that she had no real evidence for her suspicions but she ignored it in the rush of emotions. She walked round and round the paths in the garden seeing nothing but the pictures in her mind and growing more and more sure of her conclusions.

A ringing phone eventually pierced her concentration and she responded automatically by running inside the house to answer it. As she lifted the phone she had the awful thought that it might be her husband calling and she almost dropped the receiver. The last person she wanted to talk to at this moment was her husband. She could not imagine what, if anything, she could possibly say to him. She glance quickly at the caller display and did not recognize the number. Probably a sales offer. She would get rid of him quickly.

"Hello?" Even she could tell her voice was shaky.

"Is this Lynn?"

"Yes. Who's calling?" She did not recognize the caller's voice and was about to put the receiver down again when she heard something vaguely familiar in the accent.

"Look! It's Philip here. Your brother? Am I calling at a bad time?" You have no idea how bad, she thought, but good manners asserted themselves and she pulled herself together to sound semi rational.

"Sorry Philip, I wasn't expecting to hear from you. It's been a while."

"You are right, and I wouldn't be bothering you now but I am having difficulty with the plans."

"Plans? What plans are you talking about?"

"Your husband said it was all right to consult you about features and I couldn't wait until later.

I have to get the house blueprints done now or the project will need to be cancelled.

Lynn? Are you still there?"

Lynn was standing by the phone with her mouth agape and not one single cohesive response in her brain.

Was it possible that in the space of a few minutes her whole world could collapse in this way? What else would she discover about her husband that she never suspected? Had he gone ahead with plans for the house on the bay in Paros without telling her, and, worst of all, had he already involved her brother without her knowledge?

"Philip, you will have to excuse me. I can't talk right now. Please call back later."

With that she slammed down the phone and burst into tears.

The rest of the afternoon disappeared in a fog of misery. Lynn could not move from the couch into which she had collapsed after her brother's call. The shocks coming one after another were too much for her to deal with.

At some point, light-years later, she heard the phone ring again and jumped. She simply could not speak to her brother again and the same applied to her husband. She would ignore the phone but first she looked to see who was calling.

Sarah! Thank God! Of all the people in the entire world, Sarah was the only one she could bear to speak to at this moment. She picked up the receiver but found her throat too dry to answer.

"Hi Mum! Just want a word about next week. David and I leave for Paris on Wednesday but Mike won't be home from his summer job until Friday night so you don't have to be here until then.

How does that sound?"

Paris? What was that about? Lynn could not drag her concentration back from the dim dark place where she had been wandering for hours.

"Mum? Are you there? Mum, what's wrong?"

"Sorry, love! I'm not quite in control at the moment."

"Right! Stay where you are. I'll be over immediately. Stay put and don't move."

There was something so comforting in the beloved voice of her daughter that it shook some sense into Lynn. I can't let Sarah find me like this, she declared to the darkened room and she dragged herself up out of the couch and went slowly around the house clicking on lights, moving all the while like some bent-over, ancient crone devoid of muscle power and energy.

Despite her ambition to tidy herself up, she could not summon the strength to find a comb, so Sarah found her mother in such a disheveled, immobile state that she thought an ambulance would be required.

"Mum! What in God's name has happened to put you in this condition? Have you been ill? Has someone broken in? Did someone hurt you?"

Lynn began to laugh at her daughter's last enquiry. Assuredly someone had hurt her and that someone was Sarah's father but how was she going to tell Sarah that her beloved father was a cheat and a lying manipulator.

Her mother's slightly insane laughter was far more frightening to Sarah than her previous stunned condition. She moved toward her mother and held her until the wild laughter had consumed all her mother's available oxygen and what was left was a pitiful dry sobbing that pained Sarah to hear, more than anything else her mother had ever done.

An hour went by and Lynn had not yet spoken more than a whisper to Sarah. She drank the welcome cup of sweet tea after first clutching it to her chest in an attempt to still her trembling arms.

Wild thoughts swept through her mind.

Tell Sarah everything and discredit her father forever.

Call Philip and cancel any prospect of Stavros' house going ahead.

Get on a plane to Greece and confront her husband.

Call a lawyer.

Call the university anonymously and accuse Stavros of misconduct with a student.

Fall into bed, take sleeping pills and sleep for a week, or forever.

The last thought brought her to her senses abruptly. What was she thinking? Crazy thoughts or actions would not make the situation any better. This was a time for rational thought. Not today, perhaps, but soon. She must wait until the burning pain in her chest had calmed enough for her to think carefully about her next move.

Sarah had been talking quietly to her mother about trivial household items and her excitement about Caroline's inclusion in the G(irls)20 Summit in Paris. She described the hotel she and David would stay in for a few days and thanked her mother over and over for agreeing to watch Mike and the house while they were away on this unexpected holiday.

All the while, Sarah was watching and waiting for her mother to respond. The idea of calling an ambulance was not far from her mind. It was possible her mother had had a small stroke or even a heart attack.

She continued looking for signs of trauma but saw colour return to her mother's face and when she finally began to talk sensibly about the Paris trip, Sarah relaxed for the first time since she had left work so suddenly and driven to Horam like a maniac.

"Can you tell me what has happened, Mum?" Sarah accompanied this request with a keen eye on her mother's reaction and two warm hands holding her mother's cool ones.

"I won't pretend I haven't had a shock, my dear, but I can't talk about it yet. I promise to speak to you privately before you go to Paris. Now, don't worry! I will be fine. You have helped me enormously and I feel some hope that things will work out."

Neither woman believed this last statement. Lynn because she had no clue how to proceed, and Sarah because she was more and more convinced that her father's strange request for secrecy had something to do with her mother's current distress. She decided not to press the matter. Her mother would reveal it in time. She would have to be patient but she vowed that whatever, or whomever, had hurt her mother so badly, she would be the tigress who would defend and support her through it all.

Eighteen

Anna slept well but she noted how restless she felt as soon as she was dressed. She was not keen on eating breakfast, thinking her stomach was a bit unsettled after the large Italian meal of the previous night. Alina, however, knew exactly what was troubling her friend and it had nothing to do with wine or food. She insisted that Anna have tea and toast, at least, and as Anna complied, she gently quizzed her about the coming day until her concerns about Lawren's arrival had come out into the open and Alina could give her opinions.

"It's natural for you to be a bit worried about how things will go. You hardly know the man and you've invited him here to a different country to do a job for you that you are not a hundred percent sure about. You'd be crazy *not* to be worried, Anna!"

Alina's comments had the opposite result to the one she had hoped to promote. Anna ignored the negative connotations and jumped to the defense of her, admittedly rash, idea.

"I am not worried, really. It's just that he has a long journey to get here and I want him to be pleased with the estate house and the work he will do. I have invested time and energy in this project and I am anxious to get it underway."

Alina sighed. On this topic Anna was hopelessly naïve. She would just have to find out for herself if she had made a huge mistake by trusting this artist fellow. She, of course, would be watching him like a hawk. She decided to make that call to Bev right away and arrange for Bev to inspect the stranger as soon as possible. She would trust Bev's opinion. She had always had a keen accountant's eye for an imposter as proved by her solid attachment to Alan, one of the most honest and transparent men that Alina had ever met. Their happiness was Alina's recommendation for Bev's good instincts.

As the morning hours passed slowly and Anna had not heard anything from Lawren, she began to be concerned that something had delayed his arrival. There was no internet access in the estate house but Anna called George at his office and asked if he could find out if the Air Transat plane had left on time. George's new secretary called within the half-hour and assured Anna there was no weather, or other incident, to interrupt the schedule.

"He will be on the train by now," she decided, and began to count the hours until he could arrive.

Should she serve afternoon tea or make a full meal for later? He would be tired if he was not used to transatlantic crossings with the addition of the three hour train trip.

"Why didn't I send Grant to pick him up from the airport and drive him here," she chided herself as impatience began to erode her excitement and resentment crept in.

"Why isn't he calling?" Wait! Did I give him the phone number here? Did I remember to tell him to drop the zero when he reached Scotland? Oh for heaven's sake, he's a grown man! He doesn't need a mother looking over his shoulder all the time."

Alina heard this last remark and nodded her head. Yup, Anna was worried all right, no matter what she might say. This confirms my suspicions. She is way too involved with this guy. The sooner this thing, whatever it is, can be nipped in the bud, the better, as far as I am concerned.

By nightfall, Anna was truly upset. She paced up and down in the lounge imagining all kinds of dire scenarios in which Lawren Drake was injured or attacked by hoodlums or thrown in some jail cell for an infringement of laws he had no way of knowing about.

She called Grant and asked him to wait at the train station in Oban and look out for a passenger of Lawren's description carrying luggage, and drive him to the estate house as soon as possible. If Grant did find such a person, she insisted on being called immediately.

Alina held her tongue and went about preparations for an evening meal with a sly smile on her face that she concealed whenever Anna arrived in the kitchen on her round of pacing through the rooms.

"Might as well light the fires," Alina suggested. "It gets cooler at night here. The kitchen is warm enough but the lounge could use some extra heat. There's plenty of hot water if you want a bath to soothe your nerves."

"My nerves are just fine," snapped Anna, stomping away to set a flame to the lounge fire in such a manner that she entirely contradicted her words.

Anna was upstairs when the call arrived.

"I've found the gentleman, Ms. Mason. Dinna worry yersel'. We'll be at the door in thirty minutes."

Grant ended the call before she could ask what sort of condition the traveller was in.

She only just managed to control an urge to run down the gravel path to meet Grant's car and drag Lawren out by the ear, her frustration had reached a level beyond any reason and she began to suspect how inappropriate that was. She restrained the impulse and stood behind the red door until a polite knock signaled Lawren's arrival.

"So, here you are at last!" It was impossible to keep all the tension out of her voice and she saw Lawren's eyebrows shoot up as he registered her mood.

"I've been expecting you for hours now. Is everything all right? Why didn't you call to say you'd be delayed?"

As Alina watched carefully, Lawren took a step back. Clearly he had not been expecting this reaction from Anna before he even had time to put down his bag. He began to apologize, then stopped, as he figured out he had not done anything to justify Anna's angry tone.

At exactly the same moment as the harsh words left her lips, Anna had realized the mistake she had made. She had spoken to this grown man as if he were one of her primary school students of long ago. She had chastised him inappropriately and also revealed her emotions in a way she had never intended.

She blushed to the roots of her hair and turned away in confusion. What could she say to mend this situation? Had she burned every boat before the poor man had a chance to look around him?

Seeing Anna's distress, Alina took over the awkward situation and quickly steered Lawren into the kitchen. He glanced over his shoulder towards Anna as the door closed, but Anna had already fled upstairs, too embarrassed to face him.

Early the next morning, after a disturbed night of restless dreams, Anna crept downstairs and found the lounge door open, the bed returned to its daytime disguise as a couch, and no one in the kitchen.

Her first thought was that Lawren had felt so unwelcome after her attack of the previous evening that he had decided to head back to Canada. This was extreme, perhaps, but she could not have blamed him.

Depression filled her. What a waste! What an idiot she was! Now, he would never speak to her again and the painting tribute to her Aunt Helen was not going to happen.

She opened the back door to let Morag outside and looked up at the sky to gauge the weather for the day ahead, when she caught sight of a figure toiling up the lower slope of Helen's Hill.

Relief flooded her mind, then excitement, as she knew she had a chance to redeem herself.

Lawren had stayed! He meant to survey the area from the high viewpoint. He was still interested in the painting.

It took only a minute for her to don her outdoor gear and take off after him. Although it had been almost a year since she had made the climb, her leg muscles remembered and took the strain. She had grabbed two hiking poles on the way out, and used them to her advantage.

As Lawren slowly scaled the last steep section of the hill, she caught up with him. He turned and his face showed his surprise. Before he could say a word, she launched into a profuse apology that rambled on for two minutes. He said nothing in reply when she finally ground to a halt.

She waited, dreading she had embarrassed herself all over again. Still, nothing was said.

Finally he spoke. "Anna, I have only just got my breath back after that climb. Please don't apologize! The fault was mine. Come over here and sit down so I can tell you what happened and after that you can point out the landmarks from this spectacular vantage point. I saw next to nothing of the area last night and that is my fault entirely. Can we start all over again?"

Anna felt as if she was absolved of a terrible crime. Her spirits rose and she smiled widely but did not trust herself to speak.

Lawren took her expression as approval of his request and began to tell her what had happened in Glasgow. During the flight from Toronto it had occurred to him that he would shortly be arriving in the city where Charles Rennie Mackintosh had lived and worked. Years before, when he was a student at the Ontario College of Art, he had been introduced to Mackintosh's watercolour paintings and decided to do a study of his life and work. It did not take long for him to become fascinated with a Scottish artist, architect and designer who blended multiple aspects of Art Deco and Arts and Crafts in his buildings and furniture designs, in a way that was remarkable in his era.

The original fascination was revitalized when Lawren realized he could soon see one of Mackintosh's landmark structures, the Glasgow School of Art, constructed on a steep hillside in the centre of the city.

Once the idea took root in his mind, he forgot all else in the urge to see for himself a building he had studied as part of his student portfolio.

"You see, I had not even thought about Charles Rennie Mackintosh in years. I guess I never expected to see any of his works for myself. I couldn't resist taking this opportunity. I simply forgot the time, Anna. I suppose you could say I was transported in a way."

"Did you go inside?"

"Absolutely! It was quite open. Students were wandering in and out and I blended in easily. No one stopped me, even when I took photographs with my cell phone. It was as if they were used to perfect strangers admiring their unique place of work. Personally, I can't imagine how anyone could concentrate in an iconic structure where so much originality and style was incorporated in every stone, and this was one of his first commissions when he was a junior member of a firm of architects! It's amazing how well preserved it is. Obviously these Scots know good work when they see it."

Lawren stopped to take breath and Anna saw an enthusiasm and vigour in his manner that she had never seen before. He is a true artist, she told herself. Art really turns him on.

"I haven't spent much time in Glasgow, myself. It's something I've been meaning to do as my parents were born and brought up in the city."

"Well, I can recommend it. I picked up a guide book at the airport so I could find my way around and there are many extraordinary buildings within walking distance of the School of Art. They call it The Merchant City. It appears that Glasgow was a rich trading centre and the stone ornamentation on the buildings demonstrated that amply. I was very impressed."

"Perhaps you can take me on a tour one day?"

"I would like that a lot. I hardly saw a fraction of what is there and the place is full of Mackintosh works to this day."

Lawren turned to Anna and she was caught in his golden gaze while he asked his question.

"Am I forgiven? The last thing I wanted was to offend you when you have been so generous to invite me here."

"Forgiven and forgotten!"

"Good! Now I want to concentrate on this magnificent landscape! What a location and what a viewpoint!"

"I am so glad you like it. This has always been one of my favourite spots. It was Helen's also. It's only when you get up here that you see that Helen's Hill, as I call it, is part of a chain of hills leading to the mountain range in the distance and yet we can still see the sea on the west."

"Does the stream come from the lake here?"

"Yes, they call it a tarn and it's deeper than it looks. The stream flows down the hill and joins a river in the valley below the farmhouse."

Conversation ceased while both looked into the distance. Anna hesitated to say more. She had discovered all this for herself and she knew Lawren should also have that privilege. She stayed seated on the rock while he wandered around the flat area looking downward in as many directions as he could.

When he returned, he asked about the cottage he had seen and Anna told him who lived there.

171

"You'll meet Bev and Alan tomorrow. We've been invited for afternoon tea, if you are not working, of course."

"I will need to absorb some of the atmosphere of the place first. If you can show me the town or any other parts of the region you think are representative, that would be helpful."

"I would be glad to do that."

Better and better she thought. Forgiven, and now tour guide to the area. This day is beginning very well indeed.

Alina had a hearty breakfast waiting and kept the chat lighthearted over the meal. It was clear to see how things were with Lawren and Anna. 'Smitten' was the word she used in her head but would never dare to say aloud.

Alina accompanied them into Oban where the artist hoped to track down an easel of some description.

He seemed to have an entire art shop of supplies in his duffle bag but scarcely any clothes. While they waited for Grant to arrive, Lawren unpacked his paints and brushes and unrolled a large canvas. He asked to store these in the larder off the kitchen until he had decided on a place where the light was right for his painting.

"This northern light is incredible!" he proclaimed. "I can see already that it will be a feature of the final work. I can't wait to get started."

Alina went off to get food supplies in Oban while Anna and Lawren climbed up to McCaig's Folly on the hilltop above the town. Lawren was delighted with the anomaly of the structure in this location but it was the view of the sea islands that captured his attention.

"If you like, we can sail to Iona tomorrow morning. I have wanted to go there but never had the opportunity and it's a place Helen had been. We can order tickets before we go home."

Lawren nodded. He wanted to hurry down the hill and explore the town, especially the shoreline, so different from Ontario's Lake Erie or Lake Huron. The smell of the ozone filled his nostrils and signified abundant sea life in the salt waters.

Anna decided to take her companion around the town's one-way street system as that would require a walk along the sea front. When they reached the town centre, Lawren spotted a hardware store that was crowded with all manner of useful items for home and workshop. The owner, an older man dressed in a leather apron said he thought they had a used easel somewhere in the storage shed at the back.

"It's no beauty, mind," he cautioned, "but it'll serve the purpose, I'm thinking."

Anna translated this discreetly when she saw Lawren's puzzled expression.

"We'll be back after lunch, Mr. McKinley. Thank you for taking the trouble."

"No trouble, Miss Mason. Glad to help."

Alina met them at the pier restaurant behind the Columba Hotel for a late lunch. She had left her shopping at Tesco's to be collected by Grant before he arrived to drive them home.

"This place smells of fresh fish," declared Lawren as soon as they entered the doors. "And we can eat looking out at the sea. Are these the ships that will take us to Oban tomorrow?"

"That's right! There is a lot of traffic on that pier opposite. It's where your train arrived last night."

"So," asked Alina, once their plates of huge scallops and fish and chips had been consumed. "What do you think of Oban, so far?"

Lawren leaned back in his chair and looked out at the view as he replied. "I think it's one of the most beautiful places I have ever seen; small in scale of course, but varied at every turn. It's a bustling port, a beach resort, a quaint town and the surrounding countryside is spectacular."

He turned around to look directly at Anna. "I am so grateful to be here. I feel strongly that I will do very good work here. This place is inspirational!"

Anna just beamed. This was exactly what she had hoped for. His first impressions were all positive.

After lunch, a paint-spattered easel had to be disassembled to fit into the back of Grant's car but Lawren declared it was more than adequate for his purposes. He ran his hands over the A frame shape and stroked the narrow shelf where brushes were meant to repose until needed.

"It has seen years of work, but I feel the painter was a happy person who loved his task."

This was the first inkling Anna had that Lawren's psychic skills were still active so far from home. Alina had not noticed the comment as she was talking to Grant about the tickets for the Iona trip.

Anna was glad she had not had to explain. The less said to Alina about Lawren, the better.

Nineteen

The trip to Iona started well for Anna when Alina announced she had a slight cold and preferred to stay behind rather than expose herself to chilly winds on the sea, or on the island.

Anna was glad she would have uninterrupted time to get to know Lawren better and to share her feelings and information about Helen without her friend's skeptical gaze.

Anna had looked out of the bedroom window as soon as she woke up and was almost sure that the white mist she saw in the valley promised a fine day rather than a wet one.

She told Alina to stay in bed until the afternoon and then she made a picnic of chicken sandwiches, pickles, beetroot salad and cookies to be washed down with cans of ginger ale. When the food was packed in a cooler bag, inside a carry-all, together with an assortment of hats, gloves and a light-weight raincoat, just in case, she tiptoed over to the lounge door and knocked quietly to waken Lawren.

After two attempts, she peeked inside the lounge and found Morag curled up on the bed but no Lawren.

"This is getting to be a habit," she declared, as she glanced at the kitchen clock and calculated how much time she had to find Lawren and get ready for the drive to the boat pier.

She found him, cradling a cup of coffee and watching sheep, in the field across the stream on the edge of the property.

"I can't sleep late," he explained. "It's not just jet lag. I usually work at night and my hours are reversed since I arrived here."

"Don't worry about that. We'll sort something out. After today your hours will be free, but for now we need to get to the pier. The first boat leaves early."

Thanks to some speedy driving by the increasingly-useful Grant, they boarded the boat just as the gangway was about to be hoisted off the pier.

"That was exciting!" gasped Anna, but her words were blown away on the wind as the ferry got underway and forged out into the channel between the inner isle of Kerrera and the mainland. Lawren watched Oban rise out of the mist then suggested they stay on the top deck to see the views. He did not want to miss anything on this trip. Anna tied a headscarf around her hair, buttoned up her jacket, pulled on gloves and followed him, somewhat reluctantly, staying as much as possible in the shelter of the enclosed, upper-deck seating area.

Lawren did not seem to feel the icy wind fraught with a burden of moisture from the bow wave. He stood with head bare and long hair tossing all over his face. His only concession to the weather was to pull up the collar on his leather jacket and stick his hands in the pockets.

Anna watched his face. He was like a young boy let loose from school for a day's adventure. His head swung from side to side as he attempted to take in every iota of the experience, from seagulls fighting the wind to stay with the ship in case someone threw a crust into the air, to the rugged coast of Mull approaching on their port side and the green depths of the sea in between.

It was only after he noticed that he was alone on the top deck that he returned to Anna and apologized.

"I didn't mean to freeze you up here. It's so refreshing, I can hardly bear to go inside. The air tastes like salt on my tongue. Do you mind?"

"Not at all! Stay here if you want. It's not a long journey. We'll be landing on Mull at Craignure, so it says here." She waved the guide book she had found on board. "And then we go by bus the length of the island of Mull. When we get to the very tip at Fionnphort it's a short boat ride to Iona. We do it all in reverse on the way back to Oban."

The seating area was steamy after the chill air outside. Anna slipped off her jacket and sat near a window where she could watch Lawren again. It was obvious to her that he was different from any man she had known before. Somehow, he had managed to retain that childlike sense of wonder that usually escapes us as adults. Perhaps it is part of his creative nature, she thought. He was much more unguarded here than he appeared to be in London. It made him seem younger and once again she cautioned herself not to get attached to someone so much younger than herself. And yet, she was feeling things for this artistic person that were both unexpected, and deeper, than she could have imagined.

It's just that holiday feeling, she told herself. Everyone acts more freely when they are away from the drudgery of daily life.

Lawren was just as enthused by the land journey as he was on the ferry. The Isle of Mull provided everything a traveller to Scotland could want. They rocked along a narrow road that obliged cars to back up to the nearest scooped-out passing place whenever they encountered the bus. A few nerve-wracking moments occurred as they scraped past, but, as no one else on the bus seemed to find this in the least worrisome, Anna returned to watching the scenery. They travelled through Glen More for most of the way and saw mountains towering nearby with loch, rivers and waterfalls galore.

When they began to emerge from the glen and follow a coast road again, Anna enquired of a passenger how long it would take to get to the port.

"Ach, lass, it's no lang noo. Aboot a half-hour, I'm thinking."

She thanked him and translated for Lawren who had been reading the guide book to identify the mountains, although pronouncing the gaelic names was beyond his, or Anna's, capabilities. Both of them consulted the guide book so they would be primed to see everything possible while on Iona.

From Fionnphort they could clearly see Iona and it took only minutes on the small ferry to pull into the jetty and unload the passengers who scattered in a rush of feet, small and large, to see the sights, eat, shop or meet friends and family.

Lawren and Anna were left alone on the dock.

"Right, Mr. Drake! What would you like to see first? I know there's a fabulous bay on the other side of the island but it's your choice."

"I want to visit Saint Columba's Abbey first, if you please. It's such an ancient building, revered for centuries, and I think I can see it over there."

"Good choice!" said Anna. "Most of the passengers have wandered off now. We might be lucky enough to get the place to ourselves."

As she had hoped earlier in the day, the skies had cleared while they crossed Mull and a bright sun accompanied them on the walk through the tiny town to the Abbey. It was great to get moving and breathe the clear air. Anna explained how she had tracked down pictures to tell her Helen had come here with a friend. Lawren was impressed and asked how she had found out all she knew about a woman she had never met.

"Well, I didn't do it without a lot of help. George McLennan was the one who first discovered Helen's tragic early life, then later he uncovered the information about her sad marriage which was the source of her finances."

"You have told me something about that, Anna, but I suspect there's a lot more to the story. I don't need to know all the details. It's enough that you cared so deeply for this lonely woman and you want the portrait to be a tribute to her."

"She died without any family around her but she put in place a plan to benefit me, a relative she would never see, and that action simply transformed my life."

Lawren turned to see a gleam of tears in his companion's eyes. He reached down to take the bag she was carrying and said softly, "We'll make sure she would be proud of the finished product, I promise you." The squeeze of his strong fingers did more to assure Anna of his sincerity than even his words could do.

They approached the Abbey along the street of small houses that Lawren said were reminiscent of the colourful, clapboard homes in Newfoundland. He was amazed to clamber over uneven grassy knolls to reach the first of the warm-toned stone buildings in the Abbey complex.

"In Canada, or the United States for that matter, this area would be ringed with fencing and criss-crossed by concrete paths with warning signs everywhere to prevent accidents. This is so much better and the natural grassy surroundings suit the age of the buildings so much better. You can immediately feel a sense of undisturbed peace here. It's remarkable!"

Anna had to agree. Whether it was the lack of tourists milling around, or the location removed from the town but close to the sea, she, too, felt an unaccustomed peace descend on her. Even the ever-present wind had died down in the shelter of these ancient walls and the sun warmed more than their faces.

Without consulting each other, they took off on their own pilgrimage route in and out of the Abbey church and cloisters, St. Columba's Shrine and the Infirmary Museum where Anna saw a collection of ancient, Christian, carved stones that she was sure Lawren would find interesting.

Finally, she stood quietly by a magnificent celtic cross for a time, tracing the symbolism of the circles. When she turned around, she realized she had lost track of Lawren completely.

She found him standing alone, with a sketch pad in his hands and facing an inscription on the fence of the abbey graveyard.

In this sacred place are the burials of many early Scottish Kings and chiefs, as well as kings from Ireland.

"Anna, can you imagine the ceremonies that must have taken place here over many centuries and now there is nothing to be seen but lumps and bumps in the turf?"

"Yes, it's sad all right, but it makes me remember that glory fades, life is short, and we should not waste a moment."

Lawren snapped to attention as if released from a spell. "So, so true! Where do we go next?"

Anna had spotted a sign outside a store on the walk to the abbey grounds. She led them back there and Lawren was delighted to see bicycles for hire.

"Perfect!" he exclaimed. "Let's cycle to that bay you talked about."

Anna was not so sure she could keep up with someone whose usual means of transport was a bicycle, but when Lawren found a model for himself with a basket to hold her picnic bag she decided to take the chance and follow Lawren's lead, after she had insisted on further reading of the island map.

The track to Martyr's Bay cut across the centre of Iona and was simple to find. They passed fenced farmland but were not bothered by cars as the track was not suitable for heavy vehicles.

Anna missed most of the scenery. Her attention was focused on the space ahead of her front wheels. Avoiding ruts was her main concern although Lawren frequently tried to distract her by shouting out about features she should see to either side of them.

When they reached the beach it was all the more surprising to Anna. There were grass-covered dunes in places and placid brown cattle seemed to be wandering free, sampling the tall grasses there. The sand was white rather than golden and the sea was a clear aquamarine with greenish boulders scattered here and there at the water's edge. The entire scene was irresistible.

They dropped the hire bikes onto a dune and ran forward over the fine sand to inspect the boulders.

"I thought they might be covered with algae," declared Lawren, "but they are an exquisite shade of green and look at the red streaks running through them! I have to have a sample to take back with me."

A search ensued for a portable rock. This entailed walking along the shore with heads down. It was harder to spot the green stones as, once they were dry, the colour was much muted.

Eventually, Anna found a chunk the perfect size for a souvenir. She handed it to Lawren and continued to look for one for herself.

Along the bay, she found something she had not expected. A rock formation set back from the water's edge, caught her eye. Immediately she was sure this was the place where Helen and Mrs. Aitken had their picture taken on that long-ago trip together.

"Let's have our picnic here," she called to Lawren. "I am starving after all this exercise!"

Fresh-air picnics always taste better and Anna's was no exception to the rule. No conversation interrupted their munching and soon there was little left to store in the bag for the return trip.

"That was inspired, Anna!" stated Lawren with a contented sigh. "This is another extraordinary location. What's its name again?"

Anna wiped crumbs from her mouth and consulted the guide book.

"It seems to have two names. Martyr's Bay is the historical one but I like the other; The Bay at the Back of the Ocean."

"Absolutely right on!" was her companion's opinion. "Now if I only knew the species of this green rock I am carrying, the day would be perfect."

"I think I can help you, there," said Anna, with a smug tone in her voice. "It's called Iona marble, and can only be found here, or nearby. The guide book says items of jewellery are made from the polished marble."

"Now that you mention it, I think I saw some of that in the Abbey gift shop."

Anna had not found a shop in her wanderings around the Abbey and she wished she had explored further. Iona marble would make an unusual gift for her friends in Canada.

They remained by the rock, basking in the sun, replete with sun, air and satisfactory food. Anna's eyes were closed as she enjoyed the sun on her face while, unbeknown to her, Lawren sketched her in his notebook.

"Tell me why you are not wearing a wedding ring, Anna, but don't open your eyes yet."

Anna was in that sleepy state where confidences seem natural and Lawren's unexpected question helped her to bring some once-painful memories to the fore.

"I was married but it didn't work out. He died recently and I have closed the book on that episode of my life. I am much happier now. It was Helen Dunlop's intervention that shook me out of the depression that had lingered on after the divorce, and my Samba friends who helped, of course."

"You are lucky to have a close group of friends. Men find that much harder, especially the arty types I know. They are all terrified to show weakness in case it affects their reputation as elite artists. It can be lonely to belong to that group, believe me."

Anna found it hard to keep her eyes closed, as instructed, but she could imagine the expression on Lawren's face from the sound of his voice.

"Have you had occasions when you needed support?"

"Doesn't everyone at some time or another?" He hesitated, then decided to match Anna's honesty with some of his own.

"I was engaged to a beautiful girl once. I loved the very bones of her and planned to spend the rest of my life telling her so, but it was not to be. There was never another to compare with her."

Anna was shocked at the emotion these brief statements revealed. She longed to open her eyes and look at him but she suspected this action would end the confidences.

"What happened?" she asked softly.

"An old, old story, I'm afraid. She found someone she loved more. The problem was it was my best friend she chose, so I lost two incredible people from my life in one dire event."

"That must have been horrible for you, Lawren."

"True, but it's finished with now and so is this sketch. You can open your eyes, pretty lady."

She opened them, turned her head to avoid the glare of the sun and leaned forward, all in the same motion so she could grab for the sketch pad and see the sketch for which she had not given permission. Lawren just laughed and relinquished the drawing to her.

Anna saw a relaxed face with upturned chin and an expression of watchfulness. One again Lawren had captured something she recognized but seldom saw for herself. She always felt self-conscious when she knew a picture was being taken. By asking her to keep her eyes closed, he had seen the true face that was hidden from others.

"You are a remarkable artist," she stated, "but very tricky. I won't let you away with that ruse again!"

"We'll see! I have many tricks up my sleeve."

They rose and stretched, brushing sand off their clothes. Anna looked at her watch and told Lawren to run for the bikes. The Iona ferry would be leaving in thirty minutes from the pier and they had to return the bikes first.

They dashed away and did not speak until they boarded the ferry. Despite cycling faster than she ever had before, Anna heard a refrain that ran through her brain in time to the sound of the pedals turning. "Pretty lady, pretty lady, pretty lady, pretty lady."

How long had it been since she had heard those words?

Twenty

In the end, they made it to Bev and Alan's for afternoon tea, although they were tired and dusty and more than a little on the late side. They had found a local taxi cab and asked him to drop them off at the farmhouse door rather than return to the McCaig house and tidy up.

"No, no! Come in as you are! it's just a bit of tea and scones and some cake, of course. Alina is here already. Come and wash up first. I'll brew another pot for you."

Anna emerged from the bathroom first and met the interested gazes of Bev and Alina. Bev immediately whispered in a conspiratorial voice, "So that's him! Alina has told me the story. You're a dark horse, Anna Mason. Not a word from you about him. What's going on? You look very comfortable together."

"Oh, hush up, Bev! There's nothing going on and don't embarrass him, please. He's not used to being inspected by a bunch of women." Bev and Alina exchanged glances at this impassioned plea and decided to be on their best behavior while watching and listening to everything that transpired.

Lawren surprised Anna by taking over the conversation and waxing lyrical about their outing to Iona while scoffing several homemade scones with farmhouse butter and blackberry jam. He apologized for spreading crumbs on the chequered tablecloth and for emptying the tea pot, by stating that he was famished after a day in the open with Anna and really needed that pick-me-up.

Anna had never seen Lawren as a social animal and was just as astonished as Alina at this transformation. She wondered if he knew he was being inspected and had decided to be proactive.

Before Bev could ask him any questions, however, Eric arrived with his step-dad and announced they had decided on a name for Eric's border collie, one of Prince's puppies.

"Well, tell us Eric!" insisted his mother. "We've been waiting weeks for this and the poor animal thinks he is called Pup by now."

"I wanted just the right name and Dad wouldn't let me have King in case Prince was jealous."

Everyone smiled at this but refrained from comments.

"It was between Mungo and Duncan. One was a saint and the other King of Scotland long ago. Dad said Mungo wouldn't work as a name because 'go' is one of his sheep herding commands and that could be confusing for the dogs, so it's Duncan, and since he *was* a king I got my own way in the end."

Eric picked up the black and white puppy that was the image of Prince sitting patiently outside the glassed kitchen door. Eric repeated the name Duncan over and over while ruffling up the pup's fur and giving him hugs. In a moment he was out the door again with both dogs in hot pursuit.

"Would you like to see a training session?" Alan asked Lawren. "It's early days yet but Prince is the one who will teach his pup how to behave."

Once more Anna wondered if there was another conspiracy between Eric and Alan to save the stranger from too much female observation, but she was glad to see him exit the kitchen after the kind invitation.

185

"My goodness, Bev, you were right about Eric! He's almost as tall as Alan and will be taller than James in the end, I think."

"You are probably correct about that, Anna. He is doing very well here. It's a healthy life for a boy and gets him away from that computer." Bev began to collect dishes from the table but she was not about to let Anna off the hook so easily. "Now, what about the portrait; has he started, or have you been too busy showing off the splendours of Bonnie Scotland?"

"Lawren only arrived a day or so ago, as I'm sure Alina has told you. He means to start soon. He's very talented and just wanted to get a sense of the place as it's his first visit."

"Well, I have to say he's not what I expected. Alina made out he's a young guy and that's not what I see at all. There are lines on that brow and although he is slender of build he's wiry rather than thin. I see as much grey as fair hair on his head and he has the air of an experienced man, certainly not that of a boy.
But, Anna! Those eyes are amazing! I don't think I've ever seen that colour of gold before."

"Oh, stop, Bev!" Anna was doubled over laughing at this detailed analysis after only a few moments in Lawren's company. "You two are impossible! Stop trying to match make. I do like him but that's all there is."
Alina and Bev did not agree, but they knew better than to contradict Anna when it came to personal matters. Bev decided there would be phone calls or e mails to Canada later, to consult with Susan and Maria about this promising situation.

The next morning, Anna found it difficult to drag herself out of bed. Every muscle in her back and legs protested as soon as she emerged from the covers. She decided to soak in a hot bath, hoping that would relieve the worst of the damage she had inflicted on herself while rushing here and there and cycling miles over rough land.

As she luxuriated in the deep tub, her mind wandered over the events of the previous day. She had to admit she had seen a different Lawren Drake during the hours they had spent together. He was not so intimidating when separated from his easel. She thought about the way he had spoken of his former love. The words he used were brief and almost emotionless but Anna knew it took years to be able to express these feelings without being overwhelmed by the memories.

I wonder how old he is? Do I dare ask, or is that way too personal? Should I try to get a glimpse of his passport?

An urgent knock at the bathroom door shattered her quiet musings and she almost jumped up to grab her dressing gown. "What is it? The bathroom's occupied!"

"It's only me! I'm leaving for the train in a few minutes. I'll call you later when I get to the hotel.

Don't do anything foolish while I'm away! Bye."

Alina goes to Manchester today to visit Philip. She had forgotten in the busy time since Lawren had arrived. This thought reminded her that she should be looking after her guest. She pulled the bath plug and dressed quickly in a toweling robe while the warm steam lingered in the bathroom. Her hair was wet only around the margins so she toweled it dry and scrubbed at her face, thinking it would benefit from some moisturizing cream and a little make-up. She threw open the bathroom door and found Lawren standing there.

"Sorry, Anna! I didn't mean to startle you. When you are ready I would like to see the room where the portrait will hang. I want to get a start made today and I need to see the light.'

"Oh, of course! I'm so sorry! I didn't mean to neglect you. Have you had breakfast? Has Alina gone already?" She realized her nervous chatter was an attempt to cover her embarrassment over her appearance but it was too late to do anything about it now.

"Alina fed me an hour ago. Please don't rush. I have all day." With this he turned and fled back down the stairs leaving Anna in a turmoil. Why do I have to act like a school kid when he's around? What's the matter with me? Is it just the proximity of a male in the house? I really need to get a grip.

She took time to make herself presentable, mostly to restore her confidence, then sailed downstairs in her best impersonation of a person in control of her feelings.

Lawren was in the kitchen with his sketch pad, talking to Morag while he drew the scene from the large windows.

"She's quite taken to me, I think. She creeps into bed with me at night."

"Oh, I'm sorry! She shouldn't be bothering you. Just close the door."

"No, I wasn't complaining. I like her company." He paused. "Did I disturb you a while ago? I didn't mean to. I thought you were up already. I am awake so early and I presume everyone else should be."

"I think we should both stop apologizing and get to the business in hand. It's what you came here for after all."

Anna could have kicked herself at the abrupt sound of these words. There I go again, jumping from one extreme to the other. What must he think of me? I will keep out of his way today and try to get my head together before I do or say something I will regret.

"I'll show you upstairs and you can set up your easel any time. I won't bother you while you are working but I'll be around if you need anything."

Opening the door to the double bedroom she slept in, was another of those slightly awkward moments.

Anna reminded herself that she had been in Lawren's premises in London and he didn't have any such scruples about his sleeping arrangements. She watched as he walked the length of the room looking at the views on both sides of the house, assessing the direction of the sun at different times of the day. He favoured the south light from the front dormer window but returned to the larger rear window in the end.

"I take it the finished portrait will hang over the fireplace here?" Anna nodded.

"Then, it's best if I set up near the window. If you can provide some sort of drop cloth to protect the floor, it would be helpful. I will remove my work each evening so you can have your room back. I'll probably continue well into the night, as is my usual practice, but that part can be done downstairs.

I plan to work consistently for the next week unless something unforeseen happens. I hope that is satisfactory."

"Certainly! I'll get a cloth for the floor while you set up." She marched down the stairs, silently cursing her stupidity. Gone were the friendly feelings of the day before and now it was all about business between them and it was her fault entirely.

She could not wait to get out of the house before she encountered Lawren again. She left the cloth on the stairs and fled for Helen's Hill where she could think about what had happened to her peace of mind since she first met this unusual man who both repelled and attracted her.

Lawren saw Anna practically running through the rear garden when he was in the larder fetching his easel and painting equipment.

"God! I have chased her out of her own house. What was I thinking? This is becoming very awkward. I have never worked in a client's home before and I don't think I would agree to it ever again. Yesterday was so pleasant and now that's all gone. I really hoped we had made a true connection.

The best I can do now is get this portrait done as fast as possible and get out of her hair. I am obviously imposing on her kindness and generosity and I hate that."

Having lectured Morag, the only creature in the vicinity, he dragged his materials up to Anna's spacious bedroom and proceeded to pin up his canvas and assemble his previous sketches.

In moments all his attention was focused on the work at hand, and yet, he could hardly forget about Anna as her face was the first thing he saw as he examined all the drawings he had done of her.

He narrowed his eyes and looked with his inner vision. She was quite lovely, especially when she did not know he was watching her. There were classical lines there; strong features, a noble brow and that glorious coppery hair. She was a woman who had found herself in this very place and she deserved a true representation of her spirit. He reminded himself that there was no earthly reason why she would consider him anything more than an employee. He was hopeless with women like Anna Mason. Men were much easier to work with. She was far above him in material wealth and station in life. If a workman was all that he could ever be to her, then he determined to be the best workman she had ever employed.

Flexing his fingers, he proceeded to plot out the placement of the figures on his canvas with total concentration.

Twenty-One

Stavros Kyriakos was setting markers on the terrain in Aegina where the excavations were to begin, when his mobile phone started ringing.

It took a moment before he recognized the irate voice of Philip, his brother-in-law. That conversation was swift, negative, and a complete mystery. Philip did not stay on the line long enough for Stavros to decipher the reasons for his anger but he did find out it had something to do with his wife.

Still reeling from that shock, he was soon accosted by his daughter who accused him of doing something to upset her mother.

"Dad, she is furious with you. I have never seen her like this. What did you do? I have to tell you she has wrecked your office at home. Files and papers are scattered everywhere. I don't know if she was looking for something in particular but the room is a mess. She promised to tell me what it's all about except now she won't even speak to me!"

Sarah's voice had been getting louder with every statement until Stavros had to remove the mobile phone from the proximity to his ear to save his hearing.

"Hold on, Sarah! I haven't spoken to your mother for a few days now. I have left messages but she hasn't got back to me yet. Look! I have no idea what's happened. Yours is the second call in as many minutes today and now I am worried. Can you watch over your mother for me until I can sort this out?"

"I can try, but not for a day or two. David and I are in Paris with Caroline. Mum's not going to talk to me, and, frankly, Papa, I'm more than a little anxious about her state of mind."

Sarah's use of the word 'Papa', a name he had not heard since she was a little girl, brought home to him the seriousness of the current situation. There was nothing for it but to reassure her.

"Look, Sarah, I am heavily involved here but I will wrap up the essentials ASAP and fly home. Don't worry too much. I'm sure I can sort this out, whatever it is. I promise to be home before you are. I'll keep trying the phone lines in the meantime, and you do the same from France."

"I won't pretend I'm not relieved to hear you are taking this seriously, Papa. Thank you."

"I love you, Baby! Enjoy Paris and give my congratulations to Caroline."

"Will do! Cheers!"

Stavros looked at the remaining metal stakes with red flags he was gripping tightly. Suddenly the summer course work on Aegina appeared less important than what was happening in England.

Despite his confident manner when talking to his daughter, he was alarmed by Sarah's comment on her mother's state of mind.

The course started in two weeks. He began to prioritize what could be left with a deputy for a few days and what must be settled before he could take the ferry to Athens and fly home.

Then it hit him; Pauline was due to arrive in an hour or so. He could not possibly leave without seeing her. The poor girl had begged him to meet with her. She insisted there were matters to discuss before the course began and she was right about that. He sat down in the shade of a pillar in the Temple of Aphaia and sipped from the water bottle strung around his waist. He could not reach Pauline now but there were others to contact. If he hurried, and was able to make the right connections, all could be prepared for an early morning departure for Athens and home. Paros would have to wait for now but Pauline was a priority. He removed the mobile phone from the top pocket of his shirt and proceeded to punch in the numbers.

Pauline Jeffries stepped off the ferry ramp carrying a small bag and wearing a loose summer dress and a big hat.

Stavros was waiting for her on the pier and gave her a welcoming hug as soon as he reached her.

"My Lord, girl, you look glowing with good health! This pregnancy suits you. Have you come all the way from England today?"

"No, and that's part of what I have to tell you. Can we go somewhere quiet and talk?"

He watched her as they drove to the little café near the temple where they had shared many secrets and dreams in past years. She sat back with eyes closed and a beautific smile on her lovely face. Her blonde hair was blowing in the breeze from the open windows and she hummed a tune under her breath. She was quite a picture, he thought, and he smiled with a deep affection for this brilliant student of his. He couldn't help wondering what would happen to her now that she had decided on domesticity over academic ambition.

Once they were settled in the shade of the café with cool drinks and a superb sea view, she began to explain what had been changing in her life in recent months.

"I must thank you for your good advice professor. I considered everything you said in your e mails and phone conversations and I appreciate the time you gave to my problems."

"You know how much I want the best for you, Pauline."

"Yes, I do, and I owe you an explanation of my choices. I will have this child but I will not give up on our plans. I still want to replace you at the university some day and I will continue to work toward that goal. It may take a little longer now, that's all."

"Indeed! And how are you going to manage to look after yourself, and a child, while you strive for the qualifications and experience you will need?"

"That's what I came to tell you." She held out her left hand and Stavros saw a diamond catch the light.

"You are married?"

"Not quite. But I am engaged, and it is all thanks to you professor."

"How do you figure that out?"

"Remember last summer when we did the new excavations here? There were several participants from colleges in England and Greece as well as the older members of the group who just wanted to experience archaeology for a few weeks."

"Of course!"

"Well, one of them was an archaeology graduate from a college in Athens."

"Yes, I remember him; a bright fellow named Theo. Is he the one?" She could not contain her excitement and her voice rose in accompaniment to the words.

"We spent time together here, talking for hours about our futures and one thing led to another."
Pauline patted her protruding stomach. "He lives near Athens and I have been staying with his family for a week or two but he wants to get away from all the uproar in the capital so he has applied for a position as a junior curator at Fishbourne Roman Palace."

"I take it from your expression that he has been accepted?"

"Exactly! He is moving to England and we will live with my family until we can get a place of our own. I will not let you down professor. Theo and I are determined to fulfill our destinies."

"Well, I can't fault you for that. Congratulations, my dear. I wish you the best of luck in the future.

I take it you will not be attending the summer course?'

"Correct. I am returning home with Theo to start our new lives together."

"Speaking of which; I, too, must return home to attend to some business. Please keep in touch, my dear. If I can help either of you in any way, I will be happy to do so."

"You have done that already. Theo and I met during your course in this very spot."

Ah, young romance, thought Stavros with a touch of envy for the years of youth when all things are possible and all barriers exist simply to be surmounted.

They drove back to the ferry and by the time Pauline boarded for Athens, Stavros had turned his mind to the problems ahead for him in England. He began to dread what he might have to deal with when he reached home.

Lynn had exhausted every emotion and descended into a state of torpor. She could not recall if she had eaten in the last day or two, but as Mike never came home until after six o'clock and he was happy to have pizza delivered, she did not waste time worrying about feeding him. She did, however, have some fleeting worry about the state in which she had left her own cozy home. Despite having closed her husband's office door she could clearly picture the chaos she had created inside and she began to be ashamed of her furious reactions.

Not ashamed enough, she decided, to compel her to return and clean up the mess. Staying at Sarah and David's had given her the space she needed to calm her mind, somewhat. It helped to be out of the house where the trauma had occurred. Looking around in Sarah's kitchen did not remind her of the shock of discovering Stavros' betrayals. She had left her mobile phone behind and deliberately removed Sarah's handsets from their bases. She knew she was not yet in a fit state to talk to anyone and she dreaded what else might be revealed in another phone conversation.

She had tried watching television but either the words made no sense at all or everything she saw cast her back to the past; a past life with Stavros that was now infected with the disappointment and pain of the present situation. Her internal dialogue continued in an endless loop.

I blame myself. I should have carved out a career for me instead of giving up everything so Stavros could have a high position in the university. He rose far above me and I never could catch up. No wonder he looked elsewhere for romance. How could I compare with those lovely young girls who adored him?

What man would not be flattered with their attentions? He must have been so bored with just an old housewife, stuck at home with none of the intellectual conversation he craved. This is how he developed a secret life and planned to live far from me back in the land of his birth where he had the support of an extended family. But how could he bear to separate himself from Sarah and the grandchildren?

The questions revolved round and round in her brain until she could think no more.

Into the vacuum, the very worst thoughts of all infiltrated with deadly effect.

What if I can't escape from this dark place?

What if this is the beginning of the mental fog that claimed my mother's sanity?

Mike came home on Monday night without the usual pizza box in his hand. Instead of a quick 'Hello Gran!" and an even quicker exit to his bedroom's hi tech centre, he stopped and sat down beside her.

"What's up, Gran? Mum has been calling my mobile all day. She says she can't reach you."

He cast a quick glance around the lounge and soon spotted the reason. Every phone in the place was disconnected. His mother was right. Something was far wrong here. Now that he was paying attention, he noticed his normally neat and tidy grandmother was looking strangely messy.

"What can I do to help?"

Lynn focused on the young man who had appeared beside her. Only moments ago, it seemed, he was just a child and now he was taking on the responsibility for her wellbeing when she was supposed to be in his home to look after him and prevent any untoward incidents, like teenage parties, while his parents were in France.

Something about his earnest expression jolted her awake.

"I'm just tired, Mike." No lie there. She was sick and tired of the struggle to figure out what to do with the dregs of her life.

"Well then, you rest here, Gran, and I'll zip down to Heathfield and get us a decent take-out for a change. Indian or Chinese, or some of that roast chicken?"

"You choose, my dear boy."

"Good enough! I'll be back in a jiffy!"

Before she could protest, he was gone, and some of the energy in the room left with him.

For the first time in days, more positive thoughts began to invade Lynn's exhausted mind

I am letting down Mike and Sarah by thinking only of myself. I need to pull myself together. Mike will be reporting to Sarah as soon as he is in the car. I can't let this go on any longer. My family needs me. My family needs me.

Dragging herself up from the couch, she walked slowly to the kitchen and splashed cold water on her face. The shock of the water revitalized her a little and she looked around the kitchen in dismay.

Dirty cups filled the sink and a carton of milk was left out on the countertop surrounded with an assortment of sweet wrappers and empty pop cans.

Sarah will be appalled to see the state of this place, she lectured herself. Even if I can't face my own home, I can sort this kitchen out before Sarah and David come back.

With something to do, she found the energy to run water into the sink and wash dishes. By the time they were dry, her head had cleared a little.

When Mike's car arrived in the driveway she had prepared two trays so that they could eat together in front of the TV. Tonight she would not question her grandson's choice of program. She was only too grateful for his undemanding company.

Stavros took an early-morning flight from Athens airport and a taxi from Heathrow to Horam.

He ignored the expense as he had built up a disastrous picture in his mind during the flight and he could not wait one extra minute to get home and see what had happened in his absence.

The second he unlocked the front door and smelled the stale air, he knew Lynn was not there. He did not take the time to inspect the damage in his office. What did that matter anyway? He was retiring now and most of that stuff would be discarded soon. But where was his wife? Her car was gone.

As soon as he remembered his phone conversation with Sarah, he turned and headed for Uckfield taking the back lanes so he could drive faster and avoid some of the speed traps on the major roads.

He found the front door unlocked at Sarah's house and stepped inside in some trepidation. What, in God's name, was he going to find? His mind raced with horrific images from war zones and hostage cases. He feared Lynn might have gone over the edge of sanity and he might be too late to save her.

After tiptoeing around the two floors in dread of coming upon a desperate scene, he caught sight of a lone figure seated on the terrace outside. He raced down the stairs, through the kitchen and out to the terrace, calling her name.

Lynn's first impulse on hearing her husband's voice was to flee from him immediately, but she was trapped in the garden and there was nowhere to hide. She took a steadying breath and straightened her back. It was time to face whatever must be faced. Time to bring a halt to the pain and deceit. She was not her mother, or her father. She would survive.

Stavros was dismayed at his wife's appearance. She was pale and drawn beneath the surface tan and her eyes were haunted. He dropped to his knees in front of her, took her hands in his and laid his head down upon them. He was assailed by a tremendous sense of guilt. What had he done to cause this suffering to his dear wife? Did he dare ask what she was feeling?

After what seemed like minutes during which time he could feel the shudders of emotion pass through her body, he finally summoned a voice although he was not yet ready to raise his head and look into those eyes.

"Ask me anything, Lynn. I swear I will tell you the truth."

There was silence until a bird somewhere began to serenade them and the tension lessened a fraction.

Lynn spoke quietly into the air. "Tell me about Pauline Jeffries."

His head came up rapidly as the import of that question raced down his spine. Still holding her hands he sat back on his heels and began to relate the story of his connection to the student.

"Lynn, you know about Pauline. She is one of my most promising students. She is ambitious and capable and I am grooming her for advancement at the university."

He stopped abruptly. Why would Lynn ask about Pauline? What had she seen, or heard, that gave her the idea something was wrong in their relationship? With his mind now racing at top speed he recalled the e mails on his computer and saw them anew in the light of his wife's fears.

"Lynn! Listen to me. There is nothing inappropriate in my dealings with Pauline. I admit she has confided in me, especially about her pregnancy, but I just found out she is engaged to one of my summer course students and she is getting married to him soon. I have *never* crossed the line with Pauline or any other student. I would *never* do that to you."

His sincerity and passion sent a shaft of sunlight into Lynn's mind and a tiny ray of hope began to grow.

She was not ready, however, to forgive him for the other transgressions.

"What is this I hear from Philip about a house being planned on Paros? When did we discuss this as a definite move and what have you decided about *our* future without consulting me?"

"These are legitimate questions, my darling. I confess I have forged ahead without talking to you. I apologize profusely. May I get up off the ground now, my legs are aching?"

She nodded, and a ghost of a smile passed her lips. He drew a chair over to her side and sat down slowly. What he said next was going to determine their future together and he was acutely aware of the necessity to phrase his words carefully.

"The desperate economic situation in Greece has caused me to speed up all my plans. We hold a considerable amount of our finances in euros in our bank here, and the euro in Greece is under huge threat with the current unrest and dissatisfaction with government agreements to support the German bailouts. I was afraid we would lose everything if I did not purchase the land on Paros right now. I went ahead and contracted my brother Xristos to build a home for us there. He was about to depart for Turkey to work and I wanted him to stay on the property and supervise the work. That is why I asked your brother, Philip, to draw up blueprints for the site. I know I should have waited until I could discuss this with you, but I felt huge pressure to move fast or we would lose the opportunity altogether."

He could see that Lynn was not going to be satisfied with this explanation. Her wishes for the future were not being considered in this scenario and that was unforgivable of him.

"I know I promised to involve you in any house plans, Lynn, and it was wrong of me to move ahead without you. I have been aware of your desires and needs despite what you might think. I know you want to remain in England after I retire and that is perfectly understandable. I have been investigating a scenario in which both of us could get at least a part of what we most want."

Lynn turned her head to look into his eyes and her heart skipped a beat. He was the most beautiful man she had ever seen. When his full attention was on a person, he was irresistible. What could be more important than a life with him? What would a life without him be? She said nothing of this but he could see he had intrigued her.

"What do you think about this idea?" he continued. "We sell the house in Horam and build a new home on the beautiful bay on Paros."

He expected an instant negative reaction to this but he could not know how his wife's feelings about their English home had changed in the past few days. What had been a sanctuary was now fraught with horrible fears and panic.

"Of course, you will have total input in the design, if Philip can be persuaded to come back on board. He insisted that you must be a partner in this and he was right. Now, here is the vital change, my darling."

Stavros reached for his wife's hands again and gave them a tender squeeze.

"Sarah has agreed to keep a bedroom for you, or both of us, at her home so you can spend whatever time you wish living in England with the family. I made her promise not to reveal this to you until all other parts of the plan were in place. The Paros house can be rented out while I am teaching courses or either of us is in England. I think this is a compromise that can work for both of us. What do you say?"

Unspoken between them was the information that living in England for part of the year would permit Lynn to access British National Health Services if she should deteriorate in health.

She looked out into the garden while she attempted to reassemble life into this new pattern.

She noticed how much brighter and cheerful the flowers and greenery appeared now that her mind was relieved of the awful pressures her doubts had created. Perhaps there was a way out of the mess after all. Perhaps the dreams of both of them could be satisfied. Marriage was all about compromise.

A smile began to move across her face as a beam of sunlight reached the terrace.

The phrase, 'All's well that ends well', popped into her mind but she immediately countered it with the caution that she would never completely trust this man again until he had proved himself to be honest in every part of his speech and action from this point forward. Forgive and forget may be the popular maxim, she thought. Forgive, yes. Forget, eventually perhaps, but not too soon.

Stavros saw the smile and heaved a sigh of relief. He knew he had taken huge risks by excluding his wife from the decision-making process and he swore to himself that he would do whatever was necessary to restore her faith and confidence in him. Open communication was the key element he had forgotten, or, more accurately, chosen to put aside. He determined never to make that mistake again.

They truly loved each other, now, and in the past they had shared. They had always been a partnership in the old-fashioned way that was unknown to today's young folk, where equality was everything. After all, their long marriage had weathered storms in the past and they had emerged, battered and bruised, indeed, but emerged nonetheless. This time it would be the same, please God.

Twenty-Two

A new daily routine was quickly established at the McCaig Estate House.

Lawren slept late, began to paint in the afternoon, and worked far into the night. He ventured into Oban once or twice for art supplies after asking Anna's permission to use Helen's old bike which he found in the garage barn.

They rarely saw each other and avoiding talking. With different schedules, Anna found it easier to leave food in the warming oven and a note to explain what was where in the kitchen. By the next morning, the plates were empty and drying on the countertop.

Anna was left to her own devices and she enjoyed the chance to get to know the summer version of her Scottish house without the usual rushing in and out that had been a feature of recent visits.

She worked in the garden, carefully transplanting wild flowers from nearby fields. She made a raised bed from the stones scattered throughout the rear yard for the herbs and kitchen plants she found springing up here and there.

On sunny afternoons she would wander over to the stream on the edge of the property, She preferred the local name, 'burn', because of the brown peat colour of the water from the tarn at the top of Helen's Hill. Sitting on a large granite rock she listened to the burbling water and watched birds descend to sip from the shallows. If she stayed very still, they would not notice her and she could study their varied plumage.

On one of these days the birds flew off rapidly when Anna's cell phone rang. She had forgotten she had slipped it into her pocket when leaving the house in case Alina called and disturbed Lawren's concentration.

"Hi!"

"It's Alina. Glad I caught you!"

"Good to hear from you. What's been happening?"

"Well, my dear, this trip to Manchester is very interesting. Not what I expected, in some respects, but definitely interesting."

"Do tell."

"The train trip was easy. There's always someone around to ask if you don't know where to go. The hotel is good and Philip took me for dinner when I arrived."

"Aha! And how did that go?"

"Not too well, I'm afraid. He talked endlessly all through the meal about a Lynn and Stavros and how they had messed up his plans after he had obliged them by spending time on their project when he had responsibilities for the London Summer Olympics."

"Wait! That must be Lynn, his sister, who I met in England when Philip and I went to see their mother in the nursing home just before she died."

"Oh, of course! You told me about that. Did you meet Stavros then?"

"No, I never did. It sounds like Philip hasn't reconciled with his family yet."

"I'd say not from the way he was talking about them."

"So the evening was a dead loss then?"

"Just about! I think he was so nervous that his mindless chatter stopped him from running out of the restaurant."

"How did you manage to scare him that much, Alina?"

"Honestly! I hardly said a word but I did get a good chance to watch him in action. We already knew he was not too comfortable around women, and that night proved it."

"So that was the end of it?"

"Not exactly. He called and apologized the next morning and took me to his house for lunch."

"That sounds more promising!"

"Indeed! The house is huge! It's a foursquare, stone, Victorian mansion, with high ceilings and tall windows in every room and those plaster roses in the centre of the ceilings with pendant chandeliers. Fireplaces, of course, with fancy glazed tiles and several huge old washrooms with clawed-leg tubs that would take ages to fill."

"Goodness, Alina, I never knew you had studied Victorian architecture."

"Well, I had a crash course. He showed me all over the place and described everything in great detail. I didn't see the rooms where his partner lives but I did meet the housekeeper.

She looked daggers at me, I can tell you, but she produced a lovely lunch in the dining room and left us to talk without interrupting."

"I take it things went better after the meal?"

"Yes, you are right about that. We both relaxed after a glass or two of wine, from his own cellar, by the way, and I think I got to see the real Philip. He **is** a lonely soul, Anna. He said he never had much success with women. I think his mother's behavior scarred him and he was afraid of too much affection, always backing out before relationships got too serious."

"Hmmm, you must have had some sympathy for that, Alina. It's not unlike your own story in a way."

"I suppose so. Anyway, we had a real heart-to-heart in the end and got a lot of stuff cleared out of the way. He told me about his mother's mental problems and his fears for his future. I told him about my own worries about my failing eyesight. We traded our worst nightmares."

"You did? I didn't expect you to go that far so soon."

"Well, Anna, let's not kid ourselves. None of us has a whole lot of time left. We might as well cut to the chase, as it were, and see if there is any point in continuing."

"And is there?"

"I think there might be."

"Really!"

"Now, don't go jumping to conclusions, my dear. It's only a possibility. I am not head-over-heels in love like some silly girl. I'm way too old for that nonsense but I do understand how lonely his life must have been. He has work colleagues, of course, but he never had a lifelong friend like you have been to me, Anna."

"We have been lucky in that respect, Alina, there's no question about it.

So, what happens now?"

"We'll see. The handsome Nigel has invited us to dinner tomorrow with his family. Philip is busy all day and I am going to work through a list he gave me of art galleries and architectural wonders in Manchester City. We'll drive to Nigel's home later."

"What will you be looking for on this occasion?"

"*I guess I am hoping to see a more comfortable, Philip. After all, Nigel is a partner in the firm. Philip must know him, and his family, quite well. I also want to observe how he introduces me to his friends.*"

"*It sounds as if you are really checking him out as a prospective partner, Alina. I must say I find that quite surprising.*"

"*Well now, Anna Mason, I have to look out for myself these days. If you decide to pair up with a certain artist we know, I could be out in the cold with no one.*"

"*Alina! You know that would **never** happen to us. Please don't make any decisions based on that utterly false premise. We are partners forever no matter what relationships might intrude for either one of us. You are scaring me with this nonsense. I wish you would come back to Scotland and talk to me face-to-face before you do or say anything conclusive.*"

"*I apologize, Anna! I am feeling a little left out and sorry for myself, I suppose. I don't mean to alarm you. Truly, I am not in danger of running off to Gretna Green!*"

"*I should say not! When will you be back here?*"

"*A couple of days at the most. You sound anxious to see me. What's going on in the love nest?*"

"*Oh, please! Nothing is going on, and that's one of the things I want to discuss with you, my friend. Hurry home to Scotland. We have so much to talk about.*"

"*Sounds serious. I'll be there soon. Take care. Bye for now.*"

Anna closed her cell phone with a sigh. Talking to Alina had made it clear she was missing the kind of daily exchanges she was used to. Although being on her own was a pleasant change, there could be too much of a good thing. Lawren had been invisible for days now and she might not see him again once the portrait was finished. He had not shown any inclination to stay around after the work was completed.

She could not brush off a feeling of concern about how fast Alina's relationship with Philip was developing and about some of the things she had said regarding their future.

Thinking about Alina's situation from a safe distance like this brought a number of choices to the fore that she would never dare broach with Alina herself.

Alina might link up with Philip in some way, but it would not likely be in Canada since his livelihood was based here in the UK.

Would it be possible for them to be close friends while living on opposite sides of the Atlantic?

What would it feel like if Alina brought Anna's half-brother into her life in this way? Would there be uncomfortable situations, or even jealousy?

Whatever happened between them it must be Alina's decision and Anna would not stand in her way.

Having decided this, she rose from the warm rock, stretched, and headed back to the house wondering what she could make for supper. She had heard a van draw up while she was talking on the phone. If it was a delivery of groceries from Tesco she would have more choices than she had had lately. Not that Lawren had complained at all. He was probably glad to have anything cooked for him rather than find something quick and cold when he worked in his tiny studio apartment in London.

To her great surprise she found Jeanette waiting in the kitchen.

"Oh, there you are Anna. I was about to leave a note. I just popped in to tell you that Lawren and I are going antique hunting tomorrow afternoon and to ask you to please look after baby Anne for a couple of hours. I don't want to drag her around in the car as we will be in and out of shops and barns. Will you do it for me?"

"Of course I will! I would be delighted to hold that darling babe for a while. Leave me all the instructions about sleeping and feeding or I can call George if I need to."

"She'll probably nap the whole time, Anna. Don't worry about it. I have to rush now. Lovely to see you!
I'll be back tomorrow."

With a wave of her hand, Jeanette was off down the path leaving Anna with something special to look forward to.

Jeanette was right. Baby Anne was asleep in her carry cot when she arrived and she slept soundly for another hour. Anna sat happily admiring her godchild for twenty minutes or so, then it occurred to her that the house was empty and Lawren's painting was upstairs on the easel in her bedroom and she could sneak a peek at the work he had been keeping covered.

Once this idea had taken hold she could not get it out of her mind. Placing the baby's carry cot gently on the kitchen floor and closing the door behind her in case Morag should appear, she crept upstairs feeling not a little guilty, but also excited to see what progress, if any, the artist was making.

As usual, the canvas was covered completely with a large cloth. She stood in front of it, hesitating between lifting a corner to look beneath and turning and fleeing at once.

Curiosity won the struggle for control and she tentatively took the corner of the cloth between her finger and thumb and raised it to eye level.

At first she could not make sense of the portion she could see. There were landscape elements and buildings. She had expected something similar to the initial sketches she had been shown in Lawren's studio with figures in the foreground. She had to see more now to sort out the confusion in her mind.

Using both hands and moving extremely slowly and carefully in case there should be wet paint underneath, she rolled back the cloth, laid it over the top of the easel, and uncovered the whole canvas.

She stood there, transfixed, for an unknown number of minutes while her senses swirled with a multitude of impressions and emotions. Her eyes darted from one focus to another as each area of the canvas captured her attention and information about the painting built up, layer by layer.

Finally, she was forced to take a breath. Tears began rolling down her cheeks although she was unaware of them.

Guilt flooded through her. A flush crept up from her neck. She was not meant to see this work without the artist's permission. How could she possibly react normally now that she had stolen a preview?

She felt impelled to turn and run and almost did this when she realized she would have to replace the cloth with the utmost care. Lawren would never forgive her if he knew she had invaded his privacy in this way. Why had she taken this risk? What could have persuaded her to be so foolish? The painting was suddenly much less important than the artist's opinion of her. He must never know what she had done to betray his trust.

Nervous tension made the act of replacing the cloth one of the most difficult things she had ever attempted. Visions of disaster made her hands shake. She imagined the horror of smearing the canvas or denting it in some way. Lawren would know in a second that someone had interfered with his work.

Despite her fears the task was finally completed. When she had finished, her arms were quaking. She could not escape from the room fast enough.

Back in the safety of the kitchen her first thought was for the baby. The little one was awake now and Anna gladly lifted her from her carry cot and snuggled her into her arms, more for her own comfort than for that of the child.

Waves of guilt and shame still washed over her but eventually they faded, leaving behind a sensation of awe and wonder at the skill of this man who had promised not to disappoint her and now had surpassed every hope and wish she had cherished when she first conceived of the portrait project.

She would never know how he had achieved it, but Lawren had accomplished something she could only think of as magical.

What she had seen was burned into her memory. Two figures dominated the centre; her own, and one other who she did not recognize, and yet knew to be Helen Dunlop. Lawren had taken aspects of Anna's mother and blended them with photographic elements he had seen, and created a face, sadder perhaps, but still expressive of all Anna felt about Helen.

Whereas Anna's figure looked forward, Helen's was turned to the side and seemed to be looking back to the series of structures that vanished into the distance. The house was there, with the hill behind stretching to the skyline. Fading into the horizon on the painting's right side, were glimpses of a castle and a mansion Anna could not identify.

Helen held a notebook and pen in her right hand and that hand almost touched Anna's left hand. Letters were fluttering into the space between them The message was clear. They had never met in life but Helen Dunlop had passed on to her great-niece a wealth of personal information in addition to the estate property itself.

There was another more immediate effect of what Anna had seen. The portrait of herself spoke volumes. She could not ignore the love that had gone into its creation. Not just the beauty of the expression with all the hope and faith in the future that it represented, but also the tenderness of the artist's intent. It was not a true depiction of the Anna she saw in the mirror with all the lines and wrinkles of her life's experience. Rather, it was a face imagined through the eyes of love and it spoke to her of that love in a way his words might never have done.

212

She had seen inside his soul and she could no longer pretend she lacked a response. Something rare had developed between them and she would have to admit it, and acknowledge it openly. How this might be achieved was beyond her comprehension at the moment. She rocked the baby in her arms and contemplated a future that had appeared out of the air, as suddenly, and with the same effect, as a violent summer storm.

Lawren Drake's painting had changed everything.

Twenty-Three

Anna was still in a daze when she heard Jeanette and Lawren arrive. She stood up in a panic, wishing she could flee before they found her in the kitchen but she was trapped with the babe in her arms.

"There you are, Anna! So sorry we are later than we expected. How was the little one?"

Without looking at Anna, Jeanette reached over and took her child into her arms as if she had missed that weight the entire time she had been gone. She checked Anne's diaper and picked up the baby's bag saying she would be back in a minute after adjustments had been made.

Anna managed to force out an enquiry about the success of their search but she could not bring herself to raise her eyes above the level of Lawren's leather jacket buttons.

"We found a perfect frame. It will need some work but I think it complements the painting perfectly."

He stopped talking and Anna felt the tension in the room stretch to breaking point.

"What's wrong? What has happened since I've been gone? Anna, look at me!"

The command was issued in combination with the grip of his hands on her shoulders. She forced herself to meet his worried gaze, all the while knowing that he would be able to read the guilt in her face.

"It ....I'm ...." Her voice faltered and died as he searched her expression for clues.

It felt like a spotlight had been turned onto her. He was delving far further into her mind than he had any right to. She felt exposed and guilty and afraid and alarmed and inexplicably happy all at once.

Lawren simply bent forward and kissed her on the lips.

It was one of the most unexpected things that had ever happened to Anna Mason and she did not resist.

When she opened her eyes again, he was still standing there with a vulnerable look on his face that she had never seen before.

Neither one spoke for a while. They just stared at each other. In a way they were each seeing the other for the very first time.

Then the floodgates opened and they poured out feelings and apologies and regrets and frustrations and hopes and concerns and fears.

"I am older than you."

"Not that much. In any case, who cares about age? What bothers me is that you have so much more to offer than I do. I have nothing."

"No! You have talent and skill beyond belief, Lawren!"

"So you saw the painting?"

"How did you know?"

"I saw it immediately when you looked at me. Everything about you had changed."

"You don't hate me for it?"

After he had kissed her again, they sat down at the table, still holding hands, and tried to be more practical.

"What did you think?" His voice shook just a little and Anna knew she would have to be careful about her reply.

"I was overwhelmed. There is so much more there than mere surface detail. You poured your feelings into the canvas with every stroke."

"I couldn't find any other way to tell you how I felt. I was afraid we were growing further and further apart and I would lose you."

"Lawren Drake, you have undoubtedly *found* me!"

They laughed together at Anna's teacher tone then grew more serious as she asked about the painting.

"I could see that everything contributed to the story of Helen and me and this house but what were the other structures in the background?"

"They are also significant parts of her life. The castle is Stirling Castle near where she lived with her husband for many years and the large building further back is one of the Quarrier's homes near Glasgow where she was sent when a child."

"But, I never told you about those. How did you know and how did you find them?"

"Anna, you will have to believe the influence working in the night hours in this house has had on me.

I won't say I heard voices but I certainly felt things, especially since Alina left.

Sometimes I walked outside in the dark just to get my head clear and I saw owls floating by. It was as if they brought me messages. I stood under your bedroom window and looked up and I thought I saw a pale face looking back at me. Emotions I had no claim to, would well up inside me and I experienced a deep sorrow at times."

"Lawren, I can't deny I have felt strange things here also. I don't doubt you are right, but that doesn't explain your knowledge of Helen's past history."

"Oh, that is much simpler to understand. You told me about George McLennan and how he had helped you, so I looked for his office on one of my Oban trips and he filled in the details, after referring to his wife, of course. I also discovered the local library where a kind old gentleman spoke highly of you, Anna, and helped me find the illustrations."

"I knew nothing of this search. Why didn't you ask me?"

"I was afraid to break the spell we were under. Being here together, and yet apart, seemed to clarify so much that I was feeling. I hesitated to reveal what I was doing."

"My friends have a lot to answer for, I think."

"Don't be too hard on them, Anna. They have all been wonderful to me. Everyone I met in Oban knows you, and has a story about how you have helped the town's people. I had no idea you were such a benefactress."

"Please don't credit me with that. It all came from Helen and her ideas. She knew Oban much better than I do. I really just followed her wishes."

"You are too modest, by far. What about the Fairisle Knitters Cooperative? I'm sure your relative did not start that venture."

"Well, true enough! A Plus was responsible for initiating the business contact with a little help from Fiona."

Lawren turned his face away at the sound of the words, 'A Plus', but not fast enough for Anna to miss his expression of doubt.

"What's wrong Lawren?"

"It's just another reason why we are so ill matched financially. You have a thriving business as well as property in two countries."

"Did Alina tell you about A Plus?"

"Yes, she did, and, frankly, it worries me more than anything else."

"Well, you can stop worrying right now. Financial issues are not a priority for me and none of my friends would think any the less of you because you are an artist. They are not that shallow."

"I hope you are right, although I have a feeling Alina might not agree with you, Anna."

"So, you picked up on that, did you?"

They both laughed out loud. Alina had not exactly been subtle about her opinions.

"Don't be concerned, Lawren. Alina wants the best for me and I am the one to decide on what, or who, that is. It's early days yet for us.

We have a long way to go before we need to be deciding on the future."

Lawren heaved a sigh of relief. "Agreed! I need time to get used to the idea of us."

"Exactly what I meant! It's a long time since I was an 'us'. We need to get to know each other and I can promise you right now, Mr. Drake, that the process will not be speedy as far as I'm concerned. I need to go slow on this."

"Absolutely! I will not rush you, Ms. Mason, I swear."

Jeanette returned just then with a happy baby in her arms, took one quick look at Anna and Lawren side by side, made an excuse and exited the house promptly.

Anna sighed. "The phone lines will be buzzing tonight, I fear. Jeanette could not miss the look on your face, or mine, for that matter."

"Do you care?"

"Not a bit! And that, alone, proves how much you have changed me."

Two days later when Alina returned to the McCaig Estate Farmhouse, Anna was beginning to recover from the emotional shocks of Lawren's declaration of love. There had been uninterrupted hours of talk, walks up and down the lane, a visit to Bev and Alan's, (where Anna got a huge hug from Bev that conveyed how much she already knew about the situation), and a ride into Oban where they managed their first walk around in public as a couple.

Lawren wisely left the friends alone to catch up while he did some restorative work on the antique frame for the painting.

Alina could hardly wait for him to leave by the back door.

"So, tell me everything!"

"No, you first!"

218

Having settled the order of revelations, Alina summarized her trip to Manchester by announcing that Philip had agreed to join her in Canada at some future date, after the London Olympics were over and his work commitments calmed down.

Anna was doubtful about this plan because she knew Philip's visit out west to meet his half-brother, Simon, had not been a great success.

"I asked about that," said Alina. "He told me he couldn't cope with the large family in Calgary but was willing to give it a try with us, if you approved."

Anna agreed readily, and thought how fortunate it was that they had purchased a condo in London, Ontario, with two separate suites on opposite sides of the building. Privacy was assured, should that be needed. Somehow she was having trouble imagining Philip sharing a bed with Alina, but that was equally as difficult to imagine as herself and Lawren in the same situation.

"Do you think it will work out for you two?"

"I don't know yet. Philip needs to see me on my home ground just as I needed to see him on his. It won't be a simple matter for us to get closer. Each of us has been alone for most of our lives and neither of us is an easy character to live with. We've both been used to our own way in most things."

"*We* get along well, don't we?' asked Anna.

"Of course we do, but that's entirely different. I don't believe I'll see Philip again before he makes it over to Canada. He talked of an emergency trip to Greece with his sister Lynn."

"Glad to hear it. They need to get together."

" Now, enough stalling, Anna! How did things progress with Lawren and what have you done about it?"

Anna proceeded to outline the events Alina had missed. It was no surprise to her friend, as she had caught the new atmosphere as soon as she saw Anna and Lawren together.

"I can't explain everything, properly," explained Anna, "I'm still processing it myself, but I know you will understand better when you see the finished painting. Lawren says it will be ready for inspection in a day or two."

Alina looked deeply into her friend's eyes and saw the changes already there.

"Is it love, Anna?" she asked.

"I think it might be, given some time, but I can tell you I am scared stiff about the implications of that."

"Are you talking about sleeping with him?"

"That's blunt, but it is certainly a concern and I imagine even more so for you, my dear."

"Too true! You, at least, have been married before. What are you scared of?"

"Everything! He has promised to go slow but consider this; after Richard and I divorced I slept on the same side of the bed we had shared for years. It was ages before I moved into the centre of the bed, rearranged the pillows and took over the space. That story is a metaphor for the time it took for me to reclaim my life again. I had submerged myself in Richard. He was far too important to me and I was much too needy. It could be how I drove him away."

"Oh, nonsense, Anna! You were far too good for him."

"That's as may be, but the point is, I cannot risk losing the person I am now. It has been much too difficult to gain back my independence and I like me this way. I could not bear to be consumed by a man again, even one as special as Lawren."

"Have you told Lawren about all this?"

"Bits of it. There is a chance he feels the same. He's an independent person also, in so many ways, and he needs space to get immersed in his art. He will keep his studio in London. We'll have to see how it works out for all of us."

"Don't worry about me, Anna! I am already convinced he's good for you. He makes you happy and that's all I ask. Remember, we are all older and wiser than once we were. We understand about compromise and sharing and we know how fortunate we are to get even a chance at happiness later in life."

"Yes, that's all true. I suppose time will tell."

They sat on opposite sides of the big kitchen table with a tray of tea things between them. Each woman was thinking of the changes the future might bring.

Alina, was feeling more objective since she was not yet committed to Philip in the same way that Anna was to Lawren. Her conclusion, as yet unspoken, was that the men would be required to make the compromises if they wanted to blend in with a very satisfactory lifestyle that Anna and she shared. She was unsure if either of the men involved was equipped to make those compromises. Her observations of men had led her to believe they were not as flexible as women. It all depended on whether or not Philip and Lawren really needed a woman in their lives.

Anna was thinking much the same things.

"Two changes I know for sure will happen when we get home to Canada," she announced.

"What's that?" asked Alina in surprise.

"One is, I'll be looking for more glamorous nightwear to replace my usual warm pajamas and socks and the other change is that I'll be heading to the gym, just in case."

Lawren returned from the rear garden for a drink of water. He had been outside sanding old paint off the picture frame. He was met with the sound of wild laughter in the kitchen and beat a hasty retreat.

He was beginning to get the idea that these particular two women were, when together, a force to be reckoned with.

Twenty-Four

Lynn Kyriakos returned to Greece with her husband. The heat of the summer months was oppressive and not her favourite time of the year there, but they had arranged that her husband would be teaching his summer course on Aegina while she met with her brother, Philip, regarding the design for the new house on the bay.

She figured she could stand a week or so on Paros as the breeze from the sea would, hopefully, temper the heat to some degree. Spending time with her brother was an additional benefit and provided an opportunity to mend fences to some degree.

After Philip was finished she would return to England with him. He was heading to London for the Olympic Games and she would begin the final packing of the Horam house.

Lynn had managed to secure two rooms at the hotel in Parikia. She knew she was able to get rooms in the high season because her husband's family was known in the town and also because even the Greek islands were devoid of the usual hordes of tourists this year. Lynn's room was small and faced away from the sea view but this did not concern her since she would be spending her days on the bay. She made sure Philip had the better room. She hoped this might encourage him to enjoy time with them in the future in the new house, if all went well with their reunion.

The first day did not go well at all.

Philip emerged from the taxi and marched down the track to the bay without a word. They had scarcely spoken at all on the way there. Lynn was hoping it was the professional person's concentration on the work ahead that kept him silent. She had known this trait in Stavros when he was thinking of teaching or writing tasks. If Philip continued to be this taciturn, however, collaboration between them was doomed from the start.

She stood back and watched as Philip traversed the shoreline from side to side, then turned back to scan the skyline, lastly focusing on the remains of the old restaurant shack.

It was hard for her to connect this tall, tanned man with the pure white hair escaping from a wide-brimmed hat, as the big brother she had once known in their childhood home in England. Her memories of him were dim now, although once they were close, as children must be in a house where their parents are at odds with each other. She preferred not to think of those sad, distant days and she was sure her brother felt the same way. The past, they say, is another country where things are done differently. There seemed no point in resurrecting the sorrows of that time although a corner of her mind still resented that Philip had escaped the eventual turmoil and left the consequences for Lynn to deal with. Had it not been for Stavros, she could barely imagine what would have happened to her. She would certainly not be standing here on Paros, enjoying the scenery in the spot where her future home would be, some day soon.

Philip was now sifting through the debris on the concrete platform which was to be the footprint for the new house. He had removed a sturdy pair of gloves from his leather satchel and proceeded to pile a number of timbers to one side. A camera and a computer screen emerged next from the satchel as Philip traced every step of the distance between the ruin and the sand dunes at the rear and up to the entrance track to the side. He shook his head and typed notes on the screen, then measured again.

Lynn was beginning to feel surplus to requirements. Why did she need to be here when the architect had not even glanced her way once? Was not the purpose of this trip to ensure her desires for a future home were included? At least, that was what Stavros had promised when he persuaded her to return to Greece. She thought of leaving and flagging down a taxi on the road. Glancing at her watch she saw the car Philip had hired was due to return for them in an hour or so. I can survive an hour, she told herself. There are much worse places in the world to wait than right here.

She was just drifting off into a dream while snuggled into a sand bank with her hat pulled over her nose, when a hand shook her awake.

"Look here! I will have to revise my plan now that I see the actual site. Your husband may be an academic but I am guessing his expertise does not lie in mathematics."

Lynn jerked awake and instantly responded to her brother's tone with a sharp rebuff. "Don't blame him. *You* were not exactly available when you were first needed. We are all scrambling to meet deadlines and conform to a variety of changing needs. You are not the only one with problems, Philip."

Philip shrugged uncomfortably as he heard the truth. For a moment, Lynn had sounded like their mother, Isobel Purdy. He did not think it diplomatic to mention this, however, and held his tongue. Recently, Alina had been schooling him on the necessity to think before blurting out his first thoughts.

He plopped down on the sand beside Lynn and removed his hat to wipe sweat from his brow.

"Well, let's make what use we can of the time we have. Tell me what you need in this house and I will keep your requests in mind. I can't promise anything. The site is very difficult and the budget is not huge."

Lynn recognized the masculine version of an apology when she heard one, and she softened her voice in reply.

"I understand the problems, Philip. I have simple needs; a bedroom and bathroom, or toilet, on the ground floor, safe stairs to the upper level and two more bedrooms and one bathroom there."

Philip waited for the rest of the list. No female client had ever presented him with this few requirements.

"Where's your wish list then? You must have more than basic needs in mind."

"I don't feel qualified to dictate to you about this, Philip. Stavros has left it to me, and I am leaving it to you in turn. Do what you can with the site. I will be happy with the basics."

Unknowingly, Lynn had appealed to the generous side of her brother by gifting him with carte blanche; a rare event in his experience. Immediately he could see the positive benefits to the site rather than the negatives and he determined he would manage to provide rather more than the basics needs now that he had been given full rein.

The idea of incorporating advanced technologies might work on this isolated site if he could get tech companies on side as a demonstration project. There would need to be both conservation and storage for water, and full use made of solar power. He must obtain a meteorological map of the prevailing winds and the weather conditions throughout the year here. There was a question of how high the building could rise without impeding the view for others, and security in this remote location had to be considered. The entire house must blend into the location seamlessly.

He began to mentally collate glass manufacturing costs and fuel efficient appliances, local flooring and roofing traditions, recycling possibilities for waste water, refuse compacting, access for vehicles during and after the construction phases and colour choices for the interiors.

Stavros had employed his brother to head up the construction phase and Philip had been assured that he had excellent English. Supervising the local Greek-speaking workers would be his responsibility as Philip would be in England soon. There was much to be done before he left. The demands filled his mind and Lynn was once again forgotten.

She could see his dilemma. Not such a great time for brother/sister bonding, then, she thought, with a sigh. Ah well, I am used to this. I will fill the time with plans for *my* future life and let the men get on with their concerns.

Watching Philip move around the site with a small computer in his hands, she was reminded of Anna Mason. They had a similar height and stance which made sense since they had shared a father.

She wondered whether she would ever see Anna again. Their first, brief meeting in Heathfield had not provided much opportunity for talk, although Lynn felt she knew Anna better through conversation with her granddaughter Caroline, who had stayed briefly in Anna's house in Scotland when the connection between their families had been uncovered.

Lynn's thoughts turned back again to her own concerns. It was time to consider how she would function in a future she had not expected, and which would have to be created from her new circumstances.

Spending part of the year here in Greece, and part in England at Sarah's, would not be a problem for her. It was a compromise that she could adjust to. The difficulty she foresaw was in how to occupy her time while Stavros was teaching his archaeology courses in either location. She planned to include Sarah's family in their new lives whenever possible, but there would be times when Lynn might be alone. She had a new attitude to this solitude now. No longer would she sit twiddling her thumbs waiting for life to come to her. It was time to grasp life with both hands and be involved.

She cast her mind around for something she could feel passionate about. She had read this was the secret to happiness. Find your passion. She thought that might best apply when you were younger but there was no harm in trying it at an advanced age.

Housework and cooking were not going to be on her list. She had spent enough time devoted to those.

Gardening on sand did not seem to offer much distraction. Travelling with Stavros was always a delight.

They had seen the wonders of the world on their travels. He was a good teacher and Lynn had developed a deep interest in history and archaeology during their adventures in Egypt, Italy, Spain and the spectacular sites of Greece itself.

Stavros was going to be occupied with teaching in England and Greece but also with the group of academics who had dedicated themselves to redress the wrongs of stolen Greek artifacts now residing in museums throughout the world. For years no government would support that movement but lately, there had been a change of heart and gradually some of the precious fragments had been repatriated. So, her husband would remain involved with his passions. The question remained; what could she do when he was not available?

Into her relaxed mind popped a scene from years ago. She and Stavros were visiting Fishbourne Roman Palace near the coastal town of Chichester. They had wandered around the site of the largest Roman family home ever built in England during the centuries of the Roman occupation. Building materials had been imported from Rome for the mosaic floors that had now been carefully excavated. The gardens that once served to provide open views from the surrounding rooms had been restored to their original design. It was a magnificent archaeological treasure house. Teaching programs for schools and for interested adults took place on the site and plans were in existence for future expansion once the row of pre-war houses on the northern edge of the site had been purchased and demolished.

Why not take courses in archaeology from such places as Fishbourne and the many other locations, like Pompeii, where knowledgable volunteers and docents were needed? She could become qualified with Stavros' help and perhaps they could work together on site in Greece and other locations. She could never aspire to achieve his elevated levels of expertise, of course, but she could at least be on hand to assist in a minor capacity. After all, their conversations over the span of a long marriage had included details and anecdotes about just such locations. Surely she had absorbed enough not to be an embarrassment to her husband and he might just be pleased at her wish to be more involved in his work.

The idea began to take shape in her mind and she felt a growing excitement at the prospect of another new beginning. There were ways to study online nowadays. Computers could make things easier.

This thought was underscored as Philip approached her and sat down again by her side with his laptop in his hands.

"What do you think about this?'" he began, turning the screen toward her and shading it with his arm.

"This is the blueprint but I can show you a three-dimensional view also."

There on the small screen was a plan for a house. The ground level showed mostly open frontage. Philip explained that these would be sliding glass panels which could be closed completely at night or when the wind was too strong. The entrance to the house was to the side of the building and led into what the Americans called a mud room only this one had a shower stall for washing off sand. This was separated from the main living area which was definitely open plan with a kitchen against one wall, an island counter and very little else. What she thought to be a rear wall turned out to be a dividing wall behind which the master suite would be concealed.

"Other features can be added if you wish but the space allows for that. More interior walls mean changes would be very costly so we should leave it like this for now."

Lynn looked for the access to the second level and found a flimsy open staircase in the centre under a light well beaming light into the centre of the house.

"The stairs must be safe for adults and future great- grandchildren to climb," she insisted. "None of these open, glass, suspended stairs will do."

"Duly noted," said Philip. He took her on a virtual tour of the second level where the bedrooms and bathroom she had requested were laid out efficiently with space for storing linens and clothing, but she could not understand what was sketched above them where she imagined the roof should be.

"Ah, a flat roof is traditional in Greece and if I can work it out, this one will provide multiple services for the house including solar power and water storage. There should be just enough room for a seating nook by an herb and succulents garden with movable sails above for shade when required. Access will be from an outside, fire-safety, metal staircase."

As Lynn was not saying anything, Philip continued with the proviso, "This is a basic model, of course. I used standard plans for speed with a little adaptation. Much more can be done should finances permit."

Lynn was thunderstruck at the creativity the simple plan showed. She closed her mouth and swallowed before attempting any comments.

"I think it looks wonderful Philip. I can't believe you could pull this together so quickly. I am delighted with what you have done already. Thank you!"

For the first time in many decades Lynn threw her arms around her brother and pulled him into an embrace. Just a few months before, Philip had learned from Alina how comforting an embrace could be so he knew not to hold back. Words were not needed, but unspoken comfort was given and received nonetheless.

Lynn recovered first and said the only thing that came into her mind to save Philip from the embarrassment of too much emotion.

"Tell me why you set aside the old planks of wood, Philip."

He cleared his throat and looked over to where the pile was lying. "I want to use these weathered beams on the exterior so it blends into the surroundings."

"Oh, Stavros will love that idea! He used to come here with his brothers and sisters when they were all children. It will be as if those happy times are incorporated into the new home. Don't they call that good karma?"

Philip laughed, and Lynn realized she had never heard that pleasant sound before.

"I don't know, but I am glad you approve of the rough plan. I will work out the details back at the hotel and Stavros' brother can have the blueprints as soon as possible. There is much more work to do to source materials but at least a start has been made today."

Indeed it has, thought Lynn. Only one of many starts in our new lives.

"Oh, I can suggest one source, Philip. Paros is renowned for the whitest marble in all of Greece. It comes from the mountains here."

"Then that is what we will use for the flooring throughout. It will be local, clean, easy to maintain and allow for decorating options when you add colourful rugs and fabrics."

For the first time, Lynn began to visualize this new home and her excitement grew to overcome the fears she had harboured for so long.

Twenty-Five

George, Jeanette and the two children arrived early. George went upstairs to help Lawren hang the new portrait while the rest of his family assembled in the kitchen to await the remainder of the guests who had been invited to the unveiling.

Alina took Liam, and baby Anne in her buggy, out to the rear garden to visit the sheep that still managed to find a way to hop over the stone walls occasionally. Jeanette and Anna set out dishes of salads, sliced meats and fresh breads along with pitchers of lemonade and fruit juices. Champagne for a toast was chilling on a stone shelf in the larder.

"Tell me, Jeanette, what does George think about Lawren?"

"Why? Are you worried about our opinions?"

"Not really, but I am interested. I don't want to make a fool of myself and you can see he is younger than I am."

"Fear not, my dear. Every woman wants a younger husband. George is one you know."

"What? I did not know that."

"Aha! Surprised you there, didn't I? Yes, George is a full four months younger."

"Jeanette! Stop teasing me. You know what I mean."

"I am just trying to show you how ridiculous your objections are, Anna. No one looking at the two of you would ever think about age. They'd be too busy admiring your taste in men."

Anna chased her Canadian friend around the table twice before collapsing, breathless, on the padded bench in front of the windows.

"Do you know when Kirsty is coming?" Anna was anxious to see the elderly woman who had nursed her back to health when she had caught a bad flu during her first ever visit to the McCaig Estate house.

Kirsty was one of the few people who had known Helen Dunlop well enough to recognize whether or not Lawren had managed to capture her image, or her essence, in his painting.

"Bev said they were picking Kirsty up from Skye early this morning. They should all be here soon."

"Good. Who else is coming?"

"One or two more, I think."

Anna immediately picked up on the strange way Jeanette had spoken and she pounced at once.

"What are you hiding from me? You can't fool another Canuck, you know."

"Well, the truth is, there will be one or two surprises but don't even try to get anything more out of me and for the love of goodness please attempt to be surprised. I was sworn to secrecy."

Anna had to be content with this small hint. She suddenly became aware of the importance of this occasion and that awareness was swiftly followed by a self-conscious fear that she had not chosen the right outfit for the day. Making an excuse to Jeanette, she ran upstairs and locked herself into the washroom where a large mirror would reveal whether she looked appropriate for a special summertime occasion or, like mutton dressed as lamb, as the derogatory Scottish saying went.

She saw a woman with a frowning and nervous expression on her face and immediately tried a more natural smile. This improved her general appearance quite well so she continued with the inspection. Her hair was freshly washed, coloured and conditioned and a recent trim had smartened up the style. She tossed her head and saw the layers swing into place neatly. So far, so good, she thought.

The dress she was wearing was one Maria had insisted on, although Anna was initially unsure about the pattern. Now she was glad she had followed Maria's instruction as the fitted white and blue floral with a calf-length, flared skirt flattered her figure and concealed any bulges she might want to hide from view. She had pulled a long-sleeved, royal blue, cashmere shrug over the dress for warmth and that seemed to add to the more up-to-date look Maria had recommended. Anna could not see her feet in the mirror but she knew the beige platform sandals were a good finishing touch.

Lawren has rarely, if ever, seen my legs, she thought. This will be a surprise for him.

"You look just fine!" she told her reflection, with a confidence she hoped to feel for the rest of the day. "Now, go down there, stop worrying about what's happening in the bedroom across the hall, and greet your guests."

Thus emboldened, she descended the stairs in regal fashion to find Kirsty with Alan and Bev Matthews waiting for her in the kitchen. Eric was standing at the window in the grip of a wildly handsome young man who turned out to be his older brother, James. Behind them Anna glimpsed the slim figure that must belong to Caroline, whom she had seen with James on one or two memorable occasions.

Exclamations of delight echoed around the room while each person renewed acquaintance with others they had not seen for some months. Everyone had to admire baby Anne and converse with her brother Liam. Kirsty had the honour of receiving the little one on her lap and Alan quickly produced a camera to capture his mother, the oldest female there, with the youngest.

There was so much happy noise resounding around the kitchen that no one noticed George and Lawren descending the stairs.

"Attention please!" declared George, in his best lawyer voice. Everyone turned to the stairs and an expectant hush spread through the kitchen as some there realized they were seeing for the first time, Anna's artist friend about whom they had heard so much.

"I would like to introduce to you, Mr. Lawren Drake, portrait painter extraordinary. " At this juncture Lawren bowed from the waist in courtly fashion which made the audience smile.

George continued with his introduction.

"Please follow me, ladies and gentlemen, to the formal presentation of a work of art, commissioned by Ms. Anna Mason and now installed in the grand salon above for all to appreciate."

Lawren stepped down and took Anna's arm through his to lead her upstairs before the rest of the procession.

Anna was glad the waiting group could not see her face as she was awash in emotion. Everything from pride to panic was flowing over her and her heart was beating like a drum. For some reason, she was at a loss to understand, Lawren was a picture of calm confidence at her side as he whispered, "Don't worry!"

The portrait was centred high on the wall above the fireplace mantel and seemed to Anna to be much larger than she had estimated. It was still shrouded in a clean cloth and all had to wait for the unveiling until every person had found a place to stand or sit.

Anna was installed in the velvet chair by the fireplace. In front of the fireplace was a large bouquet of flowers. Lawren stood behind her with his hand on her shoulder to steady her nerves.

Without another word, George expertly flicked the cloth and the portrait was at last revealed.

The sound of indrawn breath was the only sign that anyone occupied the spacious room. Even the tiny children felt the drama of the moment and kept still.

Anna was amazed all over again. She thought she had seen the painting before but it was almost as if she had never known a thing about it until this very moment. Perhaps, she thought, it was due to the expert match of subject and antique frame that added a new dimension. The colours were more alive and the background more compelling but the figures captured attention as they were meant to do. Anna stared at herself in her perfected form with eyes and scarf of a startling blue and the figure in the painting stared right back at her. There was some secret in those eyes and she felt as if she could look into their depth forever to fathom the mystery.

Behind her in the scene, was Helen Dunlop ; the reason for the entire project. Where before, Anna had thought the figure of Helen dim and ghostlike, she now saw that it was a complement to the colours of her own portrait only in a more muted hue. The letters and Journals between them were so realistic that they might, at any moment, float out and into the room.

Her musings were interrupted by the pressure of Lawren's hands and by the clapping of a wildly delighted crowd showing their appreciation in traditional fashion.

Anna looked first at Lawren and her eyes told him everything he wanted to know. She then stood and moved against the flow of bodies pressing forward to congratulate the artist. She was searching for Kirsty who had been seated comfortably on Anna's large bed.

She bent low to whisper her request into the old lady's ear.

"Kirsty! What do you think? Is it a good enough likeness of Helen? It was so difficult to get a picture of her."

Kirsty took Anna's face in her soft, wrinkled hands in reply and spoke out against the noise in the room,

"My dear lassie, it's a miracle. He has caught her very look, the way she is glancing backward. The past was never far from her mind until the day she died." Without pausing for breath, she continued, "That man cares very deeply for you, Anna. Now everyone here can see it." Anna kissed Kirsty's cheek and turned to find Fiona standing behind her, waiting her turn.

"Oh, Fiona! Now the day is perfect! What a lovely surprise! Come and meet Lawren. How are you?
Tell me all your news."

Hours later, when most of the visitors had departed and the house had finally calmed down, Anna had a chance to ask Fiona what her first impressions of Lawren were.

"I was warned you would be asking that question," she replied, with one raised eyebrow expressing her disapproval. "You know I am not one for beating around the bush, Anna. I'll tell you what I really think. Are you sure you want to know?"
It was too late to turn back now. Anna simply nodded without taking her eyes off Fiona's stern face.

"I think ……………. those eyes are *amazing!* Sorry for teasing you. I just couldn't resist!"

"I'll forgive you in a year or two," responded Anna, as relief flooded through her. If Fiona had not liked Lawren, she would have had serious doubts about a future relationship with him. It now seemed as if all her friends had approved of Lawren. Even Alina had come around to a more accepting opinion of him.
Does this mean I should do something to consolidate our relationship, she wondered. Her instincts told her it was too soon to be making commitments but how would she know when the time was right?
Just then, Lawren came in from the larder where he had been washing and packing his brushes. He had already announced his

intention to fly back to Canada. He wanted to leave Anna and Alina with some time to themselves. There were many things to be considered by all parties before they made permanent changes to their lives.

He smiled at Fiona as he settled himself on the couch that had been his bed in the lounge.

"I have an announcement," he stated proudly. "I have a commission from George McLennan. He wants me to do a family portrait while the children are still small and he says he will recommend my work to the Oban town council members in case there are others who would like casual, or more formal, portraits."

"Excellent news!" exclaimed Anna.

"Now you have good reasons for returning to Oban, Mr. Drake," said Fiona, with a sly smile.

"Please call me Lawren," he insisted. "Anna considers you a family member and I want you to think of me that way also, in time, of course."

"I'll do that. But now I have to go see my wee house in Oban which has been deserted for months since I have been living in Inverness. I'll call you tomorrow, Anna, and congratulations to you both for everything."

With this cryptic statement, delivered with another sly look, Fiona left them alone in the lounge.

Anna breathed out a sigh of contentment and collapsed down into the comfort of the fireside chair.

"You know, I think I'll light this fire just for the added warmth," she began. "It's been such a wonderful day although I feel exhausted with all the excitement. You must be feeling something similar."

Lawren did not reply at first. He reached forward from his chair on the other side of the fireplace and retrieved a tall box of matches, lighting the fire with a few deft moves. When the blaze was just beginning to warm their faces, he looked over at Anna and said, "It has been an incredible day for me, Anna. It seems every day has been significant since I first met you. This house, this land, everything I have seen and heard has told me so much more about you."

She was intrigued and sat up to hear his interpretations. "What do you mean?"

"Well, today is a good example. You probably have no idea how well respected you are, Anna Mason.

Each and every one of your friends and acquaintances has taken the time to tell me what a great person you are and with those comments has come an implied warning that I should treat you with the care you deserve."

"Oh, that sounds embarrassing, Lawren. Did they annoy you?"

"Far from it! I speedily came to the conclusion that you are a most fortunate woman. I think a person's friends tell a significant amount about that person. If that is a reliable measure, and I believe it is, you are a woman blessed in so many ways."

Anna could not miss the regretful tone of voice in which these extravagant compliments were delivered. She reached out for Lawren's hand and quietly asked, "Why does that make you unhappy?"

"It's nothing new. You know I feel this is an unequal situation. You have so much to offer and I have very little, other than myself."

Anna chose her words carefully and reinforced them with a firm pressure on the hand she was holding.

"Lawren Drake, I never wish to hear those words again. What you are offering is beyond price. I know what a talented and unique man you are. I feel privileged to have you in my life. No matter what the future holds for us, I hope we will always be friends, at least."

Lawren stood up and walked over to the window where he could clearly see the path from the front door and beyond the gate, fields, forest and hills to the darkening skyline.

He was struggling within himself as to whether the time was right to risk a most important move forward.

Anna could feel the tension from his figure poised behind her and she chose to stay still and quiet until the problem, whatever it was, had resolved itself.

After several long moments she heard a whoosh of air leaving lungs and Lawren appeared in front of her again. He pulled the armchair over until their knees were almost touching and the firelight flickered across their faces giving them both a fey appearance.

"Anna, I have something to offer you. I don't want you to be afraid that I am asking more than you wish to give. This is a symbol rather than a commitment. The choice to accept or reject is entirely yours."

"That sounds intriguing, Lawren, but I have no clue what you are talking about."

"Right! I'll explain. Remember when we went to Iona?"

"Absolutely! It was a marvelous day. I loved it there."

"Me too!" They shared a warm smile at the memories and it gave Lawren the courage to proceed.

"Well, you know I have some claim to psychic tendencies. I had a very strong impulse when I visited the gift shop at the Abbey, to buy something unusual. I have learned to follow these impulses."

Anna could stand the suspense no longer. "Lawren Drake, will you please get to the point. I am not as patient a woman as you seem to think."

In response, he reached into his pants pocket and retrieved something small which he presented to Anna in a closed fist.

"There are two. I will wear one from this time forward, the other is for you and, I repeat, it is your choice if, when, and where."

At the conclusion of this mysterious speech he opened his fist and in the palm of his hand she saw two silver rings glinting in the glow from the fire.

Her first impulse was to cry out in alarm. Rings were a commitment and she was not sure she was ready for that, despite admittedly strong feelings for this man.

"Let me show you," he begged, in response to her silence. There is an inscription on the outer surface."

He placed one of the rings onto the middle finger of his strong left hand and she could see that there was inset, a band of darker silver with raised letters that she could not interpret.

"It's gaelic, and it says, 'Anam charaid'".

The way he pronounced the words told Anna he had taken the trouble to learn how to say them correctly and the soft syllables so close to her ear had a magical sound in the quiet room.

She felt a presence nearby. It was almost as if Helen Dunlop stood there beside them willing Anna to make a momentous decision.

"What does it mean?" she asked, with a quaver in her voice and the start of a tear in her eye.

"It means soul mate."

The words dropped into the silence like an explosion. She was immediately overwhelmed by a storm of emotions both positive and negative, and for a space of seconds she let the storm rage through her until the tiny voice of her braver, wiser self came through.

Soul mate. What more could you ask of any man than this?

She could not speak. She allowed her actions to speak for her as she tenderly picked the second ring from his outstretched palm and placed it on the middle finger of her left hand where, by some strange alchemy, it fit smoothly, as if it had always been there.

His face lit up at once and he bent to kiss her hand.

"Is this truly your answer?" he asked.

"It is," she said.

At that very moment, a log dropped in the fire and bright embers flew upward like a child's sparkler on July first.

She thought, as she fell into his arms, Helen approves.